Purgatory Reign

LM PRESTON

Purgatory Reign

LM Preston

Description: Seventeen-year-old Peter Saints' life stinks. But things are about to get much worse. First, his parents are murdered in front of him. Then another victim dies in his arms.

Visions plague Peter with warnings that something wants him for a sinister cause. It desires the one thing that Peter refuses to give—his blood. Peter carries within him the one gift or curse that could unlock a secret to destroy the human race.

On the run with Angel, a scruffy kid, Peter starts to unravel the mystery. It's the one treasure the heavens sought to hide from the world. Unfortunately, when Peter finds the answer he hopes that will save the one girl he loves, he opens the door to a great evil that happens to be salivating to meet him.

Purgatory Reign

PUBLISHED BY: Phenomenal One Press
www.phenomenalonepress.com, phenomenalonepress@yahoo.com

Cover Illustrator: Alicia 'Kat' Dillman

Paperback: ISBN 978-0-9850251-3-7

For my children and my husband, who helped me dream the impossible and gave me the support to achieve it. To my husband who wrote a short story for a class that I dug out of a box, and read to be inspired to create this great adventure.

Acknowledgments

Thanks to God for giving me this anxious energy to create and tenacious spirit of positivity with an active imagination. To my devoted Beta Readers, Jordan, Missy and my daughter, who helped me create a better story. To my husband, who created the basis and inspiration for this story. To my editor, Cindy Davis, who's been my best support in my art. To my kids and my husband, who continue to give me true and honest feedback for all of my work. I thank you.

Young Adult:

The Pack by LM Preston– Teen, blind, vigilante on a mission to save the missing kids on mars. Shamira is considered an outcast by most, but little do they know that she is on a mission. Kids on Mars are disappearing, but Shamira decides to use the criminals most unlikely weapons against them the very kids of which they have captured. In order to succeed, she is forced to trust another, something she is afraid to do. However, Valens, her connection to the underworld of her enemy, proves to be a useful ally. Time is slipping, and so is her control on the power that resides within her. But in order to save her brother's life, she is willing to risk it all.

The Pack – Retribution (book 2) - Revenge doesn't have a name, but has chosen a victim - Shamira. But she's never been the type to lie down and let someone hurt her family or her friends. In order to find the mastermind behind the threat to all she cares about, she must give up the one person who's found his way into her guarded heart, Valens. Valens refuses to back off easily, and neither will Shamira's friends. They join forces with her in order to deal with a new enemy who seeks to kill everyone in Shamira's life that dared save the missing kids on Mars.

Bandits by LM Preston - Daniel's father has gotten himself killed and left another mess for Daniel to clean up. To save his world from destruction, he must fight off his father's killers while discovering a way to save his world. He wants to go it alone, but his cousin and his best friend's sister, Jade, insist on tagging along. Jade is off limits to him, but she is determined to change his mind. He hasn't decided if loving her is worth the beating he'll get from her brother in order to have her. Retrieving the treasure is his only choice. But in order to get it, Daniel must choose to either walk in his father's footsteps or to re-invent himself into the one to save his world.

Flutter Of Luv by LM Preston - Dawn, the neighborhood tomboy, is happy to be her best friend's shadow. Acceptance comes from playing football after school with the guys on the block while hiding safely behind her glasses, braces, and boyish ways. But Tony moves in, becomes the star Running Back on her school's football team, and changes her world and her view of herself forever.

Coming 2013 –
PURGATORY REIGN (Print Release March 16th, 2013)
WASTELANDS (Bandits Series Book 2) Fall 2013

Chapter 1

Closer. Come closer. Peter's large frame leaned on the door to the gym, the one thing he actually liked about the rundown, makeshift group home. He beat his fist against the wall and listened to the kid scream obscenities while searching for him.

The bully was just who Peter wanted to see. Peter hungered to kick the bastard's brick-head the last two days for roughing up a younger kid. He didn't want the reason for the fight to be too obvious, or else Pastor Finnegan would lecture him about turning the other cheek and all. But Pastor Finnegan could save that forgiveness monologue for someone that needed it—Peter didn't. He'd given up on turning the other cheek the day his life went to crap. Peter refused to call him by that long last name, and the Pastor usually let it slide—if he was in a decent mood. Even so, the old man was hard to shake once he got a sermon started. Being the only authority figure in Peter's life for the last eight years, the old lunatic had grown on him.

The burly dark-haired boy bellowed, "Peter! Where's my money?"

Peter's jaw clenched. And he taunted Remmy with his middle finger pointed up. Then he flicked his chin with his fingers to egg the kid on further, knowing the bully would charge him. The big, dumb ones always did.

Remmy's face reddened and with balled fist he barreled toward Peter. Peter whirled and pushed Remmy's head down to the floor. Remmy's soft, bulky frame shook as his arms slid out and he grabbed for Peter's calf. Breathing easy, a sneer on his face, Peter slid out of Remmy's reach to kick him on the shoulder. Remmy's upper body jerked back and he howled; his pale blue eyes filled with fury.

Peter reached down, and snatched Remmy up by his collar with ease, then slammed him against the frame of the door. His elbow was firmly placed under the stocky bully's chin, putting just enough pressure on his neck to strangle Remmy's cough. "I'm the head dog here! You pull that move with another kid I'll kick your teeth in without nothin' to hold me back. The cash I took from you…consider it payment for me not wiping your sorry face across the floor." Peter yanked back his fist, preparing to knock punk out cold.

"Peter! You stop that. Boy. I'm warning you." Pastor Finn's gruff command froze Peter's fist in place.

Peter's eyes narrowed at Remmy's cocky grin. Exhaling, Peter pulled his fist back further and landed a blinding blow to bully's nose, knocking him out cold on the floor. Punching the maggot out was worth whatever punishment he'd face.

Pastor Finn's firm hand grabbed hold of Peter's black curly mass of hair. "You've pushed me too far this time, boy! To the cellar, and clean it, that's where you're sleeping tonight." He whipped Peter around to face him. "Your allowance for the week is cut off. Now git!"

Peter stared at Pastor Finn's tall, bulky chest. Looking the man in the face could cause him to get even a worse punishment. A serious beat down that only Pastor Finn could deliver. Who'd ever think a retired cop would want to become a pastor? The offbeat man of God could read him like the back of his hand. Today though, Peter wasn't in the mood for it.

He had to roll out. Get some air. He'd been in this dump for what seemed like forever, and was never allowed off the grounds. Some strict stupid rule Pastor Finn drilled into them. Peter had been sneaking out for as long as he could remember. And he was doing it again today. Beating the new bully up proved to be a great diversion for some fresh air.

Peter nodded at the pastor and, with a spin, headed in the direction of the cellar.

"Stay down there until after breakfast. Maybe hunger will make you remember the rules here."

Peter slowed his stride. "Right, Pastor Finn. I get the point." With a grin sliding across his smooth chocolate face, he casually walked toward the cellar.

He let out a sigh, thankful no one would follow him into the depths of the rundown parish. Peter figured if the place wasn't on so much land to hide the raggedy dump, the state would've condemn it. He dragged his hands along the jagged cement block walls leading to the basement stairs. The old lunatic used the basement as storage for all kinds of explosives, weapons, and antiques. Peter belted out a chuckle as he remembered teasing Pastor Finn about being an undercover hoarder.

Navigating his way around the stacked boxes, bins, and racks, Peter stopped just past the six-foot statue of one of the saints. He swore the old dude stole it from some real church for his rundown chapel on the other side of the huge basement—the one in which he forced all the kids he collected, or that were sent to him, to sit for two-hour sermons.

For all the old man's craziness, he was like a father to Peter—maybe even worse than a father when it came to being over protective. Pastor Finn was like a savior, parent and jailer all wrapped up into one mean package. Pastor Finn's warnings didn't spook him though, so with a shrug, Peter stretched.

Taking a deep breath, Peter knelt on one knee, let out a growl and pulled on the metal ring of the thick wood door in the cement floor. The cellar was Peter's secret treasure, and a way to steal some freedom. His heart beat furiously in his chest at the anticipation. He pushed the heavy door back. It landed with a slam and bump. Deftly, he swung his legs over and climbed down the ladder.

The cellar was dark, damp, and quiet, just the way he liked it. A torn twin mattress was in the corner, *his corner*. He'd been the only kid to ever be sent to the cellar. Mainly, because he knew how to piss off Pastor Finn. Truth was, he got a kick out of seeing the man all keyed up. Did it on purpose really, as a test to see how far the preaching man would let it go before he'd pawn him off on someone else. But the old man never did, at least not for the time Peter had been at the orphanage.

Peter kicked the mattress, and lay down until it was safe to roll out. Counting the minutes silently for a while, Peter hummed to the beat of a rap song he'd heard. The club he hung out at on his escape excursions was an outlet for the one thing that seemed to help him escape from his sucked up life—dancing.

Minutes elapsed. It was lights out upstairs. Finally, it was time. He jumped off the bed, refreshed, and kicked it out of the way. The small, slightly rotted wooden door it covered was the key to his temporary taste of independence. He sat back and with two hard kicks, the door opened. Peter squeezed his thick, muscled frame through the space and shimmied out onto the flat cement pavement.

Staring briefly into the clear starry night, he took the jagged, broken steps two at a time. The warm summer breeze teased his loose curls while he cleared the stairs. He ran quietly the quarter mile to the garage.

"Damn!" he muttered. The light was on above the garage that held Pastor Finn's babies. He really wanted to take a motorcycle tonight, but there was no way he could get one without being seen.

He consumed a deep breath, and ran the two miles to the first city street that put him in the upper South West side of Washington, DC. As he broke through the wooded area just in front of the city block, he slowed his walk to a casual swagger. He slipped a hand in his jean pocket and grasped the forty dollars he'd lifted from Remmy. And chuckled. Remmy had beaten up and stolen money from at least four kids at the orphanage. Money they earned for doing chores that Pastor Finn doled out. Most of the kids were thankful for the bit of cash they could use for candy when Pastor Finn's assistant went out to the store.

The city was fairly tame that night. Although there were people walking past him to get to the various nightclubs that littered this part of the city, it wasn't half as crowded it usually was on a Saturday night.

He'd made it out three times this month—getting in trouble just came easy to him. The teen club that opened earlier that summer was his favorite spot. He liked to dance, but only planned to chill and listen to the music instead of mingling. Getting in through the back was always easy, and his only option since he didn't have an ID. Although, Pastor Finn had taught him to drive every kind of vehicle he owned, for some reason the old fart wouldn't let him get a license.

Whatever. It wouldn't stop him. The club was tucked between several tall office buildings. A small neon light proclaimed the name—JAM HOUSE. Kids mulled around waiting in line. Peter slowed his stride to watch for the security guard that went periodically to the back to make sure the alley stayed clear.

"Petah! Petah…" A soft but insistent call closed in from a distance. Rapid steps tapped behind him.

Peter groaned and shook his head when the tingling on the back of his neck started. *Not her…not tonight.* He should've never given her any money. For some reason, him being a sucker for a hungry, dirty, crazy fourteen-year-old girl gained him an unwanted pest. He'd been avoiding her for over two months. Unfortunately, this night she'd tracked him down. Probably wandered around, haunting the spots she knew he frequented.

He hunched his shoulders and quickened his steps, glancing back angrily at the club he wouldn't be able slip into now. The nutcase spoiled that for him. Peter stepped briskly, hoping the girl's short legs wouldn't allow her to keep up with him. She walked with a slight limp. The handicap was one of the things that kept her from following him in the past. She seemed to have an uncanny ability to find him on his nights out.

Peter glanced back, and was surprised at how well she kept up. Her greasy, long, brown hair swung around her shoulders like a cape.

"Petah! I see….you! You wait for me, Petah. My fri…end." Her hand waved at him.

He questioned how she'd survived on the streets for so long. "Kiss off. I don't have no food for you today. Leave me the hell alone and go home!"

Peter pivoted, looked across the street before he stepped off into a jog just as several cars were plowing down the street. He hoped the girl wouldn't cross the street to catch up to him. The cars would deter her. He jetted in front of the first car in the cluster of speeding vehicles rushing to beat the yellow light. Someone honked, and cursed at him while they swerved around him. Peter didn't look back. He wouldn't look back at the girl's pale, sad, and desperate face. Peter had problems, issues of his own. Taking on hers, was just not something he could do.

As his foot touched the curb, he heard a blood-curdling scream. "PETAH!!!!!!!!"

A sickening thump made him jerk around. His face crinkled with fury. The car threw the sparse girl's body upwards into the air, and sped off down the street. She bounced several times on the pavement. Peter ran and knelt beside her. Blood dribbled from her lip. And he felt like garbage, being the cause of her injury.

She smiled at him. "Petah. I…knew you would come." Her dazed eyes never left his face. "Take me home, Petah."

He shook his head and searched around. Surprised the street was now deserted. Tendrils of guilt filled his chest. *Another one…my damn fault. My fault.* He slid his arms under her frail form and picked her up. Her broken body was light in his strong hands. Peter expelled a cough, choking on his shame.

"Where's your home? Your family?" His eyes watered and he blinked to keep himself in check.

"No family. Dead," she sang. "All dead. But Petah…my friend." Her hand lifted and she caressed his cheek.

He searched around briefly and hurried across the street. It didn't take long to spot a deserted, boarded up house. There were many that littered this side street of the city.

"Please don't let there be no meth addicts in here," Peter mumbled, and kicked at the window on the side away from the alley.

The girl groaned and then released a broken giggle.

Peter shook his head. "Only somebody crazy would laugh right now."

"Crazy? My name's Hanna…n-not crazy." She snuggled her head against his chest.

Peter bent slightly and squeezed them through the broken window, careful not to cut Hanna or himself. He laid her on the dusty wood floor and took a quick glance around to make sure they were alone.

"Why did you do that? Follow me?" Peter demanded. He ran his hand down her twisted arm and dirty blouse to check for injures. His eyes closed when he realized that pieces of bones stuck out at odd angles from her arm. Not to mention, her leg was a tortured mess of bones twisted with meaty red pieces of her bleeding flesh.

"I had to… They told me," Hanna whispered. "They said to protect…" she coughed out blood, "protect…Petah."

He coughed back the stale taste of vomit and gulped at the red dribble down her chin. "Girl, you crazy! Your arm is broken, you're bleeding. Don't that shit hurt?" Tingles of shivers rose the hairs on his arms, and made him tighten his fist when he realized the girl could die. Right here, and all because of him.

"I don't feel it. They take it away," Hanna hummed. "All pain…" She gazed passed him and reached up her hand. "Can I g-go home now? So, beautiful you are…so bright. I go," she whispered, seemingly to no one.

"No! No! Don't die. God…you can't." Peter grabbed her chin and forced Hanna eyes to meet his. "Look! Hey, I'm sorry. Damn. I shouldn't have run from you. Why the hell did you keep following me? Why?" His hand shuddered as he ran it down his face.

Her eyes fluttered closed, then slowly opened. "To give you this…my gift." Hanna wiped at the blood on her face. She grasped Peter's hand with strength that belied her condition. And with her index finger drew a circle, and a squiggle of lines within it. "It is done." With a gurgle and a cough, blood spurted from her mouth and she went still.

Chapter 2

While the darkness battled with the fog, Gavin relaxed back on the soft cushion of the limo. His pale, large, hand pinched the skin of his arm through his charcoal suit, a reflex that had always soothed him. He shuttered his eyes closed with anticipation.

"Sir, are you sure this is the way?" the driver asked, a sliver of fear laced in his voice.

The gentleman snorted, opening his eyes. Gavin's impatience with the meek minds of mere serviceable men was barely contained. "Keep the course."

"Yesss, sir."

So close he could *taste* it. His teeth ground together, and an insidious grin slipped for a brief moment across his face. He wouldn't falter; destroying all possible means of failure was the only way.

Tonight he would get a name. The name of the one that held the key to destroying his plans. A destiny Gavin had worked his life to achieve. Unfortunately, the answers he sought came at a heavy price. Not a price he was unwilling to pay, but a price nonetheless. For this answer, he'd have to get a strong one, one of the strongest links possible.

The road twisted around bend after bend. Several times, his driver cursed the fog of the night. Howling from the surrounding wolves didn't relent. The feral sounds made his driver jumpy, but gave Gavin peace. Fear wasn't something he'd ever experienced, but was something he'd secretly enjoyed watching in others.

His jaw grated at the latest hiccup in his plans, but he would resolve that tonight. This gift would please the one he sought to answer his question. She would do as a fitting price. The others were too meager an offering in his attempts to thwart the impending disaster of his life's work.

"Sir, are you sure it's up ahead just a m-mile?" the driver stammered.

He didn't bother answering, but continued to stare out the window for signs pointing to the house that had been there since his birth.

After another minute, the wooden sign the driver had been searching for appeared to glow in front of the headlights, and the murky fog floated across it as if in a final warning. He smirked and relaxed in his seat. "Uhum, this is it."

The limo stopped and the driver scrambled to open his door.

The man waited and smoothly stepped out of the vehicle and passed the driver. "Wait here until I return. It may be a while."

The driver mis-stepped and stood in Gavin's path."Sorry, sir. I forgot my place." The driver gulped then bowed his head. "I will wait as requested."

Gavin pivoted away and walked to the one house, the one person he knew would give him the answers he sought. The woman had lived on the outskirts of his family's estate for decades. The hard packed walkway lead up to the house. Jagged rocks pointed from the cottage style home; the wooden door with a window glowing of gold beaconed. He knocked.

Within seconds the door opened and a short, round, gray-haired lady peered up at him. Her expression wary, she stood aside and let him in. "Sir, it's been a while. What can I do for you at this late hour?"

Gavin stood in front of her, his tall stature looming over hers as his arms crossed casually in front of him. "A name. And quickly, my driver is waiting."

She smacked her tongue, wagging her forefinger. "You know it doesn't ever go that easy. These things are unpredictable. Calling the spirits always costs something."

His eyebrow bent upward. "Here's the money." He reached in his pocket, his expression bland, as he clutched his money clip. Several hundred-dollar bills were pulled from a money clip and tossed on the table. Gavin knew she wouldn't be aware of the origin of the spirit she called. It was known to hide itself into a captured benevolent host prior to collecting its price.

"Oh, this is more than enough." A kindly grin broke out on her face. She snatched the cash from a nearby table and stuffed it in her bra. "Give me a moment to ready things and I'll get you that name."

Gavin watched her move around the room, preparing the table for her summoning of the spirits. Detached, he stood while she sat at the table between them and slipped into her trance.

She hummed while she meditated for a moment. Within minutes, her body started to shake, her eyes rolled back in her head, and a bit of foam seeped between her lips. She moaned.

He knew from experience he'd only have a short time to get his answer before the greedy one would consume the spirit in which it hid and demand the price. "The name of the one who can stop me, the one I should remove from the equation."

She hissed, and her white pupils turned on him. "Peter. Peter Saints."

Her body jerked from side to side in an attempt to fight her way free of an invisible force, but it was too late, the price would be paid. For one moment, shock and fear laced her expression before she slumped to the floor, permanently silenced.

Gavin slipped his hands into his pocket, pulling out rubber gloves and a knife that he calmly unfolded. For a brief moment he stared in space while in thought.

"Peter. Peter Saints," the name left a sour taste on Gavin's tongue.

Shrugging off his jacket, he grinned. Messes, he hated to leave messes. And tonight, like all the other nights, he'd clean it up.

Chapter 3

Peter's hand burned. "No!" What the heck was he supposed to do now? He crouched beside Hanna. Too guilty to leave her there like that, he grumbled. Lifting his hand, he stared at the symbol she'd drawn with the blood from her face. "It is done," she'd said. His jumbled thoughts replayed Hanna's last words over and over. The symbol throbbed on the palm of his hand, so he rubbed at it. The blood wouldn't wipe off, it just blazed even hotter the more he touched it.

"What did you do, crazy girl? What did you do?" Peter couldn't stand her staring so Peter used his thumbs to close Hanna's eyelids. Then he rubbed the palm of his burning hand on his pants. Tears welled up in the corners of his eyes and he quickly wiped them away with his fist. The guilt bubbled up inside him like a burning river of lava. He dropped his chin.

"I won't leave you, Hanna." His voice cracked. "Not until I have to. Pastor Finn will know what to do. He'll pray over you." Peter yelled until his last breath was spent. Breathing heavily, he fought to regain control. Peter mumbled quietly, "He'll know what to do."

Peter sat there and watched her. His knees bent. He rocked back and forth. *Why does everyone got to die around me? What did I ever do to have to deal with this crap again?* Flashbacks of the car accident that killed his father badgered his thoughts. His mother's brutal death trying to save him plagued him like a smack in his face. She'd saved him that day…but for what? She ended up dying facedown in the dirt and murdered by some thugs, after she told him to run to the church nearby. He bit his lip. Sick of himself. He was sick and tired of feeling this ache in his chest, the guilt, and loneliness. All of this bad luck he probably deserved for being a major screw-up. Peter didn't need another reminder that he was a screwed up guy with a curse for causing the death of anyone stupid enough to care about him.

He rocked his body back and forth there until the stirring of daylight lit the cracks in the abandoned house.

"Hanna, I'm sorry. So damn sorry. Pastor Finn will help us. He'll bury you, give you a prayer—you know, something to help you. Help you…oh, I don't know how. He can't bring you back to life." Peter spun around and punched the wall. His fist pounded the cracked drywall over and over again.

He gulped, lowered his fist and laid his head against the wall. Taking a deep breath, Peter forced himself to look at Hanna's quiet body once again. With a nod, affirming his need for help, he walked through the broken window. The alley was still deserted. Pulling from all the strength he had left within him, he ran home.

When his foot landed on the plush grass of the parish, he searched frantically for any sign of Pastor Finn. He headed to the garage; the place Pastor Finn usually was first thing in the morning. Peter's arms pumped, his chest heaved, and his legs ached, but he wouldn't stop until he found him. The burning mark on his hand wouldn't let him forget, wouldn't let him relent until he got help for Hanna, or for himself.

The two-level, rundown garage's door was slightly ajar. Peter glided to a stop on the dew-covered grass to bang on the door. Moments, which seemed like forever, passed while he knocked fervently before he gave up and yanked it open.

"Pastor Finn! Pastor Finn!" Peter's heart pounded in his chest and his feet took the stairs two at a time.

The pounding of the pastor's heavy steps came from up above. "Boy! Peter? What are you doing here? How'd you get out? It's not time to get out of the cellar!" Pastor Finn's booming voiced yelled down the steps.

Peter collided with him and the large man held onto the railing to steady himself. Pastor Finn grabbed hold of Peter's shirt. Then he studied him quietly for a moment before his voice deepened. "Where have you been, Peter? Where?" Fear and concern filled the older man's eyes.

Peter took a moment to catch his breath. "I left. I left the grounds. But something's bad has happened. Sh-she…Hanna died!" He coughed and his eyes watered. "Because of me! My damn fault. It was my fault. You gotta help her! I always screw shit up. Always. Please…"

Pastor Finn put his hands on Peter's shoulders and shook him. "Why'd you leave? I told you never to leave here. You'll put us all in danger. Yourself in danger. I didn't save your butt for you to screw this up, boy." He yanked Peter by the shirt and down the stairs. Then dragged him, practically running, all the way to the cellar stairs where he pointed at the small door where Peter had escaped. "Sixteen years old and you think you are man enough to make it out there?" he grumbled. "This is where you got out?" He sighed. "You don't understand."

"It's my fault! Did you hear me? I killed someone! You gotta help her." Peter jerked out of his grasp and grabbed Pastor Finn's shirt, facing off with him. For once in a long while, he stared down the man eye to eye. He straightened up to his full height. The older man's gray crew cut and piercing blue eyes were filled with fear. Peter's hand loosened in shock that it was the first time he remembered that Pastor Finn looked afraid.

"I can't help the dead." He pushed Peter's hands away from him. "But I have to help you. Come with me."

Peter watched him, confused. His teeth clenched at Pastor Finn's betrayal. "I thought you were different. I have to go back. Bury her, like she deserves." Peter stumbled backwards.

Pastor Finn's hand burst forward and grabbed Peter's shirt at his shoulder. Tightening his fist, he dragged Peter around the side of the building and through the door to the basement. Peter struggled in vain as Pastor Finn's firm grip didn't relent, but tugged Peter through the basement past several tall stacks of boxes.

"You have to get out of here. Leave before they find out you are still alive," Pastor Finn demanded.

Peter shook his head in disbelief of the man's off-beat ranting. "Who? Who would care if I am dead or alive? I don't have a family, remember? They died, they all died! Why the hell I didn't die with them I'll never know." He hit downward, breaking Pastor Finn's hold on him. "Seems to me all the hell I'm good for is causing death."

Dark blue eyes assessed him, and then Pastor Finn twisted to rummage through a box in front of him. "Your mother saved you. We'd been in contact with your father and knew we had to get you to safety. It was better they thought you were dead. Easier to hide you that way."

"What the hell are you talking about?" Peter frowned. His hand started to itch and burn even hotter than before. "Ugh! God, this hurts."

Pastor Finn stopped his rummaging through the box and turned around handing Peter a bag. "What hurts? You got hurt?"

Peter lifted his hand and Pastor Finn held it. Then made a sign of the cross on his face. "This is it. The sign. It is time."

Confused, Peter's eyebrow lifted. "What time? Tell me what is going on? What is it?"

Pastor Finn pushed a black bag into his hand. "Take this. It's got money, some fake IDs, keys to the motorcycle and a gun." He sighed. "Also, directions to a safe place. Don't stop till you get there. You can only stay the night on holy ground if you don't want them to find you. But I can't promise that even with that…you'll be safe now."

"Who are you talking about? What. The. Hell is wrong with you? With everyone. Even Hanna was talking crazed!" Peter ripped a hand through his tight curls, refusing to take the bag.

"Truth is son, I don't know who's after you. All I know is that the *Decretum Venia* has been protecting you and others since your birth. They've been hiding you, only the higher levels of the order know why. You were given to me by my elder when your mother contacted them at your father's death. The *Decretum Venia* was trying to get you to me when on of your protectors was attacked. They met up with a contact at a church near where your mother was. Then you were transported here once it was safe." Pastor Finn jabbed the bag at Peter once more.

Grudgingly, Peter took the sack. "I'll do this if you bury Hanna for me. She didn't have a family." He cleared his throat. "She was homeless; I gave her some money when I snuck out a couple of months ago. After that, she found me, and I ditched her. Last night though, I tried to dodge her by running across the street and she got hit when she followed me." He bit his bottom lip, a frown marring his face. "It was my fault. I-I didn't mean to do it."

Pastor Finn pulled Peter to him in a hug and patted his back. "Son, it wasn't your fault. It was an accident. But I'll do it for you."

"Why are you telling me this now?"

"I had no reason to before. Write down where the girl is and I'll take care of it."

Peter pulled away and nodded. "Thank you. I knew…I knew I could trust you." He took a pen and scribbled down the house number where Hanna's body rested.

"There's a GPS in there too," the pastor said. "But don't do cell phones. If you have to, only if you absolutely have to, get a quick phone or use someone else's. Put the license plate that's in that bag on the motorcycle too. Never leave it on the vehicle you are driving—never. You hear? Now go! Go now!" He pushed at Peter's chest.

Peter hugged the Pastor to his chest once again. He slid the handles of the sack over his shoulders and ran to the garage.

Chapter 4

Riding the motorcycle didn't give Peter the feeling of peace or freedom that it usually did. It seemed the farther he rode, the more his chest hurt. Pastor Finn was the only father he'd known, at least since he was nine. His birth father was like a ghost. A memory he kept hidden deep within the recesses of his mind, because it was too painful to think about.

His teeth worried his bottom lip. The warm breeze on his hands soothed him a bit. He rode through the city and glanced about at the tall concrete buildings, people rushing down the streets on their way home from work as he weaved in and out of traffic. The honking horns, yelling, and construction sounds teased his ears through his helmet. Unfortunately, the elation he usually felt escaped him and at that moment the only thing he wanted was to be in his old bedroom in the attic of the orphanage.

DC was alight with the humidity and beating sun, but the tall buildings with a multitude of windows cast a shady spot here and there. He whizzed in and out of the jammed packed cars chasing the cooler areas of shade. In a hurry to get to the location Pastor Finn told him to run to before dark, he cut off a cab.

"Watch where ya goin', idiot!" The driver flipped him off.

Peter glanced back but sped past the car to get on the highway. The highway leading outside of DC and into Virginia was light of traffic, for that he was relieved. So many questions plagued his mind.

"What the hell was Pastor Finn talking about?" He twisted his neck to relieve the tension and the achiness. "My father contacted some people? The name—it sounded Latin, *Decretum Venia*? Shoulda paid more attention during class," he mumbled.

He kept driving over the bridge and onto highway Route 95 to some-place he didn't even know existed, since over half of his life was spent in the orphanage as a pseudo-prisoner of Pastor Finn. It wasn't until three years ago he'd even left the grounds. Now that he finally got to leave, he didn't want to. But if his history of causing the death of anyone he got involved with was consistent, he had a sinking feeling that if he would've stayed there any longer, everyone in there would've died. Bad luck—that was him. He didn't know what it was about him, but he was either cursed or damned stupid to think he could live a normal life.

"Screw it. It is what it is. My sucked-up life."

After two hours of driving he took the exit to some town called Spot-sylvania. He drove down the two-lane road and veered off on a side street that led to a dirt road. The dirt path ended at a cemetery. He rode to the back of the graveyard to a small rundown church.

"You kiddin', right?" He leaned, trying to balance the bike. The sky above the church looked dusty red, giving the vibe that the place wasn't quite as it seemed. "Great, a summer storm." He revved the cycle and drove it onto the porch of the one level church. Bits of white peeling paint were scattered on the porch. The door hung slightly off the hinges. Just as he got the motorcycle on the porch, the rain poured down and rumbles of thunder teased the darkening skies.

Peter snorted. "This place safe? Why did I listen to the man. Knew his ass was insane," he grumbled.

He got off the cycle and went to the door. Opening the beat up but heavy entrance, he nudged it until it stuck on the wilted floor. Then returned to his motorcycle and pushed it inside. Steadying his ride, he searched around and realized that the place was actually clean. It ap-peared like someone took care of it from time to time.

Peter went to the door and fiddled with it before he lifted it and pushed it into place. The latch caught and he locked it.

"Now what?" He stretched as fatigue hit him. "Sleep, but damn, I'm hungry." Peter bought his fist up and bit it.

His head whipped around at the sound of whining. "Who's there?" After a few moments a small dog with shaggy fur cautiously made his way toward him.

"If you're lookin' for food, you got the wrong guy. Unless you know where the food is." Peter plopped onto the floor and reached out for the mutt to sniff his hand. The dog lay next to him. He yawned, then took off his pack to sit back.

Absently, he petted the dog. With each stroke it seemed the knot in his stomach loosened. The loneliness that covered him dissipated and his eyes slowly shut as exhaustion enveloped him.

***

Peter never dreamed. Just, didn't allow himself to after the numerous nightmares he'd had when he first got to the orphanage. But now, he seemed to be trapped within a nightmare determined to remind him of those he lost.

The scent of something familiar surrounded him. Peter inhaled deeper, never getting enough of the smell of *her*. His mother, like it was yesterday. She'd hold him tightly to her chest, enveloping Peter in strawberries from the lotion she favored.

His body fought the visions, his arm waved side to side. The floor hit against his shoulder, and Peter jerked up and down, refusing to accept the reality of his dream. Then he *heard* her. There, he'd felt it—her presence next to him in the open room of the abandoned church.

"Peter! Peter. I've missed you. For so long, I've missed you," his mother's voice called to him. He could never forget the lilting tone in which she often spoke. Her Island accent was almost poetic, soothing even.

A caress went down his face and Peter jumped. "No…no. Go away. Dream, dammit, no." His eyes opened, unseeing of the room around him, caught in the daze of his dream. The dog whined nearby. Peter felt the warmth of the mutt's body on the side of his leg, but it didn't comfort him as it had earlier.

His mother's transparent tan image wouldn't relent. Long, black wavy hair fluttered, like a pool of dark water. Her body was cloaked in the peach colored dress she'd worn the night she was killed. Her face, her body, his *mother*, floated to him in the dark. Everywhere he turned she was there. Whispering of his name grew stronger and closed on him. The nearer she came, the more he fought to erase her image which blurred then cleared before coming close enough to touch him.

"Peter." Another caress. No hand, just a touch—or breath of something. Someone.

A hand on his back. "Peter."

"Peter!"

His skin crawled. Fear engulfed him. Peter's heart drummed in his chest, and his eyes jerked from side to side trying to avoid her image. "I'm sorry. Just go away. I didn't mean to kill her…Hanna. The accident. Dad's accident. Dead, everyone dead."

"No accident, Peter. It is time. Hanna was deceived, but you will meet your destiny."

He scrambled back on his hands and feet. The dog's warmth escaped him. Its faint barking gave him something in reality to hold onto. "I'm dreaming…dreaming!"

"No, you're not." She stood transparent in front of him. "Look at me. I can't stay long. I miss you. I so miss you."

"This can't be real." His fingers tensed on the floor.

"Oh, Pete, it is."

He swallowed when she used her pet name for him. His legs bent and he took several slow, calming breaths. Peter raised his hand in defense. "Okay. I believe you. God, I miss you too." His voice cracked.

"Pete, it's started. We'd fought for years to keep you hidden. But now, your name has been called." She bent forward to kiss his cheek.

It felt like a whisper of a cool breeze on his fevered skin. "I don't understand. Nothing is making sense. What—"

Her hand lifted to quiet him. "The time is here. You are in serious danger. Now like never before."

"What danger?" he croaked.

She stepped back from him. "Let it be revealed. Give him the sight." A glistening tear dropped from her eyes. "Pete…seek the signs expelled from your heart and you will know what to do," she whispered. Her hand reached out to him and she disappeared.

Peter surged forward. "No!" His chest heaved as his fisted hands fell heavily on the wood floor.

The burning on his hand intensified. "Owwwwww!" He lifted his hand. It was glowing red.

Recognition, then fear etched his features. "No, this can't be real." He could read the symbol Hanna had drawn on his hand as if it was a language he'd known all his life. "Emunah. What does it mean? A name?" He released the breath he'd been holding. *Emunah.* "Hanna's name? Naw. Then whose?"

Chapter 5

No way Peter could go back to sleep now. The floor groaned when he stood and then stretched. His skin tingled; his heart still raced as he closed his eyes, willing himself to pull it together. Gradually, calmness enveloped him and he forced every muscle in his body to relax like Pastor Finn taught him in his early days at the orphanage. This day summed up the troubled riddle that was his life and he refused to wallow in it. His hand seemed to throb in argument, but he tightened his fist in response.

The cracked walls, and peeled paint made the place seem well used. Peter felt the dog stare back at him from across the room. "Damn, what a muffed up day. If I'd known stealing money from Remmy would end me up in this bowl of cowshit, I woulda let him get away with beating up those kids."

The dog slowly made his way over to where Peter stood. It looked up at him while sniffing at his hand. "You know where there's some food, boy?"

Its tail hit Peter's leg as it passed by to prance over to the door on the opposite side of the room. Peter followed, hoping the mutt understood English. The dog looked healthy, like it was eating. If this was its home, Peter hoped it would know where he could get something to eat.

His stomach growled while he rubbed it. "I'm hungry enough to eat dog food." Peter moved the dog out of the way to push open the door. At least the hunger kept his mind off all the insane crap that had happened that day. One thing was sure, he may have been bored at the orphanage most of the time, but at least he had a place to call home. Now, not only did he have Father's memory haunting him but his mother's ghost and another one—Hanna. The poor girl he caused to die loomed heavy in his thoughts with remorse that preoccupied him also.

The small kitchen was only large enough for a stove, short refrigerator and small counter. Peter started to feel a bit like the walls were closing in on him.

"Humph." Peter's chin jutted out at the dog. "You must live here." Peter's foot nudged a dog food dish on the side of the refrigerator and willed his stomach to stop rumbling.

His hand tightened on the cold handle of the refrigerator, saying a silent prayer that there was actually edible food in there. Peter opened the door. He laughed loudly in relief of finally getting a meal, even though it wasn't much in the refrigerator.

Frowning at the rotted fruit and a half-eaten sandwich covered in mold, his eyes traveled the shelves. "Bam! Paydirt!" He reached inside and snatched several of the hotdogs still in the plastic wrapper. There was a jug of water, which he grabbed while breaking a hotdog in half. He stuffed the cold greasy meat in his mouth and lifted the jug to his lips for several greedy gulps.

"Damn, that's good." He looked down at the dog. "Here. Gotta hook you up with some food, too."

The dog gently took the meat from his hand and barked. Peter ruffled its shaggy head. It licked his hand and walked to the backside of the refrigerator. Lifting its front paw, the dog scratched at the wall.

"What's behind the refrigerator, boy?" He chuckled. "I gotta give you a name." Peter peered between the wall and the fridge. Then he wedged his foot in the middle of them before he pushed the refrigerator forward.

The dog barked and scratched the wall.

"What's this? A hidden door?" Peter tugged at his chin. "Just my luck if there's another dead body in there." He squinted at the dog. "But you ain't led me wrong yet, boy. Can't be mad at a dog that shows me where the food is." Running his hand down the door that was flush with the wall, his finger slid against a latch sunk into the surface. He raised it.

Click. The musty smell of mildew and water filled his nostrils. Taking a deep breath, he stepped forward. The dog hung back. Peter's hand beckoned him. But the dog laid near in the crack in the door.

"Oh, I see, you just gonna leave me hanging. Fine." He walked further down the hallway.

The place had dim lights tucked in the bowed ceiling that brightened as he walked. His footsteps echoed around him, but he was comforted by the dog's barking behind him.

"Scared mutt won't follow," he whispered, even though he couldn't deny the rising hairs on his neck. The walls were made of smooth cement block. He decided to walk faster since the hallway seemed to go on forever. There was nothing on the walls except a few cracks here and there.

Finally, he came to the end and turned at the corner that led to an alcove. There was nothing on the floor, no dust, trash, nothing. The walls in the alcove had a map of the world carved in it, which spanned from the top of the ceiling to the floor. Ghostly shapes and symbols similar to the one on his hand were scattered in several locations in front of the wall, hovering in front of the map.

"Either this place is haunted or something weird as shit is going on here." Peter stepped back from the wall. The symbols stood out, shifted and changed. Clear as print, he read each, which said the same thing—the word, *sanctuary.*

"Sanctuary? A safe place. For what?"

Taking a deep breath, his eyebrows wrinkled, but he couldn't stop himself from stepping closer. His finger traced the map to his current location.

"My God? That's…here. I'm at a…sanctuary?" His finger passed through the smoky symbol that hovered over the map, marking the rundown church in which he stood.

His heartbeat kicked up a notch, and his finger made its way to the other sanctuary closest to his location.

"Another one. And another." He stood there following each location until he committed them to memory. "Pastor Finn's place—a sanctuary?" The one thing going for him was his photographic memory which saved him during Pastor Finn's long history lessons and was being put to use for once.

After his finger traced the last and final location, the ghostly symbols disappeared as if blown by a hidden gust of wind. He stumbled back, a creepy bubble of apprehension sitting in his stomach. "I gotta get out of here. Now."

Peter stepped back, then pivoted and jogged out of the hallway. The desire to see what the other sanctuaries were like burned in the back of his head. The mystery that was now his life didn't seem to want to let up. Answers to what really happened to his parents ate away at his thoughts, flashin in the dark peace he'd created for himself over the years.

Seeing the dog waiting up above was a calming beacon and he couldn't help the smile that slipped on his face. "Hey boy! You waited for me. Damn, it's nice to have a real friend." He rubbed the dog vigorously before hugging the mutt around the neck.

Peter pushed the door and the refrigerator back into place with little effort. Tons of nights spent being punished by Pastor Finn kept him in exceptional shape. Push-ups, pull-ups, weight lifting, and mile runs around the compound were part of his daily payment for his purposeful habit of ticking off the stuffed-up old man. Truth was, when the pastor kicked his ass, he'd let him, simply out of respect for all the old fart had done for him. The nut actually thought he was *training* him for some unforeseen adversary. How the guy had thought he'd ever meet up with one while trapped in that rundown orphanage Peter would never know.

A bittersweet grin crossed his face as he thought of the man who'd been his only parent for the past years. He grabbed the remaining hotdogs from the fridge and stuffed them in his mouth as he leaned against it.

With a shrug, he put the thoughts aside and headed to his motorcycle. The only thing the past memories brought him was a hole in his chest and a desire to run back to the only home he'd ever known. Now though, he knew without a doubt, he could never go back. Never put them in danger.

Peter knew what he had to do now. More than he'd ever been sure of anything in his life. He had to figure out what was in these sanctuaries and what did Pastor Finn, his dead mother, and the dead slightly insane girl Hanna want to warn him about.

A quick look out of the stained window showed clear skies. He went to the front door, and lifted the latch, realizing as he looked out into the daylight that it was already noon. The dog whined and, with a twist, Peter bent in time to give the dog one final rub. "Sorry dude, but this is where we say goodbye. Seems it's something I always gotta do. But you know what? It doesn't get any easier. At least not for me, anyway."

Peter scanned the room as if making sure no one was around to hear him. "But that's between me and you. Since you look like the kinda friend I can count on."

Chapter 6

Peter had been driving for hours. The day turned to night and he still couldn't figure out what the hell he was doing. Traffic on the highway was sparse since the weekend hadn't hit. He kept his speed down to avoid cops who probably scoped out the highways.

The breeze got warmer and warmer with each mile he traveled further south. He couldn't help but have zone-out moments as he watched all the shadows of bushes on each side of the highway. Peter couldn't remember a time when he'd been out of the city except when he went with his parents. They'd lived in some nice suburb area just outside of DC and only went to the city for the museums and sightseeing. Before that life ended, he remembered being happy. He remembered having friends, playing outside, taking the feeling of innocence he had then totally for granted. He didn't know what hit him the fateful day everything had changed. From what he recalled, their car went over some bridge and into the water. His mother had pulled him as she swam from the wreckage. He'd looked back at the car, watching it sink and tried to fight against her to get to his father. Peter remembered his father's dead eyes and gashed face bobbing in the filled car.

Another truck barreled by with a honk, and he felt the vibrations on the handlebar. He'd veered into its lane while he daydreamed.

"Time I get off. Ain't no way I'm gonna make it there in just one day." He squeezed his hands tighter on the handlebars to stave off the burn of the brand. Then pulled over and onto a busy exit, blinking to stay awake.

Peter weaved through the cars in front of him and the lights in the southern city flickered by. He didn't know where he was going, but he hoped wherever it was he'd find someplace to sleep. His eyes drooped a bit from fatigue just as a car was changing lanes.

The honk of the car jerked him awake. "Ugh!" Peter fought to keep control of the steering wheel but lost the battle and veered off the two-lane street, smack into a wood electrical pole. Dizzy, he blinked his eyes when a pop sounded. Then a shock of electrical lights rained in the sky from the impact. Another crackle sounded before a small fire on one of the wires fizzled down to a crackle.

His body was ablaze with adrenaline and he flexed his shoulders before dislodging the motorcycle from his legs. Letting out a deep breath, a growl bubbled up in his chest and he kicked the crushed motorcycle over and over again. "Dammit! Stupid, damn stupid."

Peter pulled the license plate off and stuffed it in his sack on his back. He stood there staring at the demolished motorcycle and pushed the palms of his hands on his eyes. *What now? Screw! I can't get there on foot.* His arms dropped and his fist clenched while he pondered what to do.

A lady walked past him on the street. Several cars honked as they drove by. He tightened the strap on his back sack just as the lady turned around.

Hesitantly, she approached with a rueful smile on her face. "You want me to call somebody for you? The cops? A tow truck?" She studied him and the edges of her mouth pushed up further, trying to appear helpful.

Peter regarded her faintly wrinkled hair, restaurant uniform and forced smile. At that moment he really just wanted to tell her to get lost. But she didn't look like she'd leave without some type of explanation. So he figured he'd give her one. "I'm good. I'll call my dad to pick me up." He forced a smile on his face. "Thanks, though."

Her brow furrowed. "You sure you're okay? You took a hard hit. I'm amazed you're able to walk away." She stared pointedly at his forehead.

Peter's forced smile fell. He wiped off a slight dribble of blood that slid down his eyebrow. "Really. If you were so concerned why'd you walk past me until now?" he smirked.

She stammered. "I…uh, you know, getting off work late, I just um…spaced out."

His chin dipped. "Yeah, I get that. Thanks though, for stopping to help. I'll be fine." His jaw locked because he was so ticked off right now that he really just wanted to tell her to stuff her nosey face where the sun don't shine. But he held his ground to let her assess him once more. He cut an angry eye at the dead motorcycle and grumbled to himself.

"Alright then." She took a step back. "Take care. Uh, if you do need help there's a restaurant about two blocks up that will let you use the phone. You can get something to eat there until your father comes. But you may want to get off the street." She looked about briefly before her concerned eyes fell on him again. "This area's known to have gangs and um, well…you don't quite look like you are from around here." With one final sweep of her eyes, she took off down the street.

Peter quirked his mouth up and decided maybe grabbing a bite to eat wasn't a bad idea. It would give him time to figure out where he could sleep. Getting a hotel was totally out of the question considering he was sixteen, a minor, with no driver's license, or ID. Much less, he needed to lay low until he got to the next sanctuary.

He sauntered down the street at a comfortable pace, on guard in case someone else approached him. Luckily though, the few people he encountered kept their heads hung low and their subtle gazes to themselves. He saw several teenagers hanging around, but none appeared like they were interested in him or where he was going.

His eyes were drawn to the buildings that bordered the narrow side-walk. It had a homey but country appeal, the kind that made him wish he were going home instead of finding some dump to crash in. There was a lot more space between the mismatched buildings than he'd seen in the city and he admired them in between his intent observation of any hidden danger around him. They were about four levels tall, not half the size of the buildings in DC. Reminded him of Old Town Alexandria where his dad took him from time to time to visit a family friend. The buildings were a mixture of homes, storefronts which sold junk that they called antiques, and a general store.

Peter just wanted to sleep, but his stomach reminded him that he hadn't eaten since he'd stopped for gas and a burrito at the convenience store. He got to the end of the corner and waited for the light to change. The streetlight ahead shined brightly on the sign of the diner the lady mentioned. He jogged across the street and to the place called Sally's Diner that was a quarter way down just under the street lamp.

The chime of the door surprised him when he entered, causing his eyes to travel up. He waited and fidgeted with the strap of his pack. An older guy with glasses put down a mop before walking over to him. Peter whispered a silent thanks that the place was pretty much deserted, except for some grungy kid sitting alone in the corner nursing a soda.

"Hello son. Can I help you?" The older man picked up a menu from the counter that wrapped around in an ugly green haze.

Behind the counter, a middle aged, sour-faced woman silently dared him to order from the grill. The gentle faced man stood patiently waiting for Peter to respond. "Do you do steak 'n cheese subs and root beer floats here?"

The man nodded. "We sure do. Come with me and I'll get you a seat."

Peter followed the man to the booth facing the only customer. The other kid hadn't bothered to look up from his drink. The kid's head bobbed as he listened to his iPod and tapped a finger on the white table-top.

"This is good. Can you put in my order? I gotta go to the bathroom." Peter searched for a sign to the men's room.

"Sure thing." The man pointed to the edge of the pea-green counter that ended at the dingy gray wallpaper and tan paneled wall. "It's just around the corner."

Peter stepped around him, not sparing the old man a glance. Once in, he was thankful the place was clean. He did a quick wash of his face. Pulling off his sack, he took some bills out and stuffed them in his pocket. Then he headed back to his seat.

He hated being caught unaware, and since he didn't know this town, he wouldn't loosen his guard. Watchful of the other customer, he sat in his dark green vinyl booth facing the door and the kid. The smell of cheese and steak filled the air. His mouth started to water. He glanced over at the cook who'd eyed him and Peter could've sworn she was cursing him out under her breath. For a split second, he felt someone watching. And it wasn't the old man. Slowly, he cut his eyes at the boy across from him.

Peter took his time studying the kid. The boy looked to be about four-teen. No facial hair, dirty face on pale skin, black eyebrows and a scarf mid-forehead covered by a knitted cap. Peter quirked an eyebrow, and wondered if the urchin stunk. The kid must be a drug-head because there was no way Peter could see why anyone would wear a long sleeved shirt and cover their head in the summer.

The old man came up beside him to deliver a large root beer with a scoop of vanilla ice cream. It was dribbled with chocolate whipped cream and topped off with a cherry. Peter slid to the side to accommodate it.

Peter couldn't help the smile that broke wide on his face. He'd never had anything that looked so good. Quite frankly, Pastor Finn's cooking sucked, and they never had sweets, soda, or ice cream at the orphanage, since Pastor Finn thought it made the kids unmanageable.

"Ah." The old guy grinned. "I knew I could get a smile out of you." He pointed at the glass. "This is my specialty."

"Thanks for hookin' it up." Peter couldn't help but lick his lips while the guy laid a napkin and spoon beside him. He took a sip, his eyes slanted to see the kid staring at him.

A frown marred the boy's face briefly before he turned away.

Peter reached out a hand to stop the waiter. Then he tilted his head in the direction of the kid. "Hey, hook that kid up with one too. It's on me."

The boy's chin jutted up, green eyes narrowed, and then he jerked his slim form covered in baggy pants with an oversized T-shirt out of the booth. Stunned for a moment, the kid remembered he had to pay his tab, and reached into his pocket to throw several bills on the table. Eyes trained on the door, the kid walked out, kicking the door closed as the bell rang after him.

"Humph." Peter sat back and rested his elbow on the back of the seat.

The older guy shrugged. "Don't know that one. The kid's been in here from time to time in the last two weeks." The old man shook his head. "All he orders is a soda and never says a word. Writes it on a piece of paper and pushes it to the server." The man sighed. "Strange that one. I'll get the rest of your order."

Peter gestured at the line of shirts and shorts depicting beach scenes hanging on the wall. "You sellin' those here?"

The guy beamed. "Oh, yes. My daughter makes them. You know, for bike week. Lots of bikers ride through here all the time."

"Add two pair of shorts and three shirts to my bill, all in black." Peter went back to sipping his drink.

The man eyed him for a moment. "You know, your bill is going to be around—"

"I'm good for it. Just add it up." Anger slinked up into Peter's chest. How dare the guy think because he was a teenager that he would stiff him on the bill?

Chapter 7

It was late. Peter's stomach was more satisfied than he ever remembered it being. He left the diner and was scoping around for a place to sleep, lay low, and stay hidden until he figured out how the hell to get to the next sanctuary.

The streets were pretty quiet. A few people came out of a nearby bar, but Peter kept going. He walked the streets for over a half a hour, passing a cluster of plush trees and bushes until he came upon a bridge. The area appeared safe enough, but he gave it one quick once-over to make sure the place was deserted. The hard packed sand under the arch was dry. Along the sides of the bridge was thick grass. There were little lights along the bridge, but Peter was sure no one would see him under the overpass.

With one last search around, he shimmied down the hill. "I'll sleep for a while, but damn…I don't want to have to jack a car to get out of here. But I don't have no choice," he mumbled.

On his right side was a thick patch of soft grass. "Guess, that'll be softer than the floor I slept on last night."

His palm still burned. Peter wiggled his fingers to stave off the throbbing ache. He wanted to scratch it, but every time he did it swelled so he willed himself to leave it alone. Leaning back on the cement wall that held up part of the bridge, he took his sack off. Peter reached in the pack to pull out two shirts and roll them into a pillow. His neck ached so he stretched once before tucking the makeshift pillow under his head.

Sleep. Sleep. No dreaming. The nightmare from the night before taunted him for a few minutes. At last, he felt at peace and slipped into a semi-calm sleep.

After an hour or so of wrestling with dreams, he forced himself to keep his eyes closed. *Think,* he had to think. Where could he get a car in this small dump of a town? Peter's thoughts came to an abrupt halt at a sound—vague, like a foot in the grass. His eyes cracked opened. Peter swallowed, gritting his teeth as the kid from Sally's Diner eased over to his sack that rested beside him.

Peter's lips thinned. He had to time it just right; because it was no way this kid was stealing his stuff without getting his ass royally kicked.

The boy crouched. Slowly reached out his hand, and then hesitated. Peter's heart was drumming in his chest. Waiting. Just one moment. Then the boy curled his fingers around one of the straps.

A yell tumbled out of Peter's mouth. His hand jutted forward, and snatched hold of the boy's wrist. The boy side-kicked his face. Peter's jaw jerked. Coughing, Peter whipped out his foot. He kicked the boy's stomach, sending the kid flying to land on his back.

The boy leaped into a squat, eyes slanted and fist ready.

"I'm gonna kick your ass so bad, you'll be begging to live," Peter snarled and with a hop forward, delivered a front kick aimed at the boy's face.

The kid ducked, slid down to one leg and a lash out to Peter's firmly planted calf. Stumbling back, Peter recovered his balance. He grabbed the boy by his baggy shirt. Then yanked the kid forward, wrapped his large hand around the boy's throat. Peter stared down unflinching into the boy's scared but determined emerald eyes that seemed to dare him to follow through. The boy pulled out a switch-blade from his pocket and with a flick stuck it under Peter's neck.

"Get off me!" the boy hissed between rapid breaths.

Peter held his ground, then relaxed his stance and decided to back out of this. He could hurt the kid. Even out live the cut of the knife, but he didn't need to bring any attention to himself. After a moment, Peter relented, expelling a deep breath. "I'm not going to hurt you, but I could. I don't care about being cut, done that before and lived." A flicker of panic crossed his opponent's face.

Diminishing his stand before Peter's eyes, the kid stammered, "I...just needed some money." The boy cleared his throat. "I wasn't going to take much. Just enough to get out of here."

Peter nodded. "Cool. If you put the knife down, I'll let you go. I'm trying to get outta here too."

The kid gradually lowered the knife and with a flick of his hand closed it and put it back in his pocket. Peter nodded and then released the kid's neck.

Choking, the kid's hand came up around his neck. "Thanks. When can I get some cash?"

Peter's eyes traveled from the kid's face to his scuffed up shoes. "When I get out of here. What's your name?"

The boy studied him for a while as if trying to decide whether he could trust Peter. "Angel. My friends call me Angel."

Peter's head reared back and he laughed. "Ye-ah right. Just call me Pete. Okay Angel, you know where I can get a car? Lift a car? Catch a bus?"

The kid's lips pursed out. "You're talking about stealing a car? That's not a good idea here. Everybody knows everyone. And the gangs will think you are trying to steal on their turf."

Peter crossed his arms. "How's it that you planned to leave?"

The kid shrugged, and scratched his forehead on the edge of the white scarf he wore. "Hitchhike. Truck drivers are pretty safe and will give me a ride. I don't look too dangerous. That's how I made it here in the first place."

Peter snorted. "Where I come from, ain't nobody safe."

Chapter 8

Peter bent and stuffed his shirts in his sack. "So, how you been surviving out here? Sleeping?" he asked the boy.

Angel bit his bottom lip and rubbed up his arm, pushing his sleeve up his forearm to reveal pale smooth skin. "It's been hard. But I stay away from the gangs by hiding out at night. This was actually my sleeping place. Not many people come this far down at night."

"Really? Why not?" Peter reached in his pack, turned slightly and stuffed the gun in his pants. He cracked his neck to the side as he put the pack on his back.

"Snakes and gators." Angel twisted the hem of one of his baggy shirts in a knot.

Peter faked an exaggerated shiver. "Ohhh, I'm so scared." He chuckled. "I'm bigger then they are. That don't scare me."

"Good, because they are poisonous. And gators, they bite. But…well, my dad used to have lots of snakes as pets. He taught me how to respect them. I guessed they were a lot safer than my other choices. Sleep with snakes." Angel lifted his palms up, one sitting higher than the other. "Or be beat up by gang members."

Peter eyebrows bunched up, observing Angel a bit closer. "So, how old are you anyway?"

Angel eyes got wide eyed. "You first."

Peter grinned, and held his tongue for a moment. Crossing his arms, he answered, "Sixteen." He lifted his head at Angel. "Now you."

"Sixteen." Angel threw a wry grin at him, daring him to deny it.

"Naw. Ain't no way you're sixteen. Unless you got serious growth issues." Peter turned and climbed up the small hill.

Angel stayed close behind. "I am, but I've always been small. You know…um had a young face, so I'm used to people thinking I'm younger."

"Whatever. If that's your story, and you're stickin' to it, then so be it. I don't care. Once we get out of this backwater town, I'm ditchin' you." He picked up his pace, remembering where the car sales lot was between the city and the bridge. He figured that'd be the best place to go undetected while he *borrowed* a car. This went against everything that Pastor Finn taught him, but survival and following Pastor Finn's God's Ten Commandments seemed seriously unrealistic when your life serves you a bowl of shit.

"More like I'm ditching you." Angel struggled to keep up by doing a slow jog beside Peter.

"Good, we think alike." He wiped his hand down his chest and over the gun in his belt. His eyes closed briefly while he recalled when Pastor Finn first taught him to shoot. Peter exhaled.

"Am I getting on your nerves?" Angel asked, a bit out of breath.

Peter slowed, and observed Angel's short stature comparing it to his own taller, bulkier frame, and glowered. "You're smart too? But too dumb to know when somebody just wants you to shut the hell up? I'm thinking about how we are gonna get one of those cars off that lot up the street."

Angel snatched at his arm. "No! I'm telling you, that's gang territory."

Peter jerked his arm away. "I can handle them. I just need a car and I'm getting one with or without you. Your choice. You want money? You want out of here? You stick with me or you can leave now!" Peter pulled a hundred dollars from his pocket, then grabbed Angel's hand and slapped it in his palm. "I gotta better idea. Beat it. Go. We're done." He stormed off.

Angel's footsteps pounded behind him. He yanked Peter's arm again. "I'm not ready to ditch you. Somebody's got to watch out for you before you get yourself killed."

Peter jerked out of Angel's reach. "For real? Why would you care? I gave you enough money to get out, find a trucker, and a ride. So beat it." Peter pushed Angel's shoulder and was temporarily stunned by the fact the kid didn't budge. "Get lost." He threw up a hand, leaving Angel behind.

"*Estupido idiota* boy!" Angel cursed in Spanish, his voice high. Then he ran behind Peter.

Why didn't the kid get the message? What was it with kids following him? First Hanna, then this boy. He snarled, "Just stay out of the way, and if you gonna follow me, SHUT THE HELL UP!"

"Okay, I can so do that," Angel whispered.

"Good, then start now." Peter thinned his lips. His patience with the kid was definitely running out.

Peter willed himself to dissolve his anxiety. This was the first time he'd ever stolen from anybody. Borrowing from Pastor Finn's collection didn't feel like stealing since he'd always returned it. Or beating up a new bully at the orphanage didn't feel like stealing since he usually gave the money they stole from the weaker ones back to the jerk's victims. He was relieved when Angel fell into an easy pace beside him. The kid confused him. It seemed Angel was purposely acting younger, even though he'd made it clear he was sixteen. Also, the kid could fight as if he'd been trained. Something didn't fit. But Peter didn't have time to think on it as they neared the deserted car lot.

Peter put up a finger. Then bent and picked up one of the rocks that lined the grass around a tree on the sidewalk. Narrowing his eyes, focusing on the one light that hovered over the handful of cars on the lot, he aimed. The rock sailed upward and struck the light. With a pop, the light went out and enveloped the small lot into darkness.

"Why'd you—" Angel started.

Peter put his hand in front of the kid's face, startling Angel to silence. Listening for anything that would alert him that someone was near, his hand lowered and he stepped onto the lot. Angel shadowed him as he checked out car after car for a used one old enough that he could break into without an alarm going off.

He walked ahead, leaving Angel to check out the other cars. The moment Peter's eyes landed on the dark green car ahead, he heard it. *Click.*

"You're dead," someone behind Peter sneered.

Peter dipped, punched his hand up until his assailant's arm cracked. Right after came the scattered sound of metal hitting the ground. With a spin, he whipped out his gun, grabbed the guy's greasy hair, and jammed his weapon under the boy's neck.

"My arm! My arm!" the guy cried. His dark eyes pleaded with Peter.

"Broken? You shoulda thought about that shit before you threatened me," Peter ground out.

The boy's face went from pain to anger. "I got friends. They're going to kill your ass."

"Friends, huh?" Peter's frown turned into a sinister grin. "I'll kill you first then off your friends." Rage he'd been repressing all these years surged up, and the desire to off this kid overwhelmed him. But he stayed it, held back, something Pastor Finn's teachings had done for him. *Calm. Keep your head.* Yet, he didn't convey that in the hard gaze he pointed at his opponent.

The guy was sweating, but within a minute Peter heard them. A few others he surmised were backing up the thug who wanted to kill him. His chin lifted and his eyes scanned the darkness—three others. Then a scream.

"Angel!" Peter whispered indignantly. *The dumb kid's going to get caught.* He just knew it, and screwed them both.

One by one, Angel assaulted them. Peter's jaw dropped a bit. Mesmerized by the artful display, his grasp on the guy he held tightened. His opponent thrashed about and Peter pushed the gun upward till the kid started coughing.

Angel attacked from behind; hitting them with a bat Peter assumed Angel took from one of them. Blows to their legs, arms, and even the forehead of a charging opponent, were artful. Each fell from the heavy blows before they figured out where Angel was. Silent as the wind, he jumped from the car, landing a kick at the last standing boy. Then he swiped downward with his bat, knocking the boy out cold.

"Da-em!" Peter's eyebrow lifted, and he cut his gaze at his struggling opponent. "Well man, you may as well join your friends." He lifted his fist and punched the guy out.

Angel ran up to him. "We have to go. Now! They called more." He grabbed Peter by the shirt.

"You ain't said nothin' but a word. I'm right behind you." Peter snatched up the other boy's discarded gun, stuffed it in his sack and sprinted behind Angel.

They darted between parked cars. The dawn was filling the void between them and the lot they'd left behind. Luckily, the streets were still deserted. Their tennis shoes pounded the pavement, though no one was around to see them on the rocky path.

Angel pointed, a bit out of breath. "Through the woods then to the main highway. Don't stop until we get there!"

"Gotcha, can you keep up?" Peter ran faster, his bag pounding his back. The paved sidewalks and hodgepodge of connected buildings that lined the street, past in a blur. He pumped his arms harder, breath racing in his chest as he counted the pace of Angel's two steps for his one. Part of him was glad the grungy kid hung with him. It would've gotten sticky back there had he ditched Angel like he'd wanted.

They raced across the soft leaf-covered ground in the small wooded area, then through the full, leafy brush, trees and splotches of grass, until they heard the rumbling of cars whizzing down the highway. Peter slid to a stop on the damp leaves. Resting his hands on his knees, he took a moment to catch his breath. Angel stood beside him and stretched.

"So what now, Pete?" Angel tapped him on the shoulder.

"Chill with that." Peter stared at her finger. "I don't do touching—at least by boys."

Angel jerked his hand back. "Uh, yeah, me either." He shrugged, while looking outward at the passing cars.

"I'm tellin' you, I'm not too keen on flagging down a truck going at over 70 miles an hour," Peter said, standing.

"Oh, you don't have to. We can walk about a mile or so that way to the rest stop. Lots of them stop there to gas up and eat." Angel started south, down the side of the busy highway.

Peter walked alongside him, eyeing him here and there. They weaved in and out of the trees to stay out of sight while making headway to the rest stop.

Angel stopped to retie his shoe. "So, how'd you end up back there without a ride? You don't sound like you're from the South at all."

"My motorcycle kinda crashed into a pole. I met some lady who told me about the diner. What were you doing there?" He waited until Angel stood.

Angel's lip turned up like he was contemplating what he should say. "The diner was safe. The old guy gave me free food if I bought a soda, so I hung out there until the gangs moved on."

"Hmm, where are you from?" Peter sized the kid up. "You don't sound like you're from the South either. What happened to make you go to that backwater town?"

"I ran into some bad guys at my house. They did horrible things to my parents. There was no one left. I had to run, or I wouldn't be alive either."

Peter snorted. "That sucks. So, you on the run from someone? You know who?" He adjusted his pack on his back and slowed down his pace a bit so Angel wouldn't have to work so hard to catch up. It seemed as though the thick green cluster of trees would go on forever.

"You could say that. I have an idea who. My mom whispered a name to me when she was being, um—" Angel's eyes watered and he quickly wiped a stray tear away—"stabbed."

Peter's eyebrows bunched. "Sorry." He cleared his throat. "How'd you get to town? Did you have a ride?"

"Not really. I hitchhiked with some lady and her daughter. They were on their way to the beach. I made up some story that I was going to visit my dad. I told her my mom kicked me out of the house, again—for her new boyfriend. I tried to pay her to give me a ride. She wouldn't take the money though, and gave me two hundred dollars instead. What about you?"

"Orphanage," he answered, not willing to spill the sorry details of his muffed-up life and affinity to causing the deaths of those around him.

Angel chortled. "Like, Oliver and Annie?"

He landed a hard stare on Angel's face. "No. In real orphanages, when the lights go out, you don't sing. You see stars from getting your ass kicked by the older kids. And if you're lucky, that's the worst that'll happen to you."

Angel inhaled a quick breath. Sympathy filled his green eyes and he reached out a hand to pat Peter on the shoulder.

"Don't." Peter cut a glance at Angel's hand. "It sucked, but it wasn't the worst part of my life. Besides, I was lucky. A good hider, and mean survivor, I usually did the beating."

Angel's hand fell in midair. "It seems to me that before you could beat someone up, you'd have to have a good reason."

"Trust me, I had a many good reasons. From the day I stepped foot in Pastor's orphanage, I had lots of reasons to want to kick someone's ass. First night there…I let it all out." Peter glared straight ahead, his burning hand throbbing. He clenched it into a fist. The vivid image of one of the older kids, flashing a light in his face and trying to pull at his pants came crashing in. He didn't know where he'd gotten the strength, but he'd scratched the guy in the eyes, and then kicked the boy in the face hard enough to break his nose. Pastor Finn busted in the open room the boys shared. That night, he'd given Peter his own room. A small walk-in closet was only big enough for a bed and was on the backside of the storeroom. That night was the first night he'd prayed. He'd thank God for Pastor Finn. After that, he preferred to start trouble than spend it on his knees begging forgiveness for the very reason that landed him at Pastor Finn's.

Angel smiled at him, a dimple peeking from one cheek. "So where are you heading now? Are you on the run, too?"

An uneasy tremble fluttered in Peter's chest. Flashbacks of Hanna's death flooded his thoughts, and made his palms sweaty from his shame. "I've got reasons. But I'm not ready to share."

"What? You're kidding right? I just told you I've got killers after me. Uh, well maybe they are after me, and all you've got to say is that you're not sharing?" Angel drew a deep breath and expelled it with a snort before going into his native language tirade.

Peter snickered. "So you speak Spanish?"

"Yeah, I speak, Spanish, French, Chinese, German—"

Peter threw up a hand. "Whoa! I get it. Where'd you learn?"

"My mother was a linguist, a translator and from Spain where my dad met her. I was homeschooled. Either she or a tutor taught me."

He hiked up an eyebrow. "Homeschooled? Why? Humph, I guess I was too since Pastor Finn taught us everything in his beat-up school-room."

"Well, my dad traveled a lot for his job. It was just easier to keep me out of school." Angel pointed. "There's the rest stop."

The sun was up and beating on their backs. Peter's stomach was irritable again. He figured they'd get something to eat before catching a ride.

"Wanna eat first?" the corner of Peter's lip hiked up.

Angel squealed and fist pumped in the air. "Oh, yeah!"

The rest area seemed to break through the trees. A huge McDonald's sign lit up the front of the building like a beacon. High in the sky the sun ate at the morning moisture. Several trucks, cars and vans were parked or getting gas.

They walked through the paved parking lot, past the line of trucks and to the entrance of the rest stop. Peter searched around for choices in restaurants, but McDonalds and Starbucks were the only places inside to eat.

He let Angel order first. He hadn't been to McDonald's since Pastor Finn took him in, so he clued in from Angel on what to order and just ordered the same thing. Angel gave him an odd look, but he kept his eyes focused straight ahead.

Their food was ready and handed to them on trays. He fought not to close his eyes as he inhaled the sweet aroma of hamburger and fries. He found a seat in a secluded corner in the back where he could watch who was coming and going. And finally he relaxed his tensed muscles.

Peter couldn't help but lick his lips, and grabbed the Big Mac, then sniffed it.

Angel giggled. "Oh just eat it already."

Peter couldn't help but smile. Angel had him. "My first Big Mac."

"No, couldn't be?"

"Oh yeah. It is. I had McDonalds when I was a kid, but um, not once since I was in the orphanage. There was no getting out of there to get fast food. We got allowance, but what was the point, we never went out to spend it. Except when I found a way out."

A frown marred Angel's face as he stuffed fries into his mouth. "Did you escape? I mean, did they keep you hostage like in Juvenal Jail or something?"

"Naw, nothin' like that. Pastor Finn was just weird, but a good guy. He kept us all in line, preached a lot. He collected kids from all kinds of places. Kids that parents didn't want to be found, or whose parents took them there when something bad happened."

Angel took a long swallow of his Coke. "So, people hid their kids there?"

"You could say that."

"You think...maybe, he'll let me come there?" Angel's eyes looked hopeful.

"Yeah, he's a sucker. But the thing is, he doesn't take walk-ins. All the kids' parents belonged to this organization. He only takes kids that are related to those members. Or something like that. I never listened in all the classes on religious affiliations."

"Are you religious? I mean, like do you believe in God?"

Peter stuffed another bite of his sandwich in his mouth, biting on a thought to Angel's question. "I do, just ain't figured out what his beef with me is." He looked out the window, and stared at the cars, people going and coming. Uncomfortable with the spotlight on him, he asked, "So how'd you learn to kick ass like you did back there? I mean, man, you took out four thugs all by yourself. Didn't leave any to take out my frustrations on. What's up with that?"

52

"Nothing." Angel tapped his fingers on the table. "I've taken martial arts since I was four. My dad was really into it and taught me several disciplines of the art. My favorite was a dance form called Cabrera. It looks like you're dancing on your hands and before you know it—the other guy's toast when you kick him in the face. I um, even competed when I was younger. That is until my parents had a freak out due to an accident that almost killed me."

"Say what? What kinda accident?"

"Somebody opened fire at my first competition. The gun was aimed at me. Well, at least my parents thought so." Angel licked the grease off his fingers greedily.

Peter quirked up the side of his lip. "No shit? So what did they do?"

"They hid me. After that, people came to my house to teach me everything. My parents were rather wealthy, I guess." Angel's eyes got a bit watery while he tapped a french fry on his tray.

Peter's chin lifted. "Humph. Then why did you fake all scared with me when we had our scrap?"

"I was going to hurt you, but you backed off." Then Angel laughed and blinked away the unshed tear.

"Naw, I woulda won, and you know it." Peter didn't crack a smile.

"I didn't want to hurt you." Angel's eyes dipped down to his sandwich, then back up at Peter. "Well, maybe, but you would've gotten cut and beaten in the process." Angel shrugged, "So, where'd you learn to fight like that? Like a mix of Jujitsu and Hapkido?"

"I don't know. It's whatever Pastor Finn taught me. He beat my ass a lot as part of his training." Peter stuffed his last fry in his mouth. "Well, this is where we say goodbye."

Angel bit his nail, then dropped his hand to the table. "Why? We make a good team. I don't have anywhere to go. No one else. I'll watch your back."

Peter turned away from Angel's pleading. "You can't go to where I'm goin'. Once I get there you might not be allowed inside. Hell, I was told not to trust anybody. Don't know if I can trust you or not."

"I don't care if I can't get in. I'll find somewhere to sleep nearby. We can just hang together until we are both safe." He pleaded, reaching to grab Peter's wrist, "Please."

Peter's fist hit the wall. "Look, I'm tryin' to save your life here. Trust me, if you get hooked up with me…you'll die. Everyone that has, *is*." Peter stood and turned to put his trash in the dump. Slamming his tray on top of the trash bin, he glared at Angel.

"It doesn't matter. I'm already dead." Angel's solemn expression begged with his.

Chapter 9

Peter was a sucker. Yep, stupid…and a chump. Why the hell did he keep doing this? Feeling sorry for kids, and helping them, never ended well for him. Or them. Was he so freakin' desperate for a friend that he'd lead another dumb ass to their death? Peter didn't have to look beside him to affirm that Angel was keeping pace with him as if he was some kind of hero, friend, someone to be trusted.

"Let's ask that dude over there." The guy Angel pointed to pulled off in his truck. Then Angel spotted another guy. "He looks decent," Angel directed.

Peter grunted. "He doesn't to me. He looks like he's *trying* to look decent."

"Just trust me, okay. I got myself this far safely. I mean, how long've you been on the road."

"Fine, we'll do it your way. For your sake you better be right." Peter hung back while Angel walked up to the trucker getting ready to leave.

He overheard Angel tell the trucker some lie about their car breaking down on their way back to college. The guy stood about his height and was slender with cool blue eyes. Peter didn't trust him. Just a creepy feeling he got. But then, to be honest, he didn't trust anybody.

The man eyed him, then turned back to Angel and nodded. Angel waved Peter over.

"Let hell begin." Peter wiped his forearm across his face and climbed in the truck beside Angel, who sat between him and the guy driving.

At first glance the guy seemed about middle-aged, slightly gray hair and fit. Peter ignored the guy but felt the scum's eyes studying him while the truck warmed up.

"So, what're your names? I'm Jeb. Been trucking now for about fif-teen years. Right out of high school."

Angel cleared his throat. "My um, name's Paul."

Peter stifled a smile. *Oh, we playin' that game?* He remained silent.

Jeb leaned forward, pulling the gear, and said, "Your friend there doesn't talk?"

Peter felt Angel's eyes on him, but he didn't say a word. He didn't care what Angel said; this dude stunk to high heaven. He must be dumb himself to have followed Angel instead of his own instincts.

"No, he doesn't talk. His name's Sam though."

The truck pulled out of the lot, and hit the highway. Jeb chatted most of the ride. Angel muttered an answer here and there.

"So where you two from? Sorry to hear about your car breaking down."

"New York," Angel answered.

Peter slid a glance at the guy, and moved his hand under his shirt till just above his gun.

"You said you were going back to your college for the summer. What school you go to?"

"Florida State. My parents went there and um, Sam's my roommate."

"College was never for me. Trucking though, I love it. No boss, no tiny office. Just me and the road." Jeb laughed. "And, of course you both."

"So, how far down are you going?"

Peter's nerves were grating. Why didn't Angel shut the hell up? Just let the guy drive them to the next state so they could ditch him and get a new ride. He knew the next Sanctuary was in Georgia. From what he could tell they had about six more hours to go—more or less.

"I'm going to Georgia for my next stop. But I could take you all the way to Florida if you want to keep me company."

Peter's eyebrow lifted at his last comment.

"Well, um, I think we are going to stop in Georgia. I have some family there that I can get some money from."

Great, is Angel a certifiable nut to let this creep think they don't have any money? Peter bit his tongue to hold back a groan. He could feel Jeb peeking over at him.

"So, he, your friend Sam doesn't talk at all? Not a word?"

Angel fidgeted beside him, and jumped a little. Peter glanced down at Angel's leg and saw the bastard's hand brush Angel's knee as he reached for the gearshift. Peter figured the scum tried to make it look accidental, but that shit was on purpose. His fingers brushed the hilt of his gun.

"No, he doesn't. Not much." Angel cleared his throat.

Peter slipped his hand down the side of his seat and started a fit of coughing to distract the dude while he unlocked the door.

"Your friend there okay? He looks sick. I could pull over and you can take him in back if you want."

Clearing his throat, Angel answered, "Oh, uh, no. He seems okay now."

"You sure? Besides it's real comfortable in the back. I have a game system set up, a fridge of beer, and some naughty movies you could watch. If you climb to the small seat back there you can crawl into the back without me stopping the truck." The truck slowed, and they bore off onto a small connecting road.

"That's okay," Angel answered, his fist grabbing Peter's shirt.

Jeb's hand was now sliding up Angel's thigh.

Peter's hand was firmly on his gun; the truck slowed a bit more once they got on the two-lane road. He flicked the door open, slightly. Peter pulled his gun out of his pants. In a flash, Peter reached in front of Angel to plant his gun to the man's cheek. "Your perverted ass better stop this damn truck, before I shoot you right now!" Peter's arm was straight as steel. He felt Angel's rapid breaths as he pushed him further back into the seat when he added more pressure to Jeb's cheek.

Jeb swallowed slowly. "I...uh...didn't mean nothing by it. Just thought you boys wanted to relax in the back." The truck slowed to a stop on the side road.

Peter didn't trust this perv to let them go. Moving the gun steadily up Jeb's face, he yanked it back and struck Jeb on the head, knocking the man unconscious.

"Oh. My. God!" Angel was shaking.

"Let's get the hell out of here. NOW!" Peter grabbed Angel by the collar and dragged him out of the truck.

"Wait, I want to see what's in the back of the truck. We could be wrong." Angel grabbed the keys out of the ignition.

"Fine, suit yourself." Peter followed Angel to the back of the truck.

Angel opened the latch, pushed the door up, and waited briefly as the light filtered inside the back of the truck.

"Da-hem, the bastard is a..."

Angel gulped. "Killer." He lifted his hand to cover his face and gagged, a tear running down his face.

Peter wanted to vomit. A boy, who looked about thirteen or so, was - tied up, and bloody in a corner. The kid laid next to a flat-screen television that was connected to a game system. Shocking as hell were the ropes, hooks, bags, tape, and see-through vials of some liquid drug. Peter turned a bit to his left and nearly lost his Big Mac seeing the variety of vicious torture tools in clear bags hanging by hooks on the back wall.

"No way I'm letting him get away with this shit! Find his cellphone. Here, take this in case the perv wakes up." Peter retrieved the gun he'd lifted from the gang banger earlier and handed it to Angel.

Peter met Angel, who was just finishing his phone call to the cops. He glared at the man who had caused the kid's death, realizing he would have done the same to them. Peter wanted to kill him. His finger itched on the trigger and he lifted the gun.

Angel reached out to stop Peter's shaking hand. "Don't. He's not worth it. He will go to jail."

Peter dropped the gun. "Let's go. Before the cops get here."

"Can we just hide out in the woods until we hear the sirens?" Angel pleaded.

"Fine, once I hear them, we get outta here. I don't need no cops asking me questions."

Chapter 10

Gavin loved it. Seeing the cold, open eyes of the Master's offerings filled him with pride. He grinned remembering the old psychic who'd suffered at the Master's hands. Gavin leaned forward on his desk and tried to relax in the modern style room. The room, with its tall windows, oversized black desk, and walls with pictures of dragons, serpents, and weapons, was decorated by his father and reminded Gavin of his family's legacy.

The plans to his life's work taunted him. Gavin's finger teased the edge of the blueprints, and he chanted his mantra to refocus. His destiny was to change the world. He was groomed for this, born to it. It was his calling to give men the power to go beyond the physical world, to a better place—a place *he* would claim.

His hand trembled at his remembrance. He couldn't help that his mouth watered. The smell of it permeated his entire body. His mind deepened into the trance and a sneer formed on his face at the luscious memory of the supple flesh sacrificed for his last gift. He enjoyed luring those offerings into his Master's hands, then the domination of slicing, burning, tasting the essence of every offering. It was his right to save some for himself. And this last offering, he'd been saving for just the right time. The old woman had lived on the outskirts of his home since he could remember. Sharing with him her gifts, believing he was as gifted as she. But Gavin's destiny wasn't as an offering to be toyed with. His was as a ruler.

Eyes closed, he groped in the open drawer for his knife. The one he used to get into the small places on those gifts, between the little bones. Sighing in pleasure, his long fingers teased the sharp tip. Gradually, he opened his eyes and stared at the plans to his masterpiece. His reason for living—made of a metal not comprehensible by the fools surrounding him. The Extraho of Obscurum order would be rebuilt. So many of his subjects needed this rising. He'd already found many of the sacred grounds of his heritage. Killed those who would seek to fight his rise to power, but it was too late for them, everything was falling into perfect place.

A knock at the door, and then footsteps, pulled him out of his trance.

"Mr. Steele, your brother is here to see you."

His smiling secretary took a step back, appearing to physically absorb the meaning of the scowl on his face.

Gavin tapped on the desk with the tip of his knife. "Ms. Kent, that will be the last time you will come into my office unannounced. Use the intercom."

She cleared her throat and twisted her hands together as his brother, Lucien, stepped in the office behind her. His pale hair, cool gray eyes, fair skin and thick muscular form identical to his, with the exception of the eyes, placed his hands on the trembling woman's shoulders.

"You do insist on being a bully, don't you, Gavin? Take pity on the poor woman. It is her first week."

His brother's charismatic grin annoyed him further. "Lucien, what do you want?"

Ms. Kent had more sense than his former secretary. She took the opportunity given by Lucien's entry to scurry out of the office when his angry eyes landed on his brother. Humph, she just may live longer than the last one. Maybe.

"I can't find him. The kid's dead. Besides, with a name like Peter Saints, he shouldn't be hard to find. But in this case, it looks like he drowned." Lucien reached into his briefcase and threw a manila folder on Gavin's desk. With the finesse of a lion, he sat on the edge of the desk. His fingers tapped the top of the folder, and then flipped it open.

"Not possible. My source wouldn't lie. The psychic I offered was enough to appease my informant," he growled. So close, so damn close. Something was missing, and he knew it. But he would find it.

Lucien chuckled. "You always ask me to do the impossible. In this, my dear older brother, you are wrong. Nowhere does this kid exist." He tilted his blond head closer to Gavin's. "Now the other one, I think I can find that one. Someone reported a possible lead."

Slamming his fist on the desk, the knife cut his hand. Gavin withheld his pleasure at the sensation from the burning cuts of pain. His tongue whipped out to lick the dripping mess. He was too damned close. Too close to lose this one chance to gain what was promised. "Find that one, and if I have to bleed this child dry, I will find what we need. Peter Saints. All these kids will lead to him."

Chapter 11

Peter was only a day's walk away from the next Sanctuary. There was no way in hell he was taking another chance hooking up with a ride. At the last rest stop they bought extra food, some clothes, tennis shoes, blankets, backpacks and drinks. He wished they sold bikes. At least they would've made it to the Sanctuary by now. Anyway, he'd take being alive, and having a full stomach, over riding a bike.

"Is this it for the night?" Angel pointed to the base of a large tree. They were in the middle of a dense woodland between the highway and some country town on the edge of South Carolina.

"Gotta be 'cause I'm dead-ass tired." Peter rolled out a blanket on the opposite side of the tree as Angel.

"Pete?" Angel settled on his blanket and tucked his backpack under his head like a pillow.

"What?" Peter lay down and covered his eyes with his arm.

"I'm sorry I screwed up back there." Angel scooted a bit closer to Peter's blanket. "You know, with the trucker. He really did seem nice in the beginning."

"Yeah, well, he wasn't. But it's cool, 'cause neither was I." Peter felt a tug on his blanket. "Man. Personal space. Don't you dare hang out on my blanket."

"Oh, uh…no I wasn't. I'm just freaked you know. It's dark out here. No lights, and that creep. He wanted to…" Angel shivered. "And we're boys…he's a boy. I mean a grown-up."

"He's a perv. But then, there's a lot of those out there. It's not our fault he was on the prowl. The bastard. We'll be all right. Just no hitchhiking—ever. I'll steal my own damn car first."

"Me too!" Angel sat up, and leaned with his back against the tree.

Peter groaned. "Man, Angel, I'm tired as shit. What the hell is buggin' you?"

"If you weren't with me. I'd be...gosh, I'd be dead, kidnapped or worse. I mean, I could've taken him. Bought him down, but I didn't see it coming until he tried to touch my knee. Then he was rubbing my leg like he..." Angel whistled. "And he didn't even know I was a..."

"You would've been all right. Remember what you did to those gang bangers? You would've got away."

"Pete?"

Exhaling loudly, Peter hit his blazing fist to the soft grass. "What?"

"Don't ditch me. Please...please don't ditch me," Angel whispered with a hint of a sob. "I'm scared to be alone. Die alone."

Shit, it was happening. Peter's heart clenched for the kid. If he was honest, deep down, way down, in the darkest parts of his mind, he'd feared the same thing. But he didn't fear it bad enough to want what happened to those who cared for him suffered. Even though Angel was an inexperienced kid with a trusting heart, something within him told him not to leave Angel. Not to leave him alone. He couldn't explain it, but deep in his gut, he wanted to protect the kid.

"I won't. Just don't regret it when..." he groaned, giving up on warning the stupid kid. "I got your back—if you got mine."

Angel's voice radiated his joy. "I have yours too, Pete. I have yours too."

Peter couldn't sleep. Anticipation, and the hope of safety at the next Sanctuary, had him tense. He didn't know if he was supposed to take Angel there. But he knew he would make it happen. Had to. Maybe taking Angel with him was a way to actually save some damn body than to be the reason someone got killed. Damn, he shouldn't have ignored Hanna. He should've waited up, stuck around to hear what she had to say.

Truth was, the minute he met her, he'd known it was a mistake to talk to her.

The first time he'd seen her, she'd been with a man. The guy looked like her father. Then the next time, she was alone, and that was when he couldn't walk past her without giving her his cash. She'd looked near starving. He'd emptied his pockets to give her all his money. A month's worth of allowance and reward money the kids he looked after gave him when he returned what was stolen from them.

He squeezed his eyes tighter. His chest felt as if someone had punched him and the guilt flooded in like a river of molten lava. He was screwed up. Royally.

"Damn, I shouldn't have run from her." *I'm sorry Hanna.*

Groggily Angel grumbled. "Run from where? Who?"

"Nobody. You wanna tip? Don't ask me questions. Especially, when you are supposed to be sleepin'."

"Can't help it. I've been an only child all my life. I like having some-one to talk to." Angel propped up on his forearm.

Peter turned his back to him. "Sorry for you. At least you had your parents a helluva lot longer than I did."

"So what? It still hurts, and makes me feel cold and lonely inside. I have no one. Both of them were only kids…my dad was adopted. His name was even changed."

"Well I had plenty of knuckleheads around me."

"Brothers and sisters? How old?"

"Naw, not exactly, but they were as close to brothers and sisters any-one could get. We kids in the orphanage—the ones who had been there long as me—I took care of them." Peter heard Angel shifting around and could have sworn the kid got closer.

"I thought you said the older kids beat up the younger ones?"

Peter ran his hand through his mess of curls. "Those kids were conveniently moved to another orphanage when I made a promise to kick their asses if they ever messed with me again. After I beat one with a frying pan, Pastor Finn had them moved. Then he was the only one who beat me. The only one I didn't win against."

"Why'd you fight him? Did he mistreat you?"

"Naw. I liked to fight so I purposely picked trouble with him. You know, to get his attention. He gave up after a while and decided to train me to fight. When he slacked off on his lessons, I picked a fight with one of the older guys. Ones I'd wanted to smack around anyway."

Angel's voice hardened. "I used to get in trouble to get my dad to notice me too. He worked too many hours for that stupid company."

"G'night."

Angel yawned. "Goodnight…Pete."

***

It was stifling hot. And bugs were biting him. But at least daylight was upon them. And they didn't have far to go. Watching Angel rolling up their blankets, he felt sorry for him. It was obvious that Angel had no street smarts. Sure Angel didn't get hurt on his own before, but Peter could tell that it wouldn't be long before Angel found himself in trouble again. The kid was tiny for his age and didn't look dangerous at all. An easy target.

He had to give Angel credit for at least keeping to himself and staying out of trouble's way. Now he couldn't bring himself to ditch Angel even if he had to. Somewhere inside, he felt a kinship with the kid. His empathy went deep, because Angel had saved his life. Truth be told, though, something within him connected with the boy the minute he laid eyes with him. It was like a voice in the back of his head screamed…*save him.* Peter didn't listen to the voice often. Hell, he'd buried that sympathetic, sappy voice after the botched up situation with his parents, then with Hanna, but for some reason, Angel found him.

"I'm stuffing your blanket in my backpack. That way if we stop for more food you can put it in yours." Angel spoke easily, and a slight accent marred his diction.

Coming out of his musings, Peter absently scratched the heated palm of his hand. "Yeah, sure." Peter's eyes traveled over Angel's slim form hidden in all the layers of clothes he insisted even sleeping in and said, "What's up with all those damn clothes? When I first saw you I thought you were a drug addict or meth head."

Angel's expression turned stormy. "I don't use drugs. I just um…have a sickness, uh called anemia, which means I am really cold all the time. I'm freezing even when it's hot outside." He turned away and stuffed their last granola bar in his mouth.

"That so? Then why the hell you sweating all the time?" Peter crossed his arms and observed Angel closely.

"Don't worry about me, it's not like I'm your girlfriend or something. I'm a dude just like you. And guys smell. I give you your space so give me mine." Angel turned completely away from Peter and bent his legs up as he took a swig of the Gatorade.

"What the hell? No, you ain't my girlfriend. But you slept damn close enough to me last night with your scared ass that I couldn't help but smell you. I'm just sayin' maybe you need to take off some layers." Still watching, he saw Angel's shoulders tense up.

"Gotcha hint. When we get to the place we are going, I'll take off a few clothes." Jerkily, Angel stood up and put his backpack on, still refusing to look Peter in the eye. "So, um, did you ever have a girlfriend? Did you leave her back home? Last night in your sleep you said something about a Hanna…"

Peter cleared his throat, pissed at himself for spilling his guts while he was sleep, and ticked off that Angel was nosey enough to hear him. "I had a girlfriend, a little while ago. She wasn't in the orphanage, but we broke up because she didn't like me keeping secrets from her."

Angel turned around, green eyes wide. "Was her name Hanna?"

Then he gulped. Peter's eyebrows crinkled. "No, Hanna was just a friend."

Visibly, Angel relaxed. "Oh," he laughed, "I had a girlfriend named um, Anna. Their names were kind of similar, so, you know, I just wondered."

Peter nodded slowly. "Yeah, you are starting to worry me. If you didn't have a girlfriend, it's cool. Don't worry, little man, you'll get yours one day. Shyan was my first and only real relationship, and I snuck out to see her for about a year." He tucked his gun in the side of his jeans. "Up until then I just messed around with some of the girls at the orphanage, but Shyan—dude, she was freakin' beautiful. I first saw her and, hell, I can't explain it, I would've done anything for her." He started walking.

Angel fell in beside him. "That sounds so…I don't know, I guess I would've wanted to meet somebody who felt that way about me. Why'd she ditch you if she felt the same way?"

Peter frowned, not wanting to rekindle the depth of his need for Shyan. If he were honest, which seemed to be the hole he kept digging for himself, he'd admit that his desperate feelings for Shyan stemmed from loneliness. His need to be connected to someone outside the orphanage, to someone who cared only for him—that's what drove his love for Shyan. "Obviously, she didn't feel the same. At that time, I was sneaking out to see her every couple a days. The day after she broke up with me, I went to her house, you know, to lay it all out there on the line. Tell her about my parents, the orphanage…about me, but there was another asshole there, kissing her on the porch."

Angel's voice softened. "I'm sorry. Did you... Did you ask her why?"

He licked his lips, and clenched his throbbing fist. "Naw, I just turned around and headed back to the orphanage." Briefly, he closed his eyes. *It was the night I gave Hanna all my money, and she changed my life.*

"Why'd you just give up if you loved her so much? I mean, if it was me I would have fought for her."

Peter grunted. "What was the point? She went to private school, had a car, a family, more money than anyone I knew. I wasn't good enough for her. That's why I played the mysterious role. It was better that way. I was trouble. I did better just messin' around with a girl when I wanted a kiss, a feel, and to screw around. More than that, they wouldn't want me around for long. Who'd want a guy with no money, no family, and now…no damn place to live?"

Angel shrugged. "You'd be surprised. I know plenty of girls that would die to have a boy love them like that. Besides, you aren't half bad looking, in a bad boy, chip on your shoulder kind of way…uhum… that girls seem to like."

Peter shoved Angel's shoulder. "Oh, little man, girls like the pretty boys like you. Slim, green eyes, soft voice, *non-threatening*. Me, dude, I scare most of 'em off. I gotta work hard to make 'em comfortable with me. I have to speak, you know, edjamacated, not the slang that Pastor Finn won't let me use in the school."

"You mean you don't use slang all the time?"

"Naw, not at the orphanage, Pastor Finn didn't let us." Peter's voice deepened an octave, imitating Pastor Finn's voice, "Proper English only, I'm not spending hours teaching it for you not to use it!"

Angel giggled. "He sounds like my tutor who refused to speak to me if I used my Spanish accent. Do they send all those old guys to the same school for uptight prigs?"

"I guess, but Pastor Finn was groomed to be uptight. He'd served four years in the Army, then went into the police force. I guess something happened and the old fart found God or went crazy, but left the force to start the orphanage. I heard there was some dude that did it before him, but the guy got murdered."

"Murdered? Why would anyone kill a man of God?" Angel put his hand over his mouth.

Peter lifted an eyebrow and chucked at Angel's reaction. "It was a freak accident they said, but Pastor Finn didn't usually talk about it. I just overheard him being warned by one of the women that brought us supplies."

"I can't believe he was able to keep all of you there and you didn't revolt."

"Why would we? Every kid there had no one. It was only a handful of us. But every now and then a married couple came and adopted a few of the younger ones." He searched around for the sign to their exit. "Right there, we're almost there."

"Thank God. I don't know how much longer my swollen feet can walk. I feel like I'm in a marathon."

"You are." Peter smacked Angel on the back of the head, knocking his hat off and grabbing it before it fell to the ground. He ran toward the exit, looking back and cracking up along the way.

Angel's feet pounded behind him, two steps to his one with his hand on his scarf trying to keep it in place. "Pete! I'm going to…"

Chapter 12

This Sanctuary was in the middle of a farm. The place looked run-down and they had to walk at least another mile before they made it to the raggedy barn. What used to be the main house was just a shell of black wood that contained the remnants of a fire. Peter surmised it had burned down long ago since it was overrun with grass and weeds.

"Are you sure this is where you need to go? I mean, why'd you want to come to an abandoned barn? How'd you even know about this place?" Angel wiped a sleeved arm across his grimy forehead.

"I got my reasons. Remember you begged to come with me. So just shut up and follow me." Peter grinned at Angel's frown—the boy didn't look half as dangerous as he thought.

"Fine, you're right. Beggars can't be choosers."

Peter could have sworn he saw someone moving through one of the windows in the barn, on the top floor. The closer they got, he figured the place was a converted barn, because it had a front door on the side.

"Hey, wait here. I'm gonna check the place out. Knock on the door. See if it's safe," *for me to bring you with me.* Peter knew without a doubt he was bringing Angel, but he just had to make sure all was clear.

He walked up the several steps to the red door. The peeling paint and splintered wood on the barn look like it was one step away from being dilapidated. Raising his hand, he took a deep breath, and the door opened.

A woman stared back at him. She studied his face, then her eyes traveled upward to his raised hand.

Peter dropped it. "Hi, uh, ma'am. My name's Pete. I was sent by Pastor Finn of the *Decretum*—"

"*Venia*," she finished with a whisper. "I'm Rosa." She smiled. "Please, please hurry in."

"Wait, I have someone with me. His name is Angel. Can he come in? He needs a safe place also." Peter asked, his face rigid, but pleading. He studied her round face, brown eyes, salty peppered hair, and her stern grandmotherly-pursed lips.

Her eyes darted past him to Angel. "If the boy can walk up to this door as you just did, he can come in. Otherwise, I'm sorry."

Confusion clouded Peter's face, but he turned and waved Angel forward.

Angel trotted up the stairs, a grin on his face. "Thank you so much for letting me come in with Pete."

Rosa reached out and pulled them in. "You can't linger out there too long. We don't want anyone seeing you. It's not safe here, not as it was once."

"Why not, exactly?" Peter asked, determined to get some answers. "Do you know Pastor Finn?"

"Yes, I know him. We trained together with the order. I'm a protector, but a spiritual one. He's a physical barrier, although the sacred grounds he protects have been barricaded by the elders in the order by prayers."

Peter now knew this chick and Pastor Finn were certifiably insane. But he'd have to deal with it, because with everything he'd seen, been through, he felt like he was slipping too.

"But that's the least of our problems. You can only stay here two days. This place has been foreclosed on. It's being acquired by an unknown buyer."

Peter rummaged through his memories of the pastor's teachings. "If this property is owned by the same people who owned the orphanage, Pastor Finn said it was protected from purchase, forever. It's safe right?"

The woman shook her head. "Unfortunately, the properties are held by several founding families, but those lines that lead to this place—were

74

killed off. Silently, without anyone within the order's knowledge." She looked at them both gravely. "Two days, and this place will be blown up before anyone takes possession."

Angel stepped forward. "Where should we go?"

"There are other safe places, though, no one in the order knows them all. I don't even know of any other, with the exception of Pastor Finn's. My orders are to go warn him what has happened. Now, I'm afraid…we are at war." Her face looked troubled. "Excuse me, I have to prepare for our departure. There are two bedrooms on the lower floor, and a bathroom. Please help yourself to the linens and boxes of clothes in the closet." Her hand touched Peter's face briefly. "You—something about you is different." She clucked.

Peter watched her rush out of the room. His eyes met Angel's stricken ones.

"What the crap is going on here?" Angel's hand was shaking. "She's freaking me totally out."

Peter ran his hand down his face. "If I knew, I'd tell you. Let's go get cleaned up and do some lookin' around. I want some answers before we leave, and I have a feelin' they're here."

His eyes roamed the place as he strode to the stairwell leading to the lower rooms. The place didn't look at all like a barn inside. It resembled a library of sorts. Books lined the walls from floor to ceiling. Scattered around the hardwood floors were tables filled with more books and peeling wooden chairs in various forms of disarray.

"Is this place a house or an archive?" Angel whispered.

"Don't know."

"Does that lady live here?"

"Rosa? For some reason I don't think so. This place looks like people come here to study. I can't see one person making this much of a mess." Pastor Finn's stacked basement teased his memory and he now wondered if the pastor had put all that stuff there, or whether people of this weird Order that they talked about put it there for storage. Maybe this was some sort of place they came to do research.

"Who would come all the way out in the middle of a farm to do research?"

Peter scratched his chin. "I guess people who don't want to be disturbed. Why don't you hit the showers first? I'm gonna look around a bit before coming downstairs."

"Okay. I can't wait to take a shower."

"I can't wait for you to take one either," Peter snickered and pinched his nose.

"Yeah well, it's not like you smell like peaches and cream either. I just didn't want to point it out because I didn't want you to find another reason to try and leave me."

Peter threw up his hands. "Look, I'm sorry I was a bastard before. I meant what I said, you hangin' with me may get you killed, and I don't want that for you…for anyone who deals with me. But as long as you want to be here, I'll have you. Thanks for saving my ass back there. I consider you more than my road dog. You're a friend."

Angel's face brightened and his eyes watered just a bit. "Thanks Pete, that means a lot to me. I know your trust isn't easily earned. But I considered you a friend the moment you offered to buy me a root beer, and I'd save your life again. Even if it cost me mine." Angel turned and started heading down the steps.

"Wait. Angel?" Peter took off his backpack. "Can you take this and put it in the other room?"

Angel took the backpack and struggled to hang it on his arm. Giving up, he slowly dragged it down the stairs.

Peter moved on to peruse the converted barn-house. He walked beyond another open room filled with books to a hallway at the dead end.

One entire wall of the dead end was a picture of a cross, and what appeared to be hundreds of angels kneeling at the base.

He inhaled the tickling smell of old books, and mildew filled him. He turned down the dead end. Again he found more walls lined with bookcases overflowing with books stacked from the top of the cases to the ceiling. Midway down the hall, there was a breach in the line of bookcases. A huge coal-black statue of an angel stood there.

Move it. Peter's neck twitched and he couldn't seem to stop his heated hand from reaching out to touch the statue. The moment his hand connected with the cool black stone, it shuddered. With a creak, it moved. The statue slid within the side of the bookcase. A wall remained.

"What...?" Both of Peter's hands went to touch the smooth wall, and like a pebble dropped in water, the image of the wall rippled away to reveal a latch. His heart drummed in his chest. Fear and apprehension caused him to take several gulps. Before he could stop himself he unhooked the latch, similar to the one in the other sanctuary. The door slid open.

Peter's feet had a mind of their own as they stepped over the threshold. Inside was a small chamber, the size of the little walk-in closet he used to sleep in. The door behind him slid closed. He trembled and spun around in the dimly lit room.

Walls of gold surrounded him. In awe he slowly spun around to take in every crevice of the carvings within the gold.

"I keep getting deeper and deeper into some insane..." he started to choke when he saw it. The hazy, ghostly glow he'd seen in the other sanctuary hovered over the masses of angels in the lower left corner of the wall carvings. Like misty ink, his name was revealed in broken smoky pieces that moved on a breath above the inscription in the small niche. The inscription was just strange markings of lines and dots and, to the naked eye, nothing but an artful display of lines. But to Peter, it said *warriors*. Frantically, he tried to calm himself. It had to be a play on words. His eyes hadn't been right since the dream about his mother.

He forced himself to start at the top of the wall, ignoring the teasing of the mist-like words. It was his name. Floating downward on the wall. There were pictures. Religious ones, of heaven, then hell, a name of some beast, and angels named from the bible were everywhere. He'd heard of them all from his teachings and even some he had never heard of. Peter had been taught from all types of religious documents, from Egypt, to Roman and others he couldn't recall. How all of them had certain similarities he never understood, but Pastor Finn insisted the kids focus on them.

He suspected, with this place being part of the parish he'd come from, it would be normal to have a religious painting of angels and demons within. He took several calming breaths, intent on ignoring the ghostly image of his name floating to the side of him.

Heck, truth was why should his name surprise him? With a name like Peter Saints he was kidding himself to think there was any significance in his name being outlined above the gold. Only thing he couldn't deny was the fact that his name wasn't within the artful wall, it was floating like a ghost in front of him.

He closed his eyes. Heard a click on the door, and with a jerk opened his eyes as he pivoted around.

Rosa stood in the hallway. His eyes slid over to the ghostly haunting of his name, and it disappeared as if being blown away.

"How'd you get in here?" she demanded.

"Sorry ma'am, I uh, was just wondering around. I touched the statue and it moved."

Rosa studied him strangely, then moved slightly out of the doorway. "Come. Come out of there. It hasn't been entered in centuries. This place was built to keep it protected. It hasn't always been a barn. It's been many things throughout time, but that enclosure has never been revealed to any of the other protectors. Until the last twenty years, the encasement has been underground. For some reason it has risen."

Peter squeezed past her to get out. Rosa reached behind the bookcase and the heavy door slid back in place.

"Didn't Finnegan teach you anything, boy?"

"Well, I guess so, I just wasn't a good listener."

A smile broke wide on her face, and she looked happy, not like the dour woman who met him at the door. "Typical, that man can put even me to sleep once he gets on a roll. The order has been around since, oh, I don't know—forever really. Both my parents were members, hmm... I believe my entire family has always been. In the older days our numbers were strong. But as times change, we are being killed off, dying off, or losing the desire to serve."

"Was Pastor Finn always a member?" Peter wondered at how her hands caressed the books they passed as if they were treasured objects.

She sighed. "He, like the rest of us, was born into it. But he decided he could do more good being in the army, then with the police. It wasn't until his brother was killed collecting a child that he decided to replace him."

Peter stopped walking. "You mean the man that ran the orphanage before Pastor Finn was his brother?" His heart twitched. He'd considered himself Pastor Finn's favorite, and to know that Pastor Finn had never confided in him about his brother hurt him. Deeply. "He never told me...I mean, us."

She pulled him into a hug. "I knew it. I knew you. You're his Peter. He raves about you all the time."

Peter pulled back surprised and elated. "He's usually pissed off at me."

Rosa nodded. "Yes, but only because he thinks you are special. Only because, he looks upon you as a son."

His voice cracked. "A son. He uh, said that to you?" Peter couldn't help his doubt. He'd wanted it to be true, but the thing was, Pastor Finn tried to be fair to all the kids. His gruff manner would soften when he reached out to them all.

"Yes, he has. But he vowed to protect and take care of you all."

"How? I mean, why don't the kids go into the system? You know, social services when our parents died, or something happens. I mean, what if I had some distant family that would've taken me in?" His eyes traveled down the hallway, until they got to turn that led to a large kitchen. Long wooden tables were lined up as if to feed a small army. They sat in front of a serving counter that separated the kitchen from the rudimentary dining area.

"We could never let you all go into the system. Then others would find you and kill you as they had your parents." She exhaled, turning to open the refrigerator.

She made sandwiches. Rosa took her time, like she enjoyed giving the gift of food. Smiling at him, her nimble fingers deftly cutting the crust off the bread.

"It's been a while since I've been able to spoil young people." She rummaged in the fridge and took out a bowl of fruit she started to slice and place in decorative patterns on the plates.

"Do you have any?"

"Oh yes, but they're grown and have kids of their own. I visit them from time to time when I'm not traveling to teach within the Order."

"You know, some of the kids were adopted. The young ones anyway…" Peter leaned back on the smooth wood counter, and couldn't help himself as he sneaked a piece of the plump mango she'd just sliced.

Rosa pushed another juicy slice at him and started skinning a kiwi. "Those kids could easily be given secret identities. The families who took them lost children around their age and desired a child. So we could have those kids assume the identity of the child that passed away. We have members within the hospitals, police forces, political realms and such that could make a clean transition like that simple."

"I really should've listened during class," he mumbled.

"It's likely Pastor Finn didn't relinquish as many details to you kids as I am. Sometimes it's better to keep you all ignorant to your personal dangers."

He snorted. "Unlikely, if they've lived my life. All the kids there either saw their parents killed, were attacked at some point themselves, or just came home from school to find everyone gone. No explanation, not even police seriously seeking to find out who murdered our families. I researched on the internet and my parents seemed to be erased from existence. Even I was. Nothing. The only thing I found was that some unknown family all drowned in a river."

"I know it sounds horrible, and you wanted resolution, but it had to be done. The forces that are working to gather you kids are pure evil. You children are their nuggets of gold. They aim to annihilate everyone associated with the order and to take any holdings we have. You children are our future. The only ones born into this protective order, and if they take you all, we have no way to make sure that all that we've protected over the years won't be desecrated."

Absently, he grabbed half the sandwich she'd prepared from one of the two plates. Peter took a big bite and couldn't help himself from finishing it off by stuffing the rest of it in his mouth. "What do I do now? Where do I go?"

Rosa caressed his cheek. "You know. You already know. And the other one you bought with you should go on that journey with you." She flattened a hand over her heart, "In here tells me you two are going to do great things; that you are our future—to trust you. Now you just have to trust yourself. I know that both I and Pastor Finn seem weird. Oh, there are many who would call us zealots or part of a cult. We are not attached to any religious affiliation. What we are called to do has nothing to do with religion—the way people worship the Maker of all. We are called to keep the human race safe from unimaginable suffering. I do this not truly knowing why, but that it is something I must do." Her hand rose to showcase the books lining the shelves high on all the walls of the open room. "These books give immense knowledge to this old soul of mine, but they don't breathe life to what is in my heart, my soul from the moment I took in air. This—you children, our future of protectors—is why I'm here."

Peter wanted to believe every word she uttered, but his mind just couldn't wrap around it. None of it made sense, but yet, all of it felt right within the recesses of his soul.

She tsked him. "When you are ready, you'll understand. Now take your friend his sandwich. I made another for you since you seem a bit starved."

Thankful for her caring, he returned a genuine smile. "Thank you." Then he headed downstairs.

Chapter 13

Peter rested his elbow on the rail while he made his way down the stairs. The steps were narrow, the walls smooth and tanned. He was careful not to drop the overlapping plates or drinks he had squeezed against his bulky frame by his arms.

He cleared the last step. His foot landed on the carpeted floor of a small cozy room with more bookshelves. There was a spattering of large couches and overstuffed chairs with ottomans throughout the room. Spotting a table, he set down the plates and drinks. His mouth watering, he picked up a cracker spread with cheese and finished it off in one bite. Thirsty, he held the glass up to his mouth until he heard Angel coming from the back hall.

The light in the back turned off, throwing the hallway into darkness. Peter heard Angel's steps then a bump, and a Spanish tirade.

Peter grinned at Angel's antics, until he laid eyes on the stranger clearing the darkened hallway to enter the main room. Peter's jaw dropped.

"Shit!" The glass fell to the floor, and he choked. Instead of the dirty kid he'd been used to seeing the last few days, Angel stood there proudly. Long wavy black hair framed the most beautiful heart-shaped face he'd ever seen, enhanced with large green eyes. Peter took a gulp and couldn't stop his eyes from roaming down the form fitting T-shirt that did little to hide full breasts, a tight stomach and softly curved hips framed by her dark tresses.

He took a step back. "You're…you…a…dammit!"

"A girl." Angel grinned, and full lips framed now clean teeth. Her firm, slightly muscled arms bent with her pale dainty hands resting on her gently shaped hips. "I wanted to tell you, but it was safer for me to look like a boy. It's something my father told me to do if we were ever separated."

Peter couldn't stop the warm rush of longing that filled him. Ashamed, damn, he'd told her things he'd never share with a girl. He was speechless.

She took a step toward him.

"Whoa!" Peter threw up a hand and stepped back. "I told you stuff…thought you were a dude, you betray—"

Angel shook her head. "No Pete, I wouldn't betray you. You're the only friend I've ever had. My real name, entire name is, Angelica Selena Ramirez. I am sixteen, and I am your friend. Everything I told you was the truth." She hesitated. "Except when I had to prove myself to be a guy." She reached for his hand like her life depended on his acceptance. Relief filled her expression when she grasped his hand.

Stunned, he couldn't help the subtle tremble at her touch. He wanted to pull her to him and kiss her…bury his face in Angel's hair forever, but he had to stay cool. Mixing his raw feelings with their friendship would ruin everything. It would ruin him. He couldn't let anyone do to him what Shyan had, and he had a deep fear that this girl…this Angel, would do that, and worse.

Peter yanked his hand from hers, and forced a scowl on his face. "You lied to me! You think doing that shit's okay? If you were my friend and you trusted me so damn much, you would've told me you weren't a guy." He turned away and kicked the overstuffed chair. This new situation just confused him further. Damn, she was gorgeous. His heart broke a million times in his chest, he wanted her so bad. What the hell was wrong with him?

Angel took a tentative step closer, and placed a gentle hand on his shoulder.

Peter flinched. "Get off of me. Don't—"

Angel's hand snatched back. "I'm really sorry, Peter."

He wouldn't turn around, even with the sob in her voice. His eyes shuttered close and it took every ounce of strength for him to stay planted where he was. Every muscle in his body clenched tightly, but he willed himself to get his head, his desires, his want of Angel under reins. Peter's eyes squeezed tighter. He heard the clink of a plate, the scrape of a glass and a wayward sigh.

"I'll be in my room. The last one on the left, yours is across from mine." Angel stood there a moment, staring at his back. "Pete, when you want to talk, just open my door. I'll be there waiting." Silent steps glided across the floor. Her voice cracked. "I'm really sorry."

He let out the air he'd been holding in, slumped in the chair, and covered his face with his hands.

Chapter 14

He was a coward. Peter groaned and admitted it to himself. Dealing with the issues that plagued his life was hard enough. But this thing with Angel was a bit much too deal with right now.

Peter had left the basement the day before when the reality of Angel's truth was revealed. Avoiding her for the first day they got there and during the night in the house had proven to be torture. He'd spent most of his time upstairs and away from her. Bored, he'd started reading the ancient books that lined the walls. The things the books revealed were weird and a little out of his league, but one thing for sure, they were where Pastor Finn's teachings had come from. The history about the order, and some enemy fighting over hidden religious relics just frustrated him. None of his musings were answered. The books didn't reveal anything specific about the order that Pastor Finn and Rosa belonged to, their true enemy, or much less what the heck they were hiding or protecting.

Peter smacked his teeth. "Why? What did I ever do to be served up this shitty life?"

Angelique. Her name ran through his mind like a soothing wave. She'd shown up there, in that space within his heart he didn't think was worthy of acceptance.

Tonight he fought the urge to seek her out. He'd waited till late to go downstairs and made a point of not peeking in her room before taking his shower before bed. But, this fluttering in his stomach wouldn't let him stay upstairs for the entire night.

Now though, he had to fight himself to stay away from her. Peter heard her across the hall, moving about, going to the bathroom. Hell, even twisting and turning in her bed. Why hadn't he met her before

Shyan screwed his head up? He wanted Angel, but for more than a friend. Selfishly he had to admit, he wanted her for himself. He was a sick bastard, and couldn't believe that the moment he knew she was a girl he wanted to jump her bones. What would she think of him? He forced his eyes shut, but his head moved side to side on his bent arms.

Sleep had escaped him. All he kept thinking about was Angel, Hanna, the weird things happening to him, and what he had to do next. Peter knew she wanted more from him than what he was giving her. He'd seen it in her eyes, the same desire mirrored within the depths of his soul. At least he hoped that's what he saw, and not her hope for just a deep friendship. Maybe his ass had psychological issues from not having a mother, or a father? Something that made him think he could have Angel forever. Of kissing her and never letting her go. Who was he fooling, of course he had serious issues, but would she accept him in spite of them? Yeah, he'd messed around with other girls, but the hard reality was, he was the loyal type deep down. Just had serious problems with trusting that anyone would want to stick around with a screw up like him.

He was damn scared she'd reject him, and scared she wouldn't. Terrified he couldn't keep her safe if she decided to hang with him through this bullshit that had become his life. Could he love her knowing she may soon die because of him? He wouldn't let that happen, he'd die to protect her first. He'd risk anything—anything for her safety. His gut confirmed that his future wouldn't be easy, that something bad was going to happen. He couldn't put it into words but he just had a feeling of a heaviness stalking him, and a warning to keep running.

His legs slid off the bed. He rubbed his hand down his bare chest, and tugged up his shorts. Peter had to see her, make sure she was okay. His heart was conflicted. Knowing now that she was a girl, one he had seriously deep feelings for, he couldn't take the chance Angel would get hurt—or reject him when she found out what he'd been hiding. He also knew he couldn't leave her—ever, even if he tried.

Before Peter knew it, he was standing outside of her door. He peeped inside, feeling a bit like he was invading her privacy, but he couldn't move. Her room was dark. Angel was wrapped up in the covers. Peter watched her, his heart thumping in his chest with each passing minute.

As if sensing him, she sat up. "Peter?" Then she flicked the light on.

Peter had to brace himself on the doorframe to keep his features unmoving. His chest literally ached, and his fingers itched to touch her.

Angel reached out to him. "Please, come talk to me."

Peter walked slowly to the bed, and composed himself before sitting on the edge. "Angel, I don't know what to do about you." He swallowed.

She moved a wayward lock of hair from his forehead. "What do you mean? You promised you wouldn't ditch me."

Peter's breath caught. He searched her eyes, wondering if he should risk it. Put the way he felt on the line with her. "I'm not ditching you. Angel, I've been having a hell of a time figurin' out how I feel about you."

Bewilderment filled her face. "What do you mean? You don't like me as a girl?" She smiled, her hand dropping to the bed.

Peter couldn't bring himself to say it first. He had to get a clue from her. Studying her expression, he watched her eyes drop shyly to his chest. And the slight trembling of her hands when she clasped them together as though she was willing herself not to touch him again.

He reached out and lifted her chin. "How do you feel about me?"

Blinking, her eyes attempted to skip away from his gaze.

His finger lifted her chin higher. "Angel, how do you feel about me, as a man?"

She swallowed. "I…um think you're handsome."

He felt a slight quiver in her chin. "Right now, at this exact moment, I wanna kiss you. I don't want you to think that I don't, you know, feel you as a friend. I don't wanna take advantage of you…you know like most dudes would try to do."

Angel unclasp her hands, she moved her hips a bit closer so that her hip touched Peter's knee. "I know you wouldn't. But…" she bit her bottom lip and her eyes darted to his lips. "I uh, my parents were really protective and I…don't want to mess this up." Peter lifted an eyebrow. "What's wrong? Mess what up? It's all good if you don't want me to kiss you. I won't push you—ever. You know that, don't you?"

She nodded her eyes never leaving his. "Pete, I haven't ever kissed anyone."

He chuckled. "You tellin' the truth?" The embarrassment on her face spoke volumes. "Don't worry…you'll be perfect," he whispered, then leaned in and gently touched his lips to her full ones. His entire chest was on fire, he wanted to drown in her, but knew he couldn't. He had to make this good for her, for them.

Angel moaned softly, and Peter's thumb tickled her chin as he teased her mouth open. Delving inside, it felt like paradise, and when her arms trailed up his arms and around his neck, he was lost.

Peter pulled away. "Angel, damn…I could fall in love with you."

"I am falling in love with you," Angel murmured.

Pulling her to his chest in an embrace, he whispered, "Me too, me too. Thanks for telling me." He felt warm inside at her admission. If he had the guts he would've told her first. Instead he just held her tighter.

They stayed entwined for a few minutes. Peter kissed her forehead, and then buried his hands in her hair while he greedily kissed her over and over again, deeper and deeper. He forced himself to stop, and gently tugged her fingers from his hair.

"Look, I don't want to leave you tonight—or ever. Can I sleep on the couch over there? You know, while you go to sleep?"

Angel stared at him as though she wanted to kiss him again. Her eyes moved from his lips to his eyes. "Don't you want to sleep beside me?"

"Damn. Ye-ah, but I don't trust myself. I've been having a lot screwed-up nightmares, and shit I can't get out of my mind."

She lifted the covers and moved over to make room for him. "I trust you Pete, just lay here and hold me. You can talk if you want." Angel patted the pillow next to her, "Besides, we've slept next to each other for the last few days anyway."

The void she'd just filled within him wouldn't let him move away. He slid into the covers beside her, pulled her close and rested his head on the curve of Angel's shoulder. Peter traced his finger down her arm to her hand as she snuggled closer to him; her soft hips spooned in his. He closed his eyes and tightened his hand in hers. Hopefully, tonight he'd be able to get some sleep.

Chapter 15

Peter held Angel close all night. The calm he felt with Angel in his arms was something he'd been searching for since he'd been in the orphanage. It was comfort, love and only the supple softness of someone he could lose himself within. Angel was that person. She'd been where he was, no parents, no family, saved his life and cared about him on a level that no one else had.

"Angel?" Peter regretted the sliver of light that peeked through the small window in her room.

"Hmm." She pulled his hand to her lips and kissed it.

His heart melted. "You awake?"

"Yeah."

"Who tried to kill your parents? Where are you running too?"

She stiffened. "I don't really know. My mother's last words were, 'run...run from Gavin.' Gavin is the guy my dad worked for at Steele Industries."

"You ever meet the dude? Did he look like a killer? Or show up at your house?"

"No, he wasn't the one who attacked my parents. That's why it seemed weird that my mom would even say that. I only met him once though, at the company Christmas party the year someone tried to kill me at the martial arts tournament."

He couldn't resist laying a kiss on her shoulder. "What kinda vibe you get from him? Did you like him? Feel like you wanted to get away from him? Or nothing?"

Angel took a moment to think. "Humph, I never really thought about it that way. When we were at the party, Mr. Steele came up to my dad from behind. He didn't even really look at me at first. Then my dad introduced me to him, but it seemed like my father didn't really want to. I swear to you, the minute I took his hand I felt creepy. I tried to pull away, and the guy looked down at me and took my cookie out of my other hand. When I hid behind my dad, the guy told my father that children were not to eat in the carpeted room."

"What? The bastard took a cookie from a kid?"

"Yeah, but it wasn't that, he was just…cold, hateful. He didn't even smile at me like most of the adults at the party had."

"What happened after that?"

"Later that year, the threat was made on my life. My dad quit Steele Industries and we started to travel a lot. He worked hard, doing jobs he could work from home or from various locations. But it never really worked out for him to stay home, so my mother did. We packed up and moved every few years when his work dried up."

Peter moved his hand up to her cheek. And turned her around to face him. His heart ached for her as she cried. He moved forward and kissed the tears from her eyes.

"Tell me, what happened next." Peter pulled her to his chest.

"There was a break in. The men weren't even wearing masks." Her voice broken, she went on, "My dad answered the door. They were wearing jeans, some of them. One had on a suit. They asked my father, 'where is the child?'" She gulped, tossing back a sob. "He fought them. My mom pushed me back into the hallway, then told me to run and hide in the attic until they left. I did, and stayed there. I heard the gunshots— so many. The men ran through the house, looking for me for what seemed like hours. I stayed up there for two days. I didn't even leave to eat."

"Angel, baby, I'm sorry I acted like an ass. You know, like I was the only one that had shit to deal with. I won't let no one do that to you. You got that?"

She moved her head back and forth on his chest. "I know you won't. I know…"

"So, did you have somewhere to go?"

"Not really, I remember my father showing this place in Florida. He said it was a swamp, but that it was a treasure only someone like me could find. I didn't believe him, but after all that happened, I didn't have anywhere else to go. So I figured maybe I could find that place. Maybe, there they wouldn't find me."

Angel sniffed, wiped her eyes then shyly kissed Peter. His eyes closed as his heart thumped faster. This was first time she'd initiated a kiss on her own. Maybe, just maybe, this was for real, he prayed.

Peter moved off the bed and walked with his hands low on his hips. He stood in front of the picture of the sea just under the tiny window high up on the wall. His muscles in his arms clenched and he breathed out to brace himself against her response to what he was about to say.

He cleared his throat. "I don't know how much to tell you, because I don't want you to get hurt knowing this. But I gotta come clean with you so you know if you go with me, what could happen." Peter took a deep breath then traced the landscape of the sea and began to speak with his back to her. "Look, that girl Hanna you heard me talk about in my sleep. I…uh, she died because of me." He pivoted, his eyes capturing her stunned ones. "My parents, they too, died because me. Someone ran my father's car off the road. My mom and I were in it with him. My mother got me out before we drowned, but a few days later, someone shot her down. She pushed me toward a church, told me to run there and not to stop no matter what. When I broke through the doors, some guy—you know, a religious dude, asked my name. I told him it was, Peter…Peter Saints. He acted like he knew me, like that was where my mother was headin' with me in the first place."

"Peter Saints, that's a…different name." Angel tapped her chin with her finger.

"Yeah, it is. I get teased a lot because of it."

"Why do you think your parents died because of you?"

"I used to hear them saying how they had to keep me safe." Peter's hand slid down his face. "My father told my mother that someone would kill us all just to get me. They didn't hear me under their bed that night. I used to have nightmares and crawl into their room and sleep under their bed. The last time was the night before my father died."

A tear rolled down her face, but her eyes never left his. "What happened to Hanna?"

He exhaled the breath he'd been holding. "When I first saw her, I had a feeling I needed to stay away. Didn't get why, but when I saw Shyan kissin' that other dude I didn't care what my gut told me, I only knew that I felt like shit and I wanted to get rid of the money I had planned on spending on Shyan. Hanna was there, looking starved, and beggin' for food. I felt sorry for her and she looked at me like she knew me. I gave her all my cash. Now thinkin' back, the moment my hand touched hers, I knew I did the wrong thing. After that, she followed me all the time, and I tried to ditch her. But the last time." He swallowed, "The last time I saw her, she ran behind me and got killed in a hit and run."

"Oh, Peter…"

Anger at himself seeped into his chest, and he hit his fist against the wall. "Don't feel sorry for me, feel sorry for her. I did it on purpose. I waited to cross the street hoping the coming car would stop her from following me—but it didn't. I caused her death, and I'll never forgive myself for it," his voice deepened. "You see, see why you better know what you're gettin' into dealing with me. Why I really don't need to be in love right now? But, Angel, I'm tellin' ya, I can't help the way I feel about you. Something…something, in here," he hit his palm on his chest, "is telling me that I have to save you. The only way I know how is to have you with me. Do you feel the same? Am I crazy? God, I feel like it." Peter jabbed his fingers in his mass of dark curls.

Angel got up and took his hand. Her finger hesitantly touched his palm and traced the faintly puckered brand on his hand, then kissed it. "I felt the same way about you. Umm, like I was supposed to follow you. Like my soul knew you forever." Her eyes lifted to his, raw with emotion.

"Me too." He pulled her by his hands a step closer to him.

"Pete? What's on your hand? It feels hot."

He shrugged, not wanting to tell her everything yet. It was too raw to even go there after revealing everything else. He released her hands before getting up and walking to the door. "A gift from Hanna." He took one long look at Angel, then turned to leave. "I'm going to wash up and look around. I'll meet up with you for breakfast in the kitchen."

Chapter 16

The barn house was quiet. Peter went down every hallway he could find, except for the hall where he'd revealed the sacred alcove. Not seeing Rosa in the kitchen, he peered out the window.

Peter headed out of the door to talk to her. She reminded him of what he'd dreamt a grandmother would be. That is, if he had a different life—the one he'd wanted since his parents were taken from him.

Rosa spied him clearing the stairs and her face looked stricken with concern. She spun around and waved him over. "Boy, what did I tell you—being out here isn't safe for you or that other child. People may be watching. Besides, it's not good for your essence to be left around for someone to sense later."

Peter stroked his chin. "This all sounds whacked to me. It doesn't make sense."

"It doesn't have to. Now go on inside. I'll be there in a minute to feed you both. I have to finish this since it weakens every few days." Rosa's eyes searched over the high grass in front of her. "Besides, I'm putting something real special here for the new owner."

He left Rosa to her praying and dropping of oils around the outside of the house. Taking two steps at a time, he pushed through the door, and practically ran into Angel, in her usual boy's outfit. Her dark hair was hidden within the white bandana she'd worn a day ago. Baggy shirts and pants covered her form, and tennis shoes finished her camouflage.

Peter couldn't hide his disappointment. "I have to get used to this again." He pulled down the baseball cap that sat on top of her bandana.

"I know it stinks, but it's safer this way." Angel caressed his face. "I just couldn't hide it from you any longer."

He pulled her into a quick kiss. "I'm glad you didn't."

Angel's gazed scanned over Peter's shoulder. "What's she doing out-side?" Angel's eyebrows crinkled in puzzlement.

"Praying around the place to keep the boogie monster out." He belted out a laugh. "It's my damn curse to be surrounded by nuts."

"No it's not nuts, my father did it wherever we went. Except, hmm, if I remember right, he didn't do it at the place the guys broke into."

"For real? Why'd he do it?"

Angel tucked the edge of her t-shirt into her sweatpants. "To create a spiritual sanctuary."

Air rushed in his lungs. "That's what this is. It's called a sanctuary. Did your father ever say he was part of *Decretum Venia*?"

Understanding dawned on Angel's face. "This is a *sanctuary*? Both my parents are decedents of *Decretum Venia* and told me that I am too. That's why we had to run. My father believed an enemy to the *Decretum Venia* might find us."

Peter checked to see if Rosa was still outside, then pushed Angel back in the house. "Your dad was right." He led her to the open book on the table. "Do you know what *Decretum Venia* means?" He gestured to the word. "It means *Order of Grace*."

Peter's finger slid down the opened page. "So, what do you know about it? The order? Their enemy?"

Angel sat and skimmed through the book he'd given her. It was writ-ten in Latin. "I know this book. Here, there's a symbol of an artifact. Something in Tibet was unearthed."

Looking over her shoulder, his eyes read the words. "The piece was from a buried tomb." Peter flipped several pages and studied the map where the artifact was found. "Shit! The object was unearthed in a sanctuary—one buried deep in ruins in Tibet. I was studying this book the last few days, but didn't get this far." He sat down.

Rosa opened the door. "Okay kids, let's go eat. We have a lot to do before morning."

They looked up, anxious from what they'd read. Angel ambled behind Rosa while Peter took one last look at the artifact, and closed the book.

Peter walked into the kitchen, his thoughts heavy. Vaguely, he recalled the lesson Pastor Finn taught about the order, and a releasing of a secret that could open a Pandora's box of sorts. He'd seen that artifact before. But where, he didn't remember. Angel was helping Rosa set one of the large tables.

"Peter, just take your plate and head over to the table. I'll pour you something to drink while I tell you what we have to do tonight." Rosa waved him to the table.

He sat down with plate in hand. Angel trailed behind him. Peter wanted to laugh at the way she worked hard suppressing the sway of her hips. She stiffened her gait and dropped the easy smile she had with him last night. His heart warmed; he wanted to kiss her in hopes he could lose himself in her again, and just forget the nagging drive that urged him to get to the next sanctuary.

Peter nodded his head at Angel. "Hey, you awright?"

"I guess so. Wait till you hear what she wants us to do." Angel slid her gaze to Rosa who approached with a large pitcher of lemonade.

Pouring, Rosa smiled as though nothing was amiss. "Tomorrow afternoon I've a feeling the new owner will send someone to inspect the property. It's just a feeling I have, but my heart has never led me astray, so I know they will come. They cannot unearth the sacred rooms here. The books are not of consequence, but they aren't unusual and replicas can be found on the internet anywhere. Now with others taking this place over," her eyes watered, "we'll have to destroy them. The sacred room that you found Peter, they can never, ever find it. I have to destroy it."

"Destroy?" Angel looked stricken.

"Yes, destroy. I've planted bombs throughout the entire place. But I don't have what it takes to cause the chamber to retract within the ground."

Peter had a sinking feeling she expected him to be able to do it. But he kept quiet, daring her to speak the words.

"But you Pete, you can do it."

"Do what? Damn magic? I can't do nothin', not a damn thing."

Rosa's kind face transformed to a hard unrelenting stare. "You can, you will. Otherwise it will lead those that try to kill you one step closer. And cursing at me doesn't mean you aren't capable of understanding what you've been taught. If you want to live a little longer, you'll do this."

"No one's trying to kill me!" Peter bolted up from his seat, the chair falling with a bounce behind him. In his heart he knew someone was after Angel, but him—who would want to kill him? Why?

"Oh, someone wants to murder you. An entire army of the evil one's puppets would hunt the earth to destroy your bloodline."

Peter rested his fist on the table and leaned closer to Rosa, who lowered the pitcher, then wiped her hands on her apron.

He took a calming breath. "I don't even know my bloodline. My parents are dead. Dead!"

She nodded. "Your bloodline is tied to the blood of the order. They are hunting and killing all our children in hopes of finding the ones who have strong gifts which allow them to protect these sanctuaries…this history from great evil." Her finger pointed unwaveringly at Peter's chest. "For Pastor Finn to send you on the run, to a sanctuary…he knew you were special." Her eyes flicked to Peter's right hand, the hand that bore the mark Hanna had given him. "Your hand is proof something has started, something none of us may be able to stop. Only running is the answer now. Trust me, trust this." She pointed at her heart. "You have what you need to submerge that alcove. We cannot let them find it."

Peter caught Angel's shocked stare from his peripheral vision. The tickling in his chest confirmed that he had no choice. He would attempt to do it, his hand itched just as he was considering touching the statue, going into the alcove and...doing what?

Resigned, he answered, "You got me." His shoulders dropped in acceptance. "I'll try."

Rosa visibly relaxed. "Good. Time is short. You," she flicked her forefinger, "Angel, come with me to activate the bombs while Peter figures out how he's going to bury the sacred room."

Peter didn't waste any time stuffing his pancakes down, and gulping his juice. They all ate in silence, he and Angel too stunned to chat. Besides, Peter had to work hard at acting like they weren't in a relationship. He eyed Rosa, who had a serious yet worried look on her features.

"You know people came from all over the world to study here?" Rosa sighed, sadness filling her eyes. "When I was younger, my husband and I taught here in the summers."

"What happened to them?" Angel asked quietly, almost slipping into her feminine voice.

Peter cut a glance at her, and Angel's shoulders tensed as she cleared her throat.

Rosa smiled and winked at Peter. "Afraid. Over the years it's been a slow, methodical genocide of members. So subtle that we just noticed it in the last eight years. We suspect it's been going on for about two generations. But it's been purposeful. As though..." she frowned, "as though, someone was looking for something specific, or someone specific."

"Where are you going after this place blows?" Peter took his plate to the sink. Temporarily, soothed by the cool water, he washed dishes. He resolved himself to what he had to do next.

"I'll be heading north. I am catching a plane to Europe. I'm meeting with an elder in regards to planning a countermeasure to the unfortunate events that have been brewing lately."

Angel followed Peter to the sink and handed him her plate. "Where should we go? What should we do?" She watched Peter dry his hands.

Rosa came over and put a hand on Peter's shoulder. "Peter knows what you both should do. You will find others like you. Or they will find you. Someone will have to start working on building our future."

Peter crossed his arms. "You talkin' in riddles. I don't know why I'm running or what I'm running to. I feel…damn, like I'm running for nothing. Maybe…maybe we should just go to the cops."

Rosa furiously shook her head. "No! You, for all purposes are considered dead. Trust me, it's important you stay that way. The elders hid your identity for a reason. Something your father shared with them saved your life. Don't let that be in vain. Stay hidden for about a month. By then, I should return. I will meet you at Pastor Finn's." The alarm on her watch went off. "It's time. After you finish Peter, meet us in the front of the house. I'll give you a car. It's unmarked but you need to get rid of it as soon as you find other transportation." Rosa patted Angel's upper arm. "Come, we must hurry."

Chapter 17

Peter stood in front of the statue once again. Staring it down for a moment, he contemplated what he could do to make it disappear. He reached out, touching it, and within seconds it creaked. It slid back within the wall. The threshold to the alcove wasn't too intimidating, at least not like on his previous visit.

At that moment though, he felt like he belonged there and for some reason, he knew that he did. Out of thin air, tendrils of wispy mist formed and gathered in front of Peter. The wall was covered in gold. Drawings were carved into the gold with lines that lead to an imprint of what appeared to be a tomb of sort. The kind he remembered from the cemetery that looked like a mausoleum that was build into the side of a hill. He recalled it being named a Tumulus, from a distant lecture in history class.

His hand suddenly had a mind of its own. It reached out to press his heated palm against gold wall. The gold lifted where his hand lay. Needles pressed outward beneath his hand. And in an instant he felt a prick on each of his fingers and his palm.

The door moved. "Uhh! What the—" A faint tremor tickled his feet and, piece by piece, golden flecks fell from the wall. "Whoa!" His heart pounded while he fought to balance himself. The artful golden wall behind him cracked, chipped and appeared to disintegrate around him.

The floor cracked, and a vibration shook the floor. He lunged for the door. Breath flooded his lungs like a pounding drum. In a dive, he hit the hard floor, sliding across the hall. Catching his breath, he stared back into the alcove with his jaw dropped, while the walls of gold appeared to melt beyond the doorway. Gold and debris fell into a huge fissure that was once the floor.

Shaking his head, he fumbled around inside the wall, groping for the statue. His hand rubbed across its smooth surface. He quickly removed his hand as the statue started to slide toward him. The sliding door to the alcove closed and he stood back staring at the rumbling wall. Once the sound of thundering destruction dissipated, the statue returned fully into place. Hopefully any remnant of what was left in this room would never be found.

Peter stood there for several minutes dazed, his eyebrows wrinkled, hands on his hips. *Oh, yeah, I'm going loco. Certifiably insane.* He whirled around and rushed to front room.

Rosa came in rolling a suitcase behind her. "Did you do it?"

"Yeah, I did. I don't know how, but it's gone."

Angel came up the steps dragging their bags. Peter went to help her.

"We may as well get on our way," Rosa said. "The cars are parked around the back. Here's the key."

Peter reached out for the car key. "Thanks."

Rosa held onto his hand, then turned it over and examined his palm. "Beautiful. It's begun."

"What's begun?"

"Your hand is a sign of change. Power resides within it." Her eyes closed briefly and she released Peter's hand. "This symbol's ancient. Our enemy seeks to find out the mystery. Unfortunately, he'll kill us all to find it. But none of us knows the entire truth, the answer is in our blood." Rosa fingered the handheld detonator. "This bomb will ensure that they are just a bit further from the answers they seek." She touched Angel's shoulder lightly with her finger. "We must get going before they send their dogs."

They left the door wide open. Rosa pointed to the ten-year-old gray Chrysler 200. Peter hoped it wouldn't garner much attention.

"The tags? Are they legit?" Peter asked then pushed the button to open the doors.

Rosa shook her head. "They are bogus. So get rid of the car as soon as you can. Don't get pulled over either. That could make things turn for much worse. Oh, and there are gloves on the dashboard—cover that hand and don't let anyone, I mean anyone, see it. Our enemy will know something has happened to you, and you don't want them to be able to use you for their gain." She got in her car, held the detonator out of the window, then waved Peter on.

"Bye! Thanks!" Angel called.

Peter sped off with Angel waving out the window. His chest felt like a balloon of air when he hit the gas. Behind them, a thundering explosion filled the sky with black smoke. Angel jumped beside him. She yelped and her hand tightened on his arm. Something was after them, he could feel it like a palatable fog and he couldn't help but push on the gas a bit harder, hoping he'd outrun it just awhile longer.

Chapter 18

Gavin was infuriated. And when that happened, the only source of pleasure was killing—not for the Master, but solely for himself. It was something he'd started as a young child. First with his favorite pet, then with the homeless, and now…well now, with those close to him. It was what set him apart from all the others that would go before the Master.

What made him special, though, were the visions. They drove him to create a magnificent device that would transport him to another time, place, a plane some would call heaven, but to him it would be his kingdom.

He knew this newly acquired property was special. His lawyers had been researching it for a decade, feeding him contacts that were tied to the property. Gavin made sure Lucien took care of each and every one of those contacts—clean and efficient in causing their deaths. Patient as always, Gavin had put pressure on his lawyers to acquire the property due to unpaid taxes. With the treasure firm and in his reach, someone deliberately destroyed it. He gritted his teeth as a growl settled deep in his throat.

There was no time for further ponderings, shit had hit the fan and his prized acquired possession just went up in smoke. Now here he was with this whimpering woman begging him to let her go. He must take care of her before he could clean up the disaster his brother's carelessness caused. Lucien should've never left the property unsecured. But he did, now the place was in shambles and all Gavin wanted to do was punish someone for it.

The other holdings that belonged to his family had been attained steadily over the years, but this one—this special property—had been held by the others. These "others" were the enemies of his existence, of his purpose, and the barrier to his ultimate goal in life. The ones who fought to keep themselves hidden and their betrayal to his cause disguised.

Gavin stood in the dungeon, hidden well beneath the grass of his vast mansion in Virginia. He had a plane waiting. He'd have to make quick business of this plaything, so he grabbed a rope and a knife.

"Ms. Kent, I regret I won't have time to play with you properly." Gavin smiled at her, something he usually saved for those who were his personal indulgences. And Ms. Kent was just that. She'd been scheduled to visit one of his company's holdings in Bermuda. Unfortunately for her, the private plane he owned was lost, blown up—and she was already considered dead.

"Please…Mr. Steele, I…won't tell," she whimpered, tears and snot ran down her face. Her hands tied tightly with a rope, as were her legs, but the bindings did nothing to stop her body from trembling in fear. She swung softly from the hook in the ceiling, her muscles tight as she fought to balance and loosen her binds.

He tilted his head and appreciated her pale skin, blond hair and frightened blue eyes. "Stop your begging, it only annoys me my love," he said seductively. The knife felt comforting in his palm and he tossed it gracefully from hand to hand just to see the spike of terror in her eyes that made his mouth water in anticipation. Gavin headed toward her, his chest bare, and his custom-made pants hugging his every step. "Again, I apologize for having to do this so quickly." He placed a gentle kiss on her full lips. It was something about a whimpering, trembling victim that aroused him, and made his skin tingle with the hunger of their screams. And Ms. Kent served him well in that regard-—very well.

Sighing, he made quick work of silencing her forever. Finished, he stood, red and sticky, staring at his work, regretful of its sloppiness. Whistling a happy tune, he pivoted with a quick lick of his bloody fingers, and climbed the stairs to shower before his flight.

***

Gavin bit the inside of his mouth until he tasted blood. Killing Ms. Kent had only taken off the edge of his anger. Lucien better be able to clean this up for both of them or their work would all be for naught. Fulfilling his father's dream may fail if he couldn't find this Peter Saints and possibly this other rogue girl that escaped her death.

Gavin needed the girl's blood to counteract any protection around the artifact he sought. Of course if Lucien could find others like her it wouldn't be a problem, but considering how many children Lucien had to kill in his search, kids with the right mixture of blood were hard to find. The sacred artifact that could reveal his enemy's secret could be lost to them now. This property had taken him a lifetime to acquire, and his Master had led him to it, demanding a hefty price. But if he couldn't find the one relic he needed to build his device, everything he worked for would be lost.

Gavin still wondered at the importance of this Peter Saints. Although the master never indicated if the male was a boy or a man, Gavin had a feeling it was a boy. Since he'd tried to collect those whom the master had handpicked prior to this day, he knew from the few Lucien was able to capture, the master wanted kids. Those clues the master only divvied out based on the strength of the offering. The offerings had been many. Some of which had been killed in vain until Gavin had learned what the master had desired as a fitting sacrifice. Through many of the offerings given since the day of Gavin's birth, he learned his father had only scratched the surface of their enemy's secret.

But when Gavin had come into his full power, he'd taken over and had greater success capturing the master's hated ones. And by accident, they had uncovered the first one of their enemy's secret. He'd never forget the stricken look of the first young one they'd captured. For some reason, the master directed them to only go for the young insisting that the blood was not pure after a certain age and wouldn't be capable of breaching the enemy's protection.

The plane landed in the charred field. Ruble from a recent explosion littered the grass. He unhooked his seatbelt.

"Mr. Steele, would you like anything?" the tall, redhead attendant asked.

"Nothing." Gavin strode past her and out of the plane.

The captain stood to the side and followed in line behind him. Spotting his brother and the other men and woman standing on the outskirts of what looked to be the remnants of a building, he wondered why they weren't picking through the debris.

Lucien turned to him, grinning widely. "Gavin! How are you doing?"

"Forget the pleasantries. Tell me why the hell your people aren't looking through this for clues?" Gavin returned Lucien's smile with a scowl.

For once, in a long time, Gavin noticed that Lucien's eyes filled with fear. Perhaps in remembrance of the years of torture he'd endured at his brother's hands. Gavin's gaze held his. His expression was implacable as he ground out, "Don't make me ask you again, *brother*."

Lucien visibly gulped. "We can't. Literally, can't without getting sick."

Gavin's hand jumped out, and wrapped around his younger brother's neck. Just the right pressure—he added just the right amount of pain to make the point that he could kill Lucien there on the spot, before he leaned in. "Show me."

Lucien pointed to one of his men. The short brown-haired man was visibly shaken by the request, but moved forward. Gavin released his brother, and wiped his hands on his suit to calm down.

Lucien's man walked up to the heap of debris. His body wrenched from side to side as if being jerked by an invisible force.

"Tell him to keep walking," Gavin demanded.

"But…" Lucien looked at Gavin and sighed. "Keep going!"

With each step the man took, his body trembled and shook as if being pushed away. His screams didn't relent but grew higher pitched as he forced himself forward until he fell, face first, bleeding from the eyes and mouth.

Lucien stepped forward, pointed to another one of his men. "You! Walk the perimeter." He crossed his arms, his eyes cut back at Gavin. "That's not all. Watch this."

The taller man hesitated before he started to walk around the debris. He was careful to stay a distance from where the other man met his death. An expression of relief flashed on his face. "It's clear!" He took one more step, and a click tickled the silence, and blew him up into meaty pieces that splattered into the sky to land like rain on those standing around.

Gavin put his hand on his hip. "They're hiding something. They knew we were coming."

"What can we do? At this rate all my men would be dead before we could get in."

"We have to use a link, a psychic. There should be an echo here, something to let us know who was here. Then we find them. We only have a small amount of blood left from the child kidnapped last year to use. Unfortunately, someone killed the child instead of leaving it for further siphoning." His frown landed on Lucien's pinched face. "If we use what remains of that blood to break this barrier we'll need to bleed more to breech any others."

"Getting a psychic can be arranged. More of the children…well, they are getting better at hiding lately. The Ramirez girl got away and there have been no live leads on other kids since."

Gavin nodded. "You will find her, you have to now. And have my new secretary contact Terrance about sending the blood."

Lucien raised an eyebrow. "Another secretary already?"

He refused to spar with Lucien. They both had their secrets, however. Being brothers, each knew a bit of their compulsions but not the depth to which they delved. Lucien knew what had happened to sweet Ms. Kent.

"Brother, you really should widen your range for playthings, or people will begin to talk. Besides, do you think using the last of the blood for this is wise?"

Gavin waved at him. "I clean up my messes, Lucien. Can you say the same about yourself? However, about this…" He nodded at the mound of charred bricks and wood. "Someone is hiding something. Using the last bit of blood is well worth finding out what."

Chapter 19

They'd about run out of gas.

"We can't stop at the rest areas," Peter said. Cops were everywhere they'd passed along the way; so stopping for gas on the highway was a big 'not happening'.

Angel held tight to his hand. It trembled like she was afraid to let it go. "I know, but it's getting late. Maybe, we should stop at the next town." She pointed at a lit up Ferris wheel peeking above the trees. "It'd be nice to go to a carnival. I've never been to one."

He groaned. "Trust me, ain't nothin' special about them. I went when I was a kid and was pissed that I was too small to ride any of the big rides."

"Well it looks fun, and I need some fun."

"Yeah, I guess I could use some too after what we just went through."

Angel folded her leg under her. "Pete, is it me, or was Rosa really intense? When I went around the house with her she pointed out places she put little bombs. Then we went outside and dug small holes for land mines. I was trying not to freak out, because anyone with that much fire power could kill me if they wanted to."

"You shittin' me? She buried land mines? Damn."

"I know, but watching that place blow up behind us…it was…" she shivered.

"Intense, I know. It just beat home the fact that we are royally screwed. If that old lady thinks something, or someone, is after us that she has to blow up shit, then we gotta lay real low."

"Did she tell you where we could go? You know, a safe place like that? Oh, no." Angel buried her face in her hands. "That so was not a safe place."

Peter's hand tightened on the wheel. "I think it was, at least from what she said. But something's up. I gotta tell you, I'm feeling edgy. You know like some shit's about to happen. Something bad."

"What are we going to do?"

He shrugged. "I know a place, someplace we can go. Hell, I know a lot of places we can go."

"How? How do you know? Did your Pastor guy tell you or Rosa?"

"Naw…I just know."

She frowned. "How could you just know? No one just knows…I didn't when I thought that trucker was safe. I mean, I thought he was but he wasn't. I guess my gut wasn't working."

"Hmm, it was. You just didn't listen. Remember, he wasn't your first choice. The guy you approached first left, so you moved on to the perv, remember?"

"Yeah, so what? I still decided he was safe enough for us to ride with."

"Maybe, but I saw you hesitate for a minute, just before you stepped up in the truck."

"True." Angel bit her lip. "I did get a little twitch in my chest."

"Well, that was your gut, your body telling you something's not cool." He peeked at her. "You ever feel that way with me?"

She grinned. "Are you fishing for compliments?"

His mouth actually twitched thinking about kissing her. "Yeah, or maybe a kiss." He tapped his cheek. "Right here if you want."

Angel leaned over and landed a wet kiss on the edge of his lip. "You are so greedy for affection."

He stiffened. "What's up with that comment?"

"Nothing, nothing at all. I meant it in fun, but you are more affectionate than I'd thought when I first met you."

116

"Met me? The time that you were a boy? No, I wasn't feeling you like that. Are you talking about the time in the diner when you killed me with your eyes and rolled out of the diner liked you hated me? "

"Uh, no. Gosh, I did do that, didn't I?"

"Yeah, why?"

"I don't know. I was scared to bring attention to myself. I was down to my last couple of dollars and had planned on staying later than you did to…to um, steal your tip."

He laughed. "You were gonna stiff the old dude out of his tip? That's cold, damn, but desperate. So, why'd you get mad?"

"You were being nice. And stealing from you or him after being nice to me made me feel guilty. I guessed I could take your tip from him since he wouldn't miss it because the kids don't usually tip."

"So, you thought I was a punk. Is that why you tried to steal from me?"

She leaned in and kissed him again. "I knew you were," then she giggled.

"Girl, you lucky I'm driving."

"Yeah, and what are you going to do? You wouldn't beat up a girl, would you?"

He exhaled. "Naw, you got me there. I'm a sucker for girls. But a dude, oh, I'd whip his ass. Now I know you're not a guy, things have to change."

She shook her head. "They can't! You have to treat me like before so no one would know."

"I know. We'll just see how things play out." He peeped at the gas gauge. It was on empty. Looked like they would either have to ditch the ride, which Rosa warned him to do, or suck it up and take a chance in this rundown town.

Angel pointed. "That way, the carnival looks busy. We can park over there."

Peter looked around for a place to park. He drove off the two-lane road bordered with trees. A heavyset guy was directing people to parking spots and collecting money. Peter drove up alongside him.

The guy walked in front of the car, and then jotted something down on a piece of paper. He bent down to Peter's window and frowned. "Five bucks for parking, kid."

Wordlessly, Peter reached in his pocket, handed over a five-dollar bill, then grabbed the ticket the man handed him. He read the guy's name tag that said, "Ride Master, Nate."

The guy bent down and studied Angel before he slapped the roof of the car. "Park anywhere you can squeeze in."

The ground was filled with gravel for the obviously popular event and cars rode past them in search of parking on the grass. The carnival was erected in a large clearing packed with dirt that was framed in thick grass. Just a few yards of grass was clear before the tree line of a forest framed the impressive carnival. There was a sign that said, "Home of Love's Spell Amusements."

He went to the side of the oval of parked cars and parked in a secluded spot within the trees. Peter gripped the steering wheel, his eyes staring at the multiple lights that illuminated the night. "You may as well grab our bags. We ain't coming back here."

"If we leave the car, are you planning on stealing another one?" Angel climbed in the backseat and put her bag on her shoulder. Then handed Peter his.

"Seems to be the best plan. We'll hang around until the carnival closes. Hey, uh, grab the license plate off the car." He put his keys in the bag. Then tucked his gun in his pants.

Peter adjusted his backpack and reached for Angel's hand. She stepped away. "Remember I'm supposed to be a boy."

"Damn, I forgot. It's good, I'll remember. C'mon, let's stay in the tree line. We don't want no one spying us." He took a moment and search around. The place was mostly packed with teenagers and young couples. Orange lights were tucked up in some of the trees, overlaying the dark pathway to the carnival in soft color.

They broke through the trees and came in on the side of the carnival.

"You smell that?" Angel sniffed the air. "Heavenly, funnel cakes."

"Never had one." Peter kept a cautious eye on those around them. But the people seemed friendly. He nodded at several who waved. Trying not to look tense, he stuffed his hands in his pocket.

"Well, I have. They are so good." Angel's eyes seemed to glow. She moved her head to and fro looking at the lit-up rides.

Peter loved the smell, popcorn sopping with butter, sweet cornbread from corndogs, and the sugary scent of cotton candy. His hand was burning hot—he rubbed it on his cramping stomach.

They cleared the gravel path and walked onto the grass. He tugged Angel's arm, directing her away from the ticket booth and they slowly walked towards the large Ferris wheel in the middle of the carnival.

Peter couldn't shake it. This feeling like someone was watching them, with eyes on their back. Thing was, this sensation wasn't a bad one. It was a bit similar to what he felt when he first saw Angel. He stopped walking, searched past the spider ride, ignoring the screams and laughter from the riders.

"Pete? Why'd we stop? My mouth is watering thinking about that funnel cake."

He pivoted in a circle, his muscles tense. "I don't know, it's like I feel something. Someone staring at us."

"Is it a good feeling or a bad feeling, because I don't feel nothing but serious hunger."

"Me too, but…damn." He shrugged. "I'm just edgy. You know, leaving Rosa, all the weird shit happening to us, it's like we have a bad luck cloud following us. I mean, how the hell is it possible to leave a place as it blows up and be cool with it? Seems like the cops would be after us for just being involved in that shit. Hell, all the stuff that I've done in the last week could land me in jail."

"No kidding. We can't help that now. Rosa told us to run, and I believe her. I know for a fact that there are some bad people after me. And if what she's saying is true, which I don't want to believe, but seems to be, then we are both screwed." She elbowed him and smiled. "Need a kiss to make you feel better?"

He quirked up an eyebrow. "You are so wrong. Why you teasin' a dude?" Peter patted her back and started walking through the small crowd waiting for the spider ride.

She followed. "Because I can."

They made their way through the light crowd to stand in line at the funnel cake booth. Peter looked around, the feeling he had earlier wouldn't shake.

"Pete? Reality to Pete?" Angel called.

He faced her. "Sorry, just lookin' around." Out of the corner of his eye, he caught a kid watching him. The kid had broad shoulders, stood almost his height, had freckles, strawberry blond hair and dark brown eyes. Those eyes skimmed away from Peter's as the kid flicked a cigarette he'd been smoking and sauntered away.

Angel moved up in line. "I'll have two funnel cakes." She cut a glance at Peter. "Uh, add strawberries and whipped cream."

Peter pulled out the money, watching the kid slide between two tents and out of sight. He smacked the money down on the counter, hitting the girl's hand by mistake.

"What the hell? You stupid or something?" The blonde woman at the counter shrieked.

"My bad. My head's not here." Peter balled his fist, putting his knuckles on the counter.

"That don't mean you're not stupid!" The woman looked down at the money. "We don't take fifty dollar bills. They don't pay me enough for this shit," she mumbled. Her head tilted. "Sal! Sal! Can you break a fifty?"

It took everything in him not to curse this girl out. He just wanted to pay, get their damn food, and roll out of this town. Taking several breaths, he fought for calm. "Look, wait, I got a twenty." His eyes narrowed, his voice lowered. "You gotta problem with taking that?"

She landed a saucy glance on Peter, then slipped it to Angel. "You're not from around here, are you?"

"Just take my money and give us our food," Peter replied, his heated fist tightening.

Angel grabbed the plates. "Thanks, uh…miss. You can keep the change, for a tip."

Peter growled. He couldn't believe this girl. But she appeared re-lieved at keeping the four dollars, and threw the fifty-dollar bill on the counter at Peter.

She ignored him when she stuffed the money down her bra. "Next!"

Dismissed, Peter followed Angel to a nearby bench to eat. He grabbed the plate she handed him and stared at the patches of teenagers meandering from ride to ride.

"Good isn't it?" Angel elbowed him with her mouth full.

Chewing, he swallowed a wad of food then mumbled. "Uh-hum." His gaze was plastered on the tent ahead. A big sign that said "Your Future Awaits, Free Readings" was lit up in front of the dark burgundy drapes. A few kids stood outside the tent, kidding and joking while pushing a girl inside.

Peter's head was so jumbled with visions of Hanna, his mom, and snips of the ramblings from Rosa that he couldn't even taste his food. He tossed the plate in the trashcan, the food unfinished. He leaned on his knees, resting his forearms across his thighs while he watched the man at the Octopus ride nod in his direction while talking on the phone. The guy glanced around then left, walking past them and toward the cars.

"Oh, I could so eat another one." Angel got up and tossed her plate in the trash then turned to Peter. She softly slapped his arm. "C'mon, we can ride some of them. It'll pass the time while we figure out where to sleep and how to get out of here without the car."

Peter swallowed. He knew Angel was trying to make light of their situation, but he was so tense he felt like he would snap. At that moment, he didn't know what the hell he was going to do, and felt like he was leading Angel to her death. He couldn't protect her, not the way he wanted to, but he couldn't leave her either.

Chapter 20

"Lucien, use the blood sparingly. It's the last we have until you finish the job and get the girl." Gavin's hard stare nailed his brother, who was on the phone with the doctor in the trailer on the edge of the property.

Gavin had purchased the medical trailer along with his other holdings that produced metals for use in building, developing medical supplies, and exotic structures for all over the world. It was put to good use at the mines his company owned worldwide. Made the workers feel safe, and gave him an excuse to have medical doctors on the payroll.

"Doc said he can do it on two of the...uhum, volunteers." Lucien's ready smile curled higher. "The psychic is over there now feeling for the echoes. We also got a license plate of two cars registered here. The owner tried to hide the registration in various names, but one car was registered here in Georgia. It's gray. I doubt they could get much farther than my network without having to gas up or stop somewhere for the night. The other car is black. The tags on that one are dead. So it's just a matter of me calling in some of my guys on State Patrol to be on the lookout for it and the other car. If either of them stopped for gas, or even in the town my people know they are coming. "

"Did you send the specs to everyone?" His jaw tightened at Lucien's smile. His brother irritated him with his easy charm. "Don't make the same mistake that let the girl slip through our fingers." He hated his brother for that. Always easy to smile, grin and charm his victims. For Gavin, it was harder. Most people shied away from his harsh mannerism.

"No problem, big brother, I've learned my lesson. I've ordered this stuff done before you even landed." Lucien's finger flew over the keys of his phone as he texted a message.

Gavin watched the psychic at work. He ground his teeth against the memory of Lucien's last disaster. The missing girl, the one he felt in his bones could've been a suitable donor for his waging war on the others…the Order of Grace, they called themselves. Those that have for years tried various ways to thwart the rise of the Dragon.

First, Lucien bled out the boy that was their last donor, a special one. Someone the Master handpicked for them, one he'd been able to find. Then his brother's botched job of the capture of his former employee's daughter. A mole of many, his enemy planted within his very own company to collect secrets on Steele Industries. Lucien paid dearly for that mistake. Gavin's eyes traveled to the severed pinky on Lucien's hand, one of his punishments for Lucien's carelessness. The cuts that scarred Lucien's back were too many for Gavin to count, but were reminiscent of his artwork of torture on his younger brother. Only because of the master's demand had Gavin allowed Lucien to survive the discipline he'd enacted when all Gavin truly wanted was to consume Lucien's essence within him.

"Sarah's ready for us." Lucien led the way to the psychic who stood stone-faced waiting for them. "The echoes have been found. I sent out pictures of the vehicles and tags to everyone in the order. We'll get them."

Gavin regarded the psychic's outstretched hand then landed his cold blue gaze on her young face. He figured her to be in her early twenties, a recruit of Lucien's since her eager eyes sought Lucien's at Gavin's harsh greeting. She had no true idea of the two men she trifled with. The master had masked their true nature from those with the gift of second sight. It helped them to manipulate those with gifts they needed in order to do the master's bidding. However, there were some with the sight that were privy to the Dragon's purpose—created for it—and used to draw others with the gift of second sight unknowingly into the master's traps. This Sarah was just that, one trapped.

Gavin worked at softening his gaze, the woman visibly relaxed. His finger teased his chin. "So, Sarah, what treasure have you found for us?"

Eager to show off, she answered, "There were three people here. An older woman, she's been here a long while. Her echoes are the strongest, as if this were her home or something. She's also one of great spiritual strength, and more than likely put the spiritual barrier around the perimeter."

"The others?" Gavin asked.

Lucien directed the doctor to them.

Sarah tapped her lower lip with her finger. "One is a female, teenaged. The other is a male. They don't have strong echoes, like they haven't been here very long. But," the young woman twisted her dark curly hair around a finger, her eyes fluttering closed for a moment as if seeking the correct words, "the male, he's strong, even more so than the woman. It's as if...if he is full of power, and energy I can't explain. His echo, although a light touch, has a strong presence. The girl's is there but hidden as if I'm hearing it behind a thick wall, like a gentle tap."

"Descriptions." Gavin could barely contain his excitement. They were close, extremely close.

She shook her head. "Nothing. A barrier was erected. I can't picture any of them."

Lucien spoke up. "The doctor here said Ralph and Mike are ready."

Gavin turned to the gray haired physician, for whom he had much respect since the man had done anything they'd asked him to perfection over the years. "Is there any of the donor blood left?"

The doctor shifted nervously from foot to foot. "The blood transfusion on both men took the last of it. Lucien assured me that you knew this before I started the procedure on the second man."

He glared at Lucien. "You better get the replacement."

"I just got off the phone with one of my guys." Lucien met Gavin's glare with a calm assurance. "He's checking out a strong lead."

"Are there any conditions that would make these host unable to penetrate the spiritual barrier?" Gavin asked the doctor. "Did you use enough blood to mask them and make the protection placed here believe they are one of the Order of Grace?"

"Yes, they both got a full transfusion. It'll still take about two hours for them to recover, but I'll suggest we wait until the morning to be safe since this is the last of the blood."

Time, he was running out of it if he wanted to find the artifact that started this, or at least another that would give him answers. Too bad the blood only worked for barriers, if only…if only it could unravel the mystery the Master sought to uncover.

Chapter 21

Peter moved up in line behind Angel. "You know I'm not feelin' this, right?"

"I know, but we are doing it. We need a thrill ride to take our minds off of the crap we had to deal with the last few days, don't you think?" Angel's stride stiffened to appear more male.

Peter smiled at her now obvious work at trying to mimic his male mannerisms. "Just relax it. Now that I know the deal, it looks like you are tryin' too hard at it."

She scowled at him, but truth was now, it just looked plain cute and made Peter want to pull her to him in a kiss. Angel was a good distraction for him, but also a serious danger. He didn't know who was after her, but taking her to the sanctuaries worried him. Hopefully, in time he could confide more in her, but he didn't want to make her even more of a liability. It was decided, he wouldn't tell anyone else where the other sanctuaries were—not even her.

"C'mon. Whoa, see that?" She pointed at the loop on the roller coaster. "That will take your mind off anything. You ever ride one of these?"

His lip quirked up in a grin. "Naw, but I can handle it. You?"

"Yeah," a faraway look clouded her eyes, "with my mom."

Peter moved up behind her in line. "Your dad was too chicken to ride?"

"No, he was just too worried. For some reason, now that I think about it, the last few years we went out of the house together, he was like…I don't know, it seemed like he was guarding us."

"From what you told me, he was." Peter reached in his pocket and got their tickets.

The man running the ride stared at him. His tall, brown eyes looked over at Angel, then back to him. "Tickets."

Angel snatched the tickets out of Peter's hand and shoved them at the man. He grabbed her hand, held it tightly and slid her closer to him. "Not from here?"

Angel's brow furled. "Uh, no."

The guy snorted and let her go. Then his hand stopped Peter. "You either? How long you staying?"

Peter shrugged away from him. "None of your business," he stated and followed Angel to the ride.

"Have a nice stay here…you hear?" the man called back, then took tickets from a small group of kids.

Peter caught the guy observing them just a bit too closely. A tingle of trepidation teased up his back, and he gently nudged Angel forward as she got on the seat. Peter hauled himself up and dared not look at the man again.

He swallowed back his apprehension. "That guy over there, the one that took the tickets—what kinda vibe you pick up from him?" Peter wanted to make sure he wasn't just being paranoid. Honestly, he knew he was, but who the hell wouldn't be a little edgy with all the crap that happen to him in the last few weeks.

Angel fidgeted in the seat. "Vibe? Hmmm, he was a creep, especially when he held my hand. So, hated it. He made me wonder if he knew I was a girl." She did a fake shudder. "Yuck."

They didn't have much time to ponder on the guy, but Peter couldn't help it, he had to touch her. He tickled the inside of her palm with his finger and she jumped, smiling at him as they climbed in the air.

"Stop it. I'm trying to act 'boy' here you know."

"No one can see our hands."

128

Angel visibly seemed to melt and laced her fingers in his, her eyes slipping closed for a brief moment and she let out a soft sigh.

"Angel, you know what?"

"Hmm." Her eyes opened slowly.

"Hold on!"

The drop pushed the air from his lungs to his throat. Peter yelled, exhilarating adrenaline poured through his body and he felt high from the joy tickling his stomach. Angel's hand squeezed his fingers.

"Ye-ah!" He pumped his fist in the air as they zoomed on the first loop.

"Ugh!" They made a sharp turn; Angel's shoulder rammed into his.

The ride came to a jerky end and Peter slipped his hand from hers. They climbed out of the ride and headed toward the back of the carnival.

The psychic booth no longer had a line. A man stepped out with a turban on his head to smoke a cigarette. Peter's head hung low. He and Angel walked past the guy. Peter's shoulders tensed, he so didn't want to stop and talk to anyone. He had to find them a way out of this place.

"Hey, you, wait. Come here," the man called.

Angel stopped, and turned when the guy walked up to them.

"Sir, I don't want my fortune told." Angel shoved her hands in her baggy jeans.

"I didn't ask you. But I need to. Your aura…Something's off." He reached out and pulled her hand into his.

She tugged it away.

Peter stepped up next to the guy and grabbed the guy's wrist. "Get off!"

The guy's face flooded with shock. He let out a startled scream and snatched away his wrist like he was burned. He stood back, staring at his wrist. "You…you're a… Get out of here. There is something evil—more evil than you know, hunting you." The guy's body trembled. He stepped back, visibly shaken. "And it's close, too close." His eyes danced in the sockets, and he jerkily twisted around, searching. "It knows you are here," he whispered. With a push at Angel, the guy obviously avoided Peter. "Go now!" The psychic hurried back in the tent.

Peter and Angel hesitated a moment before they moved off. They both stumbled when the psychic rushed out of the tent dragging his bag behind him like the devil himself was following. The back of Peter's hand hit Angel's arm while they watched the man hurry away.

"What the hell was that?" Peter mumbled.

They strode to the back of the carnival to the woods beyond to find a place to sleep for the night.

"I don't know, but I don't like it." Angel followed alongside Peter, her eyes furtively looking around to make sure they went unnoticed. "Good thing most of the people are leaving. I saw security following people to the cars."

Peter put a hand on Angel's back and led her through the woods. They'd got a bit of distance and heard the crash of waves. He trudged ahead to see if there was a beach through the trees while Angel tagged along behind him.

Two steps later, the hairs on his neck stood on edge. He turned around at Angel's yelp. His stare hit the hard features of the man with his arm around Angel's neck, and a gun firmly to her temple.

"Yeah, that's right boy," he nodded at Peter. "Lift those hands up in the air. I wrote down the plates off your car, kid. I know someone that's willing to pay a lot of money for both of you—dead or alive."

Peter's teeth ground together, feeling helpless at the surprised fear in Angel's. He recalled the guy named Nate from the parking lot, then later at the ride.

"What makes you think that? You sure we're who you're lookin' for?"

The guy sneered. "Oh yeah, I got notice to look out for a car like yours. Lots of money was tied to that car you drove in here. That's why I was writing down every tag number that came to this park. I'm sure you two are who they want. No doubt there. The tags and picture of the car was sent to anyone in the know, and with a half a million-dollar price tag. I'm going to enjoy turning you over."

"Seriously, we stole that car awhile back from some girl. Man, it ain't ours." Peter fought to hold a steady gaze.

The guy raised his gun a bit higher. "I don't give a shit whether you're who they're hunting for or not, I'm turning your asses in—dead, if I have to."

Angel's leg slowly lifted. Her elbow hit the man in the stomach, giving Peter his signal to charge the guy. Angel lifted her knee and pounded down on the assailant's sandaled foot. Peter plowed a punch to the man's face. Angel yanked out his gun arm and cracked it on her shoulder.

Peter roared as the assailant landed a punch to Angel's face. She dropped, her head hitting a rock. Peter yanked the gun from his pants. Attempting to dodge the assailant, Peter slipped. The guy was on him. Pounding Peter's face with thick meaty fist, the guy grabbed for Peter's neck. Peter stumbled from the man's weight. He fell backwards. The guy's heavy form straddled him. Punch after punch jarred Peter's face from side to side. Nate leaned in to get a better hit. Peter's body became trapped under the man's heavy bellied form. Blood. Spit. And anger rolled off him.

Peter's gun was just out of his reach. Adrenaline pumped in his chest. He swallowed the blood in his mouth. And suffered through the blows. His weapon, just had to get to his weapon.

All at once, the smoking kid from earlier stood behind Peter's attacker. The kid lifted a metal pipe high behind Peter's assailant. One. Two. Three hard strikes to the guy's head. Then a splatter of blood and teeth.

One more jab. And the man fell unconscious, pinning Peter between him and his backpack.

"Push him up and I'll kick him off you," the boy said. His foot pushed the man off Peter, letting out a curse at the effort.

"Thanks, dude." Peter used his feet and hands to tilt the guy over and off him.

"Save it, we have to move." The kid's eyes jumped around. "Let's get out of here, cops everywhere."

Peter stood, adjusted his backpack. "Gotta get my uh…friend. Can you grab his backpack?"

"No problem." The kid followed and waited.

Peter took Angel's arms out of her pack, and lifted her into his arms. The kid picked up the backpack and put it on. "I'm Kyle, by the way."

"I'm Peter." He nodded.

"Can you run with him, 'cause, I'm hearing sirens now?" Kyle started to jog toward the sound of crashing waves.

"Yeah." Peter adjusted Angel in his arms as he ran behind Kyle.

"You have to keep up," Kyle called back.

Peter sped up. "Done." He sprinted, but couldn't shake the eerie vibrations that caused him to shiver slightly. They'd almost died tonight. Angel almost died. Her limp weight was a trigger for the heaviness that settled on him. He couldn't lose her —she was all he had now. Pathetic he knew, but she was…special. With his tainted past, he didn't deserve her, and she didn't deserve this. Why this kid showed up out of nowhere he didn't know, but he was happy he did.

"Almost there, just on the other side of the trees," Kyle's voiced between rapid breaths.

Angel moved and a groan escaped from her busted lip. "Pete?" she coughed, then snaked her arm around his neck.

"Shh, you'll be okay right. You'll be okay." He sneaked a kiss knowing Kyle was looking straight ahead. For what it was worth, her sigh made him feel better. Made him feel like maybe, just maybe they would be okay.

Chapter 22

They broke through the woods and their feet pounded headway toward the beach. Sprouts of grass snaked from side to side on the sand, and Peter's feet dug into it as he followed Kyle who started to slow down. A busted up trailer that was a bit tilted, looked like a mirage in Peter's dim world.

"My cousin won't be coming home tonight. She's working her other job," Kyle said. The handle of the door jiggled and he pushed it open.

"Thanks. You know, for what you did back there." Peter bent over a bit to help Angel stand.

Angel's arm draped around Peter with her other hand on her forehead. "God, my head hurts so bad."

Kyle held the door so Peter and Angel could enter.

"I got some Tylenol in the bathroom. Wait here, I'll be back." Kyle went to the back of the trailer. The home shook a bit from his heavy steps.

Peter pressed his hand on the large bump in the back of Angel's head and pushed her down on the couch. Then he sat beside her, his leg rubbed against the wood sticking out the slit in the frayed upholstery.

"Did you beat the scum up bad for me?" Angel winced and forced a grin on her face.

"I tried, but his heavy ass fell on me. I was trying to get my gun when Kyle hit the bastard with a pipe." Peter grabbed the pill bottle from Kyle.

"I'd been spying on ya'll since you got here. City folk don't usually stop in this town." Kyle sat across from them, grabbed a box of cigarettes off a nearby table, and leaned back as he inhaled.

Peter's lip turned up in disgust at the curl of smoke, and coughed. "Man, d'you mind? That shit stinks."

"So you say, but it relaxes me. Especially since I just saved your asses and you're sitting in my home. Deal with it." Kyle cleared his throat, before taking another drag.

"Were you scopin' us out trying to rob us? I appreciate your rescue but I don't get why. You don't come off as the good savior type." Peter leaned forward, his arms resting on his thighs.

Kyle smirked. "You got me all figured out, huh?"

"I know people, and when I first saw you earlier tonight you were following us. How do I know you aren't workin' with that dude back there?"

"No, not my style. But I do need a favor. And guess what, I'm in a good mood. You'll get something out of it for your trouble too." Kyle smashed his cigarette butt in plate sitting on the table. He stood and grabbed some keys from a shelf.

Peter got up, and looked down at Kyle's slight form. "What, what you want from us man—money?"

"A way out, I uh…have a situation. I'm not from this backwater slum. I came in several months ago to crash with my cousin."

"Where's she?" Peter asked.

"Working, you know, she's got a gig stripping at the local bar."

"So, what's that got to do with us? You helped us, I thanked you, 'nuff said." Peter crossed his arms.

"I got to get out of here. I have my reasons, but it's got to be tonight. We can borrow my cousin's car. It's legal and will get us pretty far as long as we keep it up on oil. And I don't want a situation with any cops."

Peter's muscles tensed while he sized Kyle up. "What you running from? Trust me—coming with us, is not a good idea if you're trying to live, dude. Did you get what happened back there?" Peter poked Kyle in the chest.

Angel pulled herself up and slipped between them. "Pete, let him come. He saved us, he has a car, and we can always drop him off later."

Peter growled. He didn't trust this guy. Sure, the guy helped him, but the fact that he'd followed them, conveniently saved them, and wanted to dodge out of town didn't add up. But what choice did he have? They couldn't go back to the other car— that ride was hot now.

"Fine. Just don't get cozy with us. You want to risk your life hangin' with us, it's your bad." Peter picked up his backpack and Angel's. "We gotta roll, like now."

"No problem, I can handle myself. Let me get my stuff." Kyle pushed passed him to the door behind him.

"Wait, you gotta cell phone you plan on bringing?"

Kyle looked at him like he was stupid. "Yeah. Who doesn't?"

"Leave it. I can't roll with them. If you don't want to leave it, then you ain't coming."

Snorting, Kyle waved his hand and disappeared into the room behind them.

Peter turned to Angel. "I don't trust this dude."

Angle smiled. "You don't trust no one, remember?"

"No, I don't, but I got my reasons. I'm not supposed to take peeps with me. You know what happened wouldn't have if you were not with me." His hand wiped down his face.

"You're kidding, right? That guy was probably looking for me. Re-member," she peeked over his shoulder, and then whispered, "I'm the one who's on the run from her parent's killers."

Kyle came up behind Peter and Angel jumped back. "Talking about me behind my back? It's cool, I get it. But you need me if you want to get out of this town alive, right?" Kyle tossed his cell phone on the ratty couch then walked around Peter to the door.

They followed him down the shaky wooden stairs to the roughed-up dark green Dodge Magnum with rust spots splattered on the hood.

"This all you?" Peter threw the packs in the seat before climbing in the front passenger seat.

Angel hopped in the back and slid off her pack.

"Don't put your bags there, pull up the latch under the seats and push them in." Kyle stuffed his under the driver's seat, and then threw a small bag in the back with Angel. "Yeah, the car's the last thing my *loving* parents left me before their escape." Kyle started the car.

"That right?" Peter rolled down the window and rested his arm on the frame. He narrowed his eyes, distinctly remembering Kyle pointing out the car was his cousin's. The liar. "I sense a bit of saltiness in that."

Kyle whipped the car from side to side, kicking up sand before they hit the rock paved road. "You could say that. They kicked me out…well, moved out, I came home and the place was empty. I stuck around for a few months, then came here to crash with my cousin a few weeks ago."

Peter drummed his hand on the door. "Let me get this straight. Your parents just disappeared, didn't come home, left no note and cleaned the place out?"

"Yep, that's about it."

They drove down the gravel road, draped in trees, with the moonlight flashing behind them.

"Why would they want to do that?" Angel asked and leaned up on the seat.

"They thought I had a slight…um, drug issue."

"You were using?" Peter frowned.

"No, just selling. I dabbled with the weed, but that's it. Didn't like the walking zombie look the rest of the shit gave people."

Peter groaned. "Why the hell would you do that? You had a family man. Something I didn't have, and you screwed it up to sell drugs?"

"What the hell you care for? It's my hell, not yours, dude. Besides, my parents weren't shit to write home about. My mom stayed at home to raise me, but was popping all kinds of prescription drugs. A hypochondriac who always had some illness or another that kept her up on her dope. That is, 'til the docs caught on to her game, then…well, I was persuaded to help with her habit. The one my dear dad didn't notice since he was whacking on his secretary most nights."

Peter shrugged. "You're right, I don't give a damn. I got my own issues." He stared out onto to the dark road. Kyle came to a stop at the crossroad where the rocky road collided with a paved one.

"Besides, I gave them lots of reasons to leave. It's all right, I got my liquor to help me forget about it." He laughed.

"You ain't funny, man." Peter checked the street both ways when Kyle maneuvered the car onto the paved road.

"What do you know about funny?" Kyle stopped at the first light since they got into town.

The houses were spaced apart. Gravel paved streets that lined the homes were virtually empty, and the lit porches flickered with glowing lights from the fireflies.

Peter inhaled the fresh scent of honeysuckle and, in a brief moment, the heaviness of hopelessness taunted him. The next sanctuary was near, but should he take Angel? And he didn't want to take Kyle anywhere. The kid seemed unstable. Kyle was obviously a high school dropout with substance abuse issues and a muffed-up family. Hell, who was he kidding? All of them had serious issues, but at least for now, no one was hunting for Kyle—not yet. If he stayed with him, Peter was sure Kyle would be on the hunt list too.

Peter rested his chin on his closed fist, its throbbing warmth now a comfort, a reminder that maybe—just maybe—he had a real purpose in this world. That even though he didn't have his parents, hell no one now besides Angel he could trust, that he could turn his life around. He could live, one day that is, live a normal life. One day, maybe, have a family of his own.

Peter smacked his teeth. "Who am I kiddin? Stupid ass dream," he muttered.

His heart was beating fast, but he couldn't tell why. Didn't know why all of a sudden everything was spooking him. Just as he finished berating himself for his paranoia, Angel tapped his shoulder.

Sirens lit up the night. Peter's eyes flew to the mirror.

"Dammit! Cop, what the hell did you do?"

Kyle chuckled. "Guess I ran that stop sign back there. We were almost to the highway. I'm thinking I can outrun him."

"Shit! Shit! This can not be happening." Peter's fist hit the door. His feet pounded the floor and he bent to push his backpack firmly under the floorboard. "You settin' us up, man?"

Angel scrambled to do the same. "What are we going to do? If they ask for ID, I don't have none."

"Don't worry, the only person they expect to have ID will be me. And I got ID—fake, but clean." Kyle pulled over to the side of the road.

Peter looked longingly at the highway sign to Rt. 95, *so close....so close. This might end it all.*

Chapter 23

Gavin watched Lucien talk to his men. The psychic studied him carefully. He felt it, he always did. Since they couldn't get a reading off him other than body language they never felt threatened—at least not with their second sight. A gift from his father, he supposed, before the man was ruthlessly murdered on his eighteenth birthday. His father had a spirit man shield Gavin and Lucien since he had great plans for them. Gavin curved the side of his lip in a sneer. His memories of his dear old dad, who most considered an eccentric genius on the edge of madness, were vivid—especially those on the night the master demanded he kill the man.

"They are close," Lucien boasted, pulling Gavin from his thoughts.

"Are they detained?" Gavin didn't bother turning towards Lucien. His eyes studied at the rubble in front of them.

"Well, one of my contacts said his guy almost had them but someone hit him from behind. They couldn't have gotten far. They are about eight hours from here by car. I'm sending backup in the helicopter to help with the search."

He slanted his eyes at Lucien. "You're telling me your guy failed, Lucien?"

"No, he didn't. He's on the job." Lucien's forced grin widened. "I have good news from the psychic and the doctor."

He'd let Lucien's redirection pass this time, but his eyes narrowed to remind Lucien that he was aware of the tactic used. "It is?"

"The psychic confirmed that once our guys got past the barrier, she can break it for good. And then she can direct our men to any artifact with a strong spiritual imprint."

"Perfect. Let's get started right away." He reached out to touch Lucien's shoulder.

Ever so slightly, Lucien flinched, and then blinked. He visibly stilled his obvious fear of his brother. "Good, I'm on it."

Gavin was starting to feel a bit of relief. If they could just find something here, any remnant that would reveal an imprint of their powerful enemy, it could set things in motion to find the other hidden locations of his enemy. A masterpiece that slivered light on the depth these servants would go to hide their existence—their secrets. Had an accidental meeting with his ancestors not taken place, the depth of his nemesis's deceit would have gone undetected for another millennia. That historic moment where something was revealed to the master, something so well hidden that only someone with the bloodline tied to the secret was able to unlock.

"They are in. She's ready to talk." Lucien's smug look of success affirmed Gavin's hopes.

It had started, the wheels of fate were turning in his favor, just as the master promised. Just as his father preached, his time had come. "Good, Lucien."

They walked to the psychic who held a sly look like she knew she had the upper hand. Gavin grinned back at her, allowing her to think she did, he knew either he or the master would fix that smirk. Make it permanent before he tasted her spoils. She looked as though her blood would be sweet with energy of a transient, powerful spirit. All the sweeter if he was able to taste of it before the master used her. But now he'd let her enjoy the upper hand.

"So what good news do you have to share? I knew someone as gifted as you would come through for us," Gavin said smoothly.

She glowed under his praise. Lucien, never one to share his future playthings, moved forward to kiss her hand.

"I told you she was special, Gavin. I knew it the moment I laid eyes on her."

"Indeed." Gavin put his hands in his pocket. "Please, share your news."

"Your men were able to fracture the breach, and I destroyed it. Now I feel remnants of something spiritually ancient. Pieces of it are buried rather deeply underground, but a small piece must have gotten separated from the rest." She sniffed the air, her hand teasing her necklace. "I sense it strongly, but the item itself is protected. If I, or you, were to touch it…something bad would happen. However, I believe if one of your men, uh, the men that broke through the barrier, found it, then they could touch it and maybe I can connect to it through them."

Lucien pulled the surprised young psychic into his arms and planted a kiss on her lips. "Yes! Thank you." He winked at Gavin just above her head as he held her in a brief hug.

"Yes. You've done well. You have such a talent."

Still glowing from Lucien's kiss, her hand covered her mouth briefly as she collected herself. "It's what I do."

Lucien walked toward his men, then turned and waved at her. "Come. Come. It's time."

Gavin's eyebrow lifted, his arms crossed, and his finger tapped his thin lips. "Yes, talented." He would use her in the final transformation. He'd steal her broken body from Lucien's pleasure after the master was done with her.

Thoughtful, he hummed lightly. If this place held any of the sacred remnants that initiated the master's search, which would mean he and someone of their blood would have to touch the item at the same time in order for the secrets held to be revealed. If the psychic wanted to chance touching such item, who was he to stop her? It would prove a valuable experiment. However, he had a feeling Lucien's men wouldn't be able to deceive such an object of power.

The beginning of his master's quest was caused by chance. It had been the fatal accident of one from his enemy's camp, and Gavin's great ancestor's good fortune who set this entire hunt in motion. Both of them, his ancestral grandsire and one from the Order of Grace, on an archeological dig that changed his master's ignorance of their deceit forever. An accident, unknown to both as their hands touched the sacred item buried under Tibet sand. A weapon that only those on the spirit realm knew could cause great suffering to the victim and to others linked to the dragon. It had sparked an awakening—an awareness of sorts—in his master. Since that moment, the master clung to all in his bloodline. Some of his ancestors were given the gift of the dreams.

Those dreams set him apart from Lucien, they made him special and set him aside as the master's vessel. Lucien was born as his servant. Generations passed from father to son, father to daughter, the dreams for building the masterpiece were passed on. But Gavin wouldn't let the opportunity skip him as it has the others, he would please the master and rule both realms. Earth and the Heavens, and Peter Saints' blood would help him do it.

Chapter 24

For the first time since Peter met the guy, Kyle was spooked. He rubbed his hands together and rocked slightly in his seat. Each second, while they waited for the cop to come to the car was torture.

"Look, it'll be nothing. Trust me, the ID I have is clean." Kyle reached over and knocked on the glove compartment in front of Peter with his fist. Then he shuffled inside to grab a torn black wallet, just as the cop came up on his side of the car.

A light flashed through the window. Peter froze his expression into serious concern when the cop with the wide rimmed hat peered through the window. The officer's eyes caught his and, for a brief moment, Peter saw his disquiet. With a flick of his wrist, the cop turned his light on Angel, who scrambled back in her seat.

"Son, hand over yer license and registration please." The officer's chubby hand waited for Kyle's documents.

"Here you go sir," Kyle said smoothly.

Peter saw the slight shudder of Kyle's hand and gritted his teeth. The guy was hiding something. For sure it was something that would get them in trouble.

The cop stood erect and walked back to his car.

Kyle looked back at Angel. His eyes fell on the small bag on the seat and he whispered, "Shit, put my bag away."

Peter gritted out, "What the hell's in the bag, man?" Bad enough his background could get them in jail for years, but if Kyle had the stuff he thought he did, they were all royally screwed. He said a silent prayer, knowing he shouldn't, that he was seriously unworthy of any of God's favor, but he didn't know what else to do.

"Don't worry about it," Kyle stared at him. "You know nothing."

The cop returned. Angel fumbled with the small bag, and then dropped it, looking up to see the cop walking alongside the car. She kicked the bag under the seat, while Peter and Kyle held their breath.

"Boys, step out of the car," the officer demanded, his expression stern and unflinching.

Peter's hand throbbed, his head hurt, and his heart beat against his chest so hard he swore it would pop out. This was it; they were going to jail, or worse. He figured worse, because no matter what, he knew he had to keep running. Had to get to the next sanctuary, with Angel, or else they'd be found out. Peter had a sick feeling at all the horrible things that would happen to Angel if they were separated.

He and Kyle stared at each other briefly. Angel, the bravest, opened the door first.

"Hand's up, son," the cop ordered, with his hand on his gun.

Peter grabbed the door handle and got out of the car. He stood stiffly with his hands up and fisted in the air. Sweaty drops slivered down his forehead and over his face while he waited for Kyle to get out of the car.

"Um, officer..." Kyle opened his door. Slowly he rose. "What's the problem?"

The cop took out his gun. "All of you, get on the ground behind the car. Lay flat on your stomachs with hands out."

Kyle's gaze collided with Peter's while Angel quietly slumped on the grass. The police car's light cast a glow on her white baggy T-shirt as she lay perfectly still. Peter nodded at Kyle. He slipped to his knees, then to the ground.

Peter's eyes followed the policeman as Kyle finally dropped to the pavement between he and Angel. The cop went to the car, flashing his light under it, checking the trunk and peering furtively around like he was scoping out the area for others.

"Kyle...Kyle? What the hell is in that bag?" Peter kicked Kyle's leg.

"My stash. Weed, liquor and my smokes." Kyle tilted his head at Angel. "But Angel took care of it. So we're good."

Angel shook her head. "I didn't get a chance to put it in the hidden compartment." Her eyes started to water.

"You dumb ass!" Kyle hissed.

"Watch it! Angel's not responsible for your shit. If we get out of this, I oughta kick your ass for this," Peter sneered. A lump of terror dropped from his chest to his stomach. Panic taunted him and he reached over to rub Angel's back, more to calm himself than just her, "It'll be all right. If we have to, we run." His eyes slid to the wooded area behind them. "Through the woods, you follow me, don't worry about Kyle. We're leavin' his ass."

Sniffing, she wiped the tears from her face. "I'm tired, Peter. Just tired of running."

"Don't...don't say that!" He stared at her anxious eyes, pushed his fear down...down deep—*for her*. He'd been through some shit, hell, he'd caused some major crap to screw up in his life, but Angel didn't do anything to deserve this. To feel this way—not like he had. "Do it for me? For us."

Angel swallowed and nodded.

"Give me a freaking break! He screwed us, and I know I'm not going out without a fight." Kyle's eyes narrowed at Peter. "Even if the fight is with you, dude."

The cop made his way to them, his gun ready in his hand. He glanced around as if making sure he wasn't being watched.

Peter's eyebrow lifted at the strange behavior and moved his hand to brace himself to run. Angel also repositioned herself while Kyle watched her.

"Look kids. Today's your lucky day." The cop waved the gun at them. "Get up and get out of here. Fast! Take the car."

They hopped up. Peter led the way to the car. "I'm driving!" Kyle and Angle hurried behind him.

The cop followed and closed the door behind Peter as he stood watch outside. "Son, I got a call about some guy getting beat up. But here's the thing. There was another call, one from…the *order*." His gaze stilled as a car passed. "That call said to detain you. And if those guys want you, ain't nothing good gonna come out of it. They'll be coming for you, but I can't do this." The guy shook his head. "Can't do what they want me to do to you kids."

"Thanks, sir." Peter cleared his throat, his hands tightening on the wheel. "Who's after us? What's the order called?"

"The dragon's after you." The cop jumped as his phone rang. He peeked at the number. "Now go! Before they get here!" He hit the side of the car.

Without a moment's hesitation, Peter sped off.

Chapter 25

It was time. Gavin watched the men who were filled with new blood stare at the shiny, black remnant the psychic pointed at.

Sarah held up her hand. "Take care with it. It looks like a piece of something that was made out of marble. The power radiating from it is ancient. So much so, it vibrates off my skin." She shivered.

Gavin's eyes met Lucien's, and he nodded.

"Go on, have one of them touch it," Lucien spoke softly to her like a lover. Gently tucking a wayward strand of hair behind her ear, he rubbed her arm to soothe her.

Encouraged, she whispered. "Touch it."

Lucien frowned at the hesitant man. "Brad, you heard the lady."

"Now," Gavin hissed. Pinching the inside of his arm, he could hardly contain his excitement. Either he would get answers, or will enjoy watching Brad's death. Whatever happens, he'd know what to do next.

Brad's trembling hand reached down into the debris.

Resolute, Gavin observed. He suspected this wouldn't end well for Brad, but at least they'd have the other man filled with blood to lead the ceremony until Lucien caught his two prizes who were still on the run.

As Brad's fingers connected with the smooth rock, dusted in gold. A show of relief waved over his features. He blinked, then grasped the entire jagged rock in his hand. Terror exploded onto his features. A sick humming sound escaped from his thin lips that appeared glued shut.

"Humm…hummm….hummm." Brad's eyes rolled back in his head. The veins on his arms, hands, face and neck appeared to throb, then grow. His mouth opened in a bloodcurdling shriek that escalated higher and higher with each pulsating beat of his heart. His skin appeared to bubble as boils popped out of all over his body between the throbbing veins which had grown so bloated they cut through his skin. And he never stopped screaming.

"Stop! Help him!" Sarah cried and buried her face in Lucien's outstretched arms.

Lucien patted her back and grinned at Gavin.

Gavin sighed as Brad's head cracked to the side. His body dropped to the ground, forever silenced.

"Well, Sarah, any other ideas?"

Sarah was crying hysterically. Between hiccups she said, "No...no. I-I thought it would work." She sobbed, "I kill-k-k killed him."

Gavin moved her chin so her eyes lifted to his. "Not you, but those who cursed this place." He leaned closely to her, almost touching her lips. "But you can do something about it, Sarah. You can pay them back. At a ceremony...only for the most gifted spiritual talents."

She nodded. "I can?"

His lip turned up, "Yes, and Lucien will be there with you."

Sarah's love-filled gaze slid to Lucien's. "You will?"

Lucien's lips gently touched hers, as if she was the most precious person in the world to him. "Of course I will."

She nodded. "I'll do it."

"Trent! Take her to the car." Lucien pushed her in Trent's direction.

They watched her walk slowly toward his man. Sarah took a quick look back at Lucien. He nodded in return. She smiled then let Trent help her into the limo.

Lucien's smile dropped as he turned his attention to Gavin. "Ceremony brother? So soon?"

"I'll give you until I can bring the council together to get the Ramirez girl and the boy that's with her. If what Sarah says is true about the echo left behind, I suspect the boy is Peter Saints." Gavin rested his hands on his hips. His ominous gaze held his brother's eyes.

150

Dragging his hand through his hair, Lucien answered, "A couple of fucking days! Gavin…shit!" He stilled as Gavin's eyes darkened. "I can make it happen. I swear it."

Gavin took a step toward his brother. With lightning speed, he grabbed his brother's hand and twisted his wrist downward.

Lucien gasped, holding back a sob. "They'll be there."

"Make sure you don't disappoint this time. My patience is depleting." Gavin increased the pressure until he heard the crack. A grin bloomed on his face, at Lucien's muffled cry. He released Lucien's wrist and walked smoothly past him to the waiting limo.

Chapter 26

Peter's eyes were glued to the road. They'd been on the highway an hour. The chug-chug sound of a helicopter appeared, made a circle, then came back. He said a silent prayer the copter wasn't sent for them. The cop had put their plates and Kyle's ID into his system before he seemed to get a change of heart. No more than ten miles over the speed limit should keep them off cop radar. But would that keep them off the dragon's radar? That was what the cop said, at least what Peter thought he'd heard. He had to be wrong. This was madness. Madness. His eyes blinked several times as he fought for control of his trembling hands.

His head hurt and chest was cramping, but he had to get as far away from that town as possible. The other sanctuary was close—real close. And now, he really didn't have a choice but to take Kyle with them.

"What the hell was that crazy cop talking about?" Kyle nudged Peter with his elbow.

Peter frowned. "Don't touch me, man. You got somewhere you want us to drop you?" He held his breath, hoping against hope Kyle had somewhere to go. Anywhere away from them.

"No. Look, I have to come clean." Kyle's fist hit the dashboard.

"Like telling us that your fake ass country accent ain't real?" Peter sneered.

Kyle leaned forward and buried his head in his hands. "My parents didn't leave me. They disappeared. It doesn't make sense that they would've cleared out the house and left *together* to get away from me." With a lift of his head, he continued, "My father was into some weird stuff. He used to curse at my mom and blame her for their problems—for not being the woman he should've married. He wanted someone that understood his history. But he married her against his family's demands."

"So…" Peter pushed harder on the gas. He frowned, spying a car speed off a nearby exit. "You think your parents were kidnapped or killed."

Kyle nodded.

Angel leaned forward. "Mine were too."

"What? No, that's not possible." Kyle twisted toward Angel.

"It is. Men murdered my parents—but I got away."

"Same with you, Peter?" Kyle asked.

Peter grunted. "I don't know. Mine died and that's all you need to know." He stared at the car that was about a mile behind and gaining. "We done sharing now?"

"This shit's weird. How'd we all, like, meet up and have the same issues? Dead parents? I mean…seriously dude, that just don't happen."

"Fate?" Angel asked.

"Hold up, we didn't follow you man, you did the followin'. So why us?"

Kyle reached under the seat and grabbed his bag. Stuffing his hand inside, he visibly relaxed when he pulled out a cigarette. He lit it up, took a drag and held rested his hand on the door. "I don't know. I just felt like you were safe. You know, that you were cool. I watched you all night. I saw you get out of your car and followed you the entire time. Something told me I had to hang with you."

Peter snorted. "Safe? Man, we ain't been safe in forever. You should've cut your odds and stayed away. Now…" He spied the car behind them speeding up. "Shit!"

"What?" Angel asked.

"We're being followed."

Kyle leaned his head out the window. "No, I think the prick's just speeding."

"Uh-uh. Get the gun out of my bag." Peter pointed at the floor as he slowly increased the speed.

"You're at eighty miles per hour." Angel leaned forward. "You ever drive this fast before?"

A grin slipped to Peter's face, memories of taking Pastor Finn's babies out drag racing flashed in his mind. "Yeah, once or twice."

Kyle pulled out two guns. He lifted his arm and handed one to Angel. "Damn, I underestimated you dude." Kyle chuckled and he looked out the window. "Damn!" He lifted the gun. And jumped a bit when another car sped out in front of the one gaining on them from a service road.

Gunshots from the other car popped around them. A bullet connected with the trunk. Peter swerved.

"Shit, they're shooting!" Kyle hollered.

"Kickin' up speed—NOW!" Peter slammed on the gas. Butterflies of adrenaline pumped over his skin. His fingers squeezed the wheel. Blood rushed to his head, and tightened behind his ears as it drummed to the beat of his racing heart.

The roar of the engine built with each stomp of his foot on the accelerator. Kyle's arm rested on the window frame as he fired at the car gaining behind them.

"Yeah, this is friggin' sweet!"

Angel leaned out the window behind Peter, taking slow precision shots at the wheels of the cars chasing them. "Too fast to get...a clear shot!"

"He's gaining! Coming up on your side Kyle, handle it." Peter veered his car in front of the red car racing up alongside of them.

"Done." Kyle fired continuously at the first car to squeeze alongside them.

Peter peeked at the driver—angry eyes, black hair and a gun, then yelled, "Hold on!" as he swerved into the side of the car.

"Ahhhhh!" Angel screamed. A loud thump sounded in the car when her upper body hit the door. "My gun's gone out the window," she groaned.

The red car wrenched to the side, and lost ground as Peter accelerated out of the jerk, smoke kicking up behind the car, rubber burning. His mouth watered as he glanced at the rearview mirror.

Kyle braced his back against the dash, his foot secured on the seat while he fired at the red car that was catching up. "I got a gun in the bag on the floor! Hurry, the other car firing up next to us."

"Damn! Damn! Damn!" Sweat broke out on Peter's forehead. He ate up road behind what looked like a family van up ahead with a travel bumblebee on top. *A family in there, God, please don't let me hit them.*

Peter pushed the car harder and onto a small bridge. It started shaking. Quickly, he changed lanes just as the red car attempted to block him. The back of his car clipped the other car.

"Yeah baby!" Kyle's shot pierced the wheel of the attacking vehicle.

The other car fishtailed, its back striking the van, which jerked around. The family's van hit the front of the red car, which veered over the side of the bridge and into the water.

Peter released go of the breath he'd been holding, and eased off the gas just a bit. "Close, too damn close."

"What you doing! The other bastard's coming—and fast!" Kyle attempted to hold steady, his gun aimed.

Angel's back pressed against Peter's seat, her gun aimed out the back window. "That family...they look okay." She sighed. "Thank God."

"Not yet! Those bastards are getting too close." Peter pushed the gas harder. The other car caught up, its dark blue hue gleamed with a slice of moonlight from the trees as it weaved back and forth on the road behind them.

Peter adjusted in the seat, swiped his arm across his sweating fore-head and leaned forward seeing a tractor trailer ahead. "Grab on to something, I'm gonna try somethin' wicked."

The black car surged forward, bumping the back of their car. Angel fell back, her head colliding with Peter's when the car jerked forward. His vision blurred temporarily. He struggled to control the wheel. But the car veered. Peter gulped, pushed harder on the wheel. He slid into the next lane, driving alongside the tractor.

"Now! Hold on now!" Peter rammed the front of the car into the wheel of the tractor causing the front end to bend and bow with the cab. Peter prayed there wouldn't be too much damage to his car. He whipped the steering wheel around and swerved out of the way of the truck's front, then burned rubber at top speed, the truck and his pursuers behind them. He heard the pursuing car's crash with the cab of the truck. Peter grinned.

He peeped at the collision behind him, blinking when the other car crashed into the semi's trailer. A grinding sound let him know him that the car had barely made it out of the incident intact.

Breathing hard, Peter whooped. "Da-yum, that was some bad-ass dri-vin' right there, man!"

Kyle's fist hit the roof. "Yeah," he blew the tip of his gun, "and shooting."

"Alive…I'm alive." Angel let out a loud breath and slumped back in the seat. With shaking hands, she put on her seat belt. "Will the car be okay?"

"Maybe." Peter slowed to a legal speed, and decided to get off the main road for an hour or so. It would take longer to get to the sanctuary in this direction, but maybe they'd be better hidden away from main roads.

"We're almost to a safe place. Rough road ahead though. The wheels on this will get us there." Peter took the next exit and followed the two-lane road for a few miles before he turned into the woods.

"Dude, you know where the hell you going? 'Cause driving through the woods to Grandma's house don't seem to be the answer," Kyle snickered.

"Trust me, I know this place is safe." Peter slowed the car. It bumped up and down and they hopped in their seats from driving over scattered rocks, grass, and bushes. Large, green bushy trees flanked each side.

"Pete, there's no road here, how do you know this is the right place?" Angel asked, doubtful.

"I just know." He briefly closed his eyes, the ghostly images on the map from the first sanctuary appeared in his head as if he were standing there. Frowning, he leaned an arm out the side of the car while clearing a patch of trees, and pulled to a stop.

Peter looked ahead at the open patch of land ahead. The ground was cleared of trees, but had dead leaves, weeds, and rocks of all sizes in a large circle. In the middle of the white rocks stood a single headstone with no words engraved on it. His hands tightened on the wheel and he stared. No one uttered a word for several minutes.

"Are you sure this is right? I mean, this place don't look safe. There's no shelter." Angel unbuckled her seatbelt.

"This is crazy." Kyle opened his door, put his foot on the ground and rested his elbows on the frame of the open door.

Peter got out, walked over to the small break in the circle of rocks. "I'm starting to think that's just what I am…crazy, screwed up insane."

Chapter 27

Peter knew it, this was it. His hand was on fire. This was the next sanctuary, but different—much different than the others. It was purposely hidden, as if it was only meant for someone unique to find it. He circled around, looking up at the overhanging trees, smelling the wild flowers. If not for the moonlight the place would be completely hidden. It was like some unknown force was confirming that this was the place. Somewhere he was meant to be. Even though his skin still tingled from their close escape, for some reason—here, in this place, he felt peace.

Peter raised his hand; the puckered, red scar glowed and turned warmer as it burned. Why it still pained him, he didn't know. But now it had become an old friend, something strange that comforted him. Alone, crap, he'd been alone all this time. His eyes traveled from one rock to the next. Every rock seemed to glow in the moonlight, calling to him to step deep within the center of the decorative circle they created around the tombstone in the middle. The head stone, plain, silver, beaconed him and slowly, hesitantly, he took one step, then another.

The tombstone's curved tip stood just at his hip. He bent forward to touch it. Closing his eyes he searched his mind, his gut hoping for direction. No answers came. No assurance that what he was doing made any sense. He rubbed his hands from the top to the base of the tombstone. Nothing. Nothing happened.

Kyle walked up behind him. "Uh, what you doing, dude?"

"Yeah Pete, you okay?" Angel asked.

Peter exhaled, frustrated. "I don't know. I mean, I do…just, give me a minute awright?" His hand didn't cool off, but burned hotter, brighter, throbbing as he rubbed it toward the center of the cold stone.

Sharp needles, small pricks of his blood, trickled as something cut through the brand on his hand. "Ummm, I…" The ground trembled.

"What the…" Kyle exclaimed.

Peter's eyes never left the rocks buried around them. Click! Metal needles felt as though they pulled blood from his hand, with each suck the rocks shifted, groaned, adjusted, then sank deep within the ground.

Angel cried out, struggling to remain standing. "Pete! What's happening? Oh-my-God!"

Trees surrounding the circle moved, crowded, and enclosed on them, making a fence of thick trees and bushes so dense they were thrown into complete darkness.

Kyle stumbled to his knees beside Peter, his shoulder grazing Peter's hip. "What's happening? What did you do?"

The siphoning needles retracted within the tomb. The surrounding ground shook and started to rise.

"Back! Back…get back!" Peter snapped out of his daze, grabbed Kyle by the shirt and stumbled backwards into Angel. They fell onto the soft dried leaves as the tombstone rose up out of the ground about twelve feet up, topping off a large mausoleum made of gray, marbled stone. A wrought iron door, covered in metal roses dusted with fresh dirt, stood waiting for them to enter. Small windows, with bars in front concealed what lay inside.

Kyle's jaw dropped. "Whoa, that's sweet."

Peter nodded. "Yeah." He wiped the blood from his hand on his black jean shorts, and he stood up.

"I don't know about this." Angel crossed her arms.

"Trust me, it'll be okay." Peter looked back at the car. "We should get our stuff out of the trunk. If we get in, we can hang out for a day or two."

Kyle headed to the beat up vehicle. "If that, I only bought enough food for two days—for me."

"Stingy ass," Peter chuckled. He walked to the car with Angel behind him. "We have enough for two days—for all of us." His elbow jabbed at Kyle.

"Oh, we friends now? You sharing? Guess shooting up some bastards and covering your back earned me Brownie points." Kyle put on his backpack and grabbed his small bag from the floor.

Peter shook his head. "No drugs in here. Leave that shit in the car."

Kyle smirked. "Sanctimonious prick."

Peter grabbed Kyle's shirt, lifted him up on his toes. "Don't piss me off. I gotta lot of shit I'm dealing with right now and would love to kick someone's ass to blow off some steam." He pushed Kyle back.

Stumbling, Kyle righted himself. "Fine, I'm leaving the stuff, but if anything happens to it, you're replacing my liquor and cigarettes. Hell, we have guns, a little liquor and weed won't make a difference in jail time."

"I don't care about the jail time. I've seen what that shit does to people. Especially drugs. And one thing I'm not gonna do is let someone, or something else, control me. I got enough bad ass dreams without trippin' off of some drug." Peter grabbed Angel by the hand and pulled her to the entrance.

Kyle came up to them, giving them a funny look. "What's up with the hand holding?" He cleared his throat. "That's not my thing."

Peter dropped Angel's hand. "It's not ours either."

Angel fidgeted with her shirt and shook her head at Peter pleading silently for him not to tell.

"Something's up with you two," Kyle smirked, "and I can't wait to find out what it is."

Peter's eyebrow lifted, but he ignored Kyle as he concentrated on how to open the metal door.

"I mean a grave in the middle of nowhere that pops the hell up out of the ground—dude, I'm thinking zombies, vampires, all kinds of horror-fried shit down there."

Peter's hand pulled back. "Can you shut up, man? I'm trying to open the door here," he grumbled.

"Yeah, soon as you open this door. Your ass is going first though," Kyle snickered.

Growling, Peter squeezed his fist and reached for the latch. With a creak, it slid back and the door opened on its own. He was the first to step through. Sunken lights lined the creases from the wall to the ceiling, and a stairwell led down into the ground. The door automatically closed behind Angel and he heard her yelp from the shock.

He waited. "Angel, walk beside me."

"Jesus! Leaving me to bring up the rear and save your ass if something goes off?"

"Kyle, shut up and come on." Peter tugged Angel's sleeve. She was shaking a bit. He just wanted to huddle her close and bury his face in her hair. But with Kyle with them, he'd have to be careful.

Cobwebs covered the walls. Peter waved a hand through several of them as they stepped deeply into the structure. He hoped he'd done the right thing; bringing them to this place could be one big mistake.

Chapter 28

The driver pulled up to the sprawling mansion, one of Gavin's favorites. It was mainly used for sacred gatherings. Ones where transitions took place, blood was lost, and spirits were called during elaborate ceremonies for the dragon. It was where he and Lucien were conceived. Their mother was a descendent of *Extraho of Obscurum*, as was his father, and she even gave birth to them in the sanctum below ground. Pure bloods were they, he was told from an early age. It was believed that only one of both parents who were descendents could be gifted with the sight.

Both he and Lucien vowed to delay their marriages to their intended for as long as possible so they would have time to realize their purpose. It has been foretold that the child born with the sight—the hunger to create the Transfero of Lux Lucis—would be born of a pure blood and would terminate its sire.

This southern country estate was framed by a raging blue sea, palm trees, and thick green grass. By initial observation it was similar to the other mansions that scattered the area. It was a two level white house with a rounded screened in sunroom on the side, a pool that peeked out on the back edge, and perfectly trimmed bushes.

The car door opened and Gavin stepped out as the doorman came to assist. "Welcome Mr. Steele. Is there anything I can get for you? Your room is ready with all you require," the dour-faced older gentlemen answered.

"No, I'm going to the Private Bungalow. Guests will be here soon, so prepare the other house for them."

Gavin walked the pathway to the small cluster of buildings that resembled miniature cottages with decorative stucco fronts framed in colorful rocks. Manmade water features framed the sides and back, which led to another pool that looked like a grotto of plush plants with an impressive waterfall for privacy.

He pushed the button on his key and the door to the larger home opened onto a dark wood floor with an ornate inlay of a sword with a curled dragon wrapped around it. His feet landed loudly and he shrugged off his jacket to lay it on a nearby white overstuffed chair. The marble columns lined the steps to a sunken gathering room.

Gavin sauntered along the side of the stairway to push the elevator button just beyond the stairs. The elevator stain glass doors opened and he unbuttoned his shirt while he waited. He swung his shirt over his shoulder as he walked into the office. The wall was decorated with his designs for his masterpiece. The machine he planned to build that would change his life. While looking at them, he changed into his loose black pants, and shirt.

The book was on his desk where he'd left it. Its page opened to the clue, the one thing that set him apart from the others before him. He'd figured out how to ask the right questions, how to get answers from the master that his father and other ancestors didn't. He sat and traced the words that jumped off the page at him.

One of pure heart, one of light will reveal a truth to one of darkness. Together they touch, and reveal the secret sanctums of their blood to hide.

The others had missed an important piece to their transition—this excerpt proved it. It was what drove him to research anyone affiliated with his enemy and, through the use of the dark arts, to gain answers, he'd realized his adversary had places they considered sacred. Places that were once traveled by those of light. Those places held powerful echoes of ancient energy. He'd had to use two psychics to reveal that to him. As he and Lucien kidnapped and held the decadence of the Order of Grace they called themselves, they'd extracted blood from all of them they'd captured. The old and the young were drained, studied, and mutilated until Gavin got his answers. Gavin called in the dragon's spiritual leaders, and found that with the younger children's blood they could infiltrate certain protected items—even holdings.

He knew then that he was close—so close. Gavin's masterpiece some would call a time machine, a mad idea for a man to believe, was possible.

"Peter Saints, you are the one. Your blood—it calls to him, and you will lead us to the answer," Gavin sneered. "You will give me my victory, or die in the process."

Chapter 29

Peter cleared the last step. Another door met them. Pure, white, it was made of muted rock, without a handle.

"So Houdini, what you got up your sleeve now?" Kyle snorted.

Peter closed his eyes, took a calming breath, and fought not to grab Kyle by the neck and choke him. Angel rested a hand on his shoulder. She leaned in, her breath tickling his ear, then whispered, "You know what to do, Pete. I trust you."

He quirked up a lip, because that's just what he needed, her affirmation. Peter lifted his heated hand, placed it on the door and leaned in. He closed his eyes as part of him—part of his soul—willed this door to grant him entry, safety, a refuge. He felt a tremor, faint, but consistent. Then something, something powerful filled him, refreshing it washed through him, a connection as prickling needles found his hand and pierced it, drawing blood with fine needles. He released a moan.

"Damn! What's that?" Kyle exclaimed.

"Pete!" Angel pulled his shirt, tugging him back against her.

He fought her, and held firm until the needles, which seemed invisible to the naked eye, retreated. Blood from his palm and the base of his fingers smeared the thick white door as it slid down into the floor, slowly revealing a dusty, cobwebbed filled chamber.

Kyle released a long breath. "Whoa! This is freaking amazing."

Peter nodded, and licked his lip as he said a silent prayer that bringing Kyle with them was a good idea. Peter stepped inside, the others followed.

"This place. It's like a…"

Peter put a finger to Angel's mouth to quiet her. Then he pulled away as if she burned him when he caught Kyle studying him strangely. "We don't know what it is, but it's where we can lay low for a few days until we have to get food."

He looked around the chamber, then up at the small, flat, light encased in the ceiling. It had rounded cement walls, no windows, no creases in the wall, just a circular cylinder of rock. Peter pivoted as Kyle went over and touched the wall. Angel sat and rummaged through her bag.

Just as Peter turned back out the doorway through which they came, his jaw dropped slightly. The wall was closing in from both sides of the archway. He dived at it, missing just as matching cement doors slammed shut. Peter's hands were braced against the wall. Annoyed, he pounded on the wall with his open palm.

"Uh-um, was that the only way out?" Kyle grumbled.

Peter shook his head and walked to Angel who stood with a flashlight. "It was the only way I knew to get out of here."

"Great, just freakin' wonderful." Kyle threw his hand in the air.

Peter grabbed him by the shirt and slammed him against the wall. "I'm gettin' real tired of your bullshit and complaining." His finger jabbed into Kyle's chest. "Remember you came—uninvited."

Kyle pushed Peter back. "I saved your sorry lives. Remember?"

Growling, Peter pushed his fist against Kyle's chest as he released his shirt. "How can I forget—your ass keeps reminding me!"

The floor shuddered. Peter grabbed Angel by the arm. His eyes cut at Kyle, who appeared freaked out.

"Dude, what the hell is happening now? The floor's—"

"Falling!" Angel shrieked as the floor turned slowly then dropped.

They all yelled as the floor plummeted and twisted. Deeper and deeper, it plunged within the ground. The small light above them flickered while pulling further and further away till they were pitched into complete darkness.

Peter flew into the wall. Firmly, he held onto Angel as her back rammed his chest. His arm snaked around her waist while he braced himself against the cement. Legs spread, muscles tightened, Peter called Kyle's name.

He groaned. "Cracked my skull, but it seems to be slowing down."

The place was pitch black; Peter couldn't see anything. "Flashlight? Angel?"

Angel's shaking hand grabbed his shirt. "I dropped it."

Suddenly, the floor jerked, and the room stopped moving. There were several clicks as the rounded room locked into place. Still there was no light. Angel bent and fumbled for the flashlight. Peter slid from behind her. She hit the light against her palm several times before it sprang to life.

"And there was light," Kyle remarked with a click to his teeth.

"Not funny man—not funny."

Overhead, inky darkness appeared to gobble up the meager beam from the flashlight. He gulped and nausea settled in his stomach. Now he didn't have a clue what to do. He flicked the beam on the wall and stepped around to inspect for a clue to an opening.

Angel cut on another flashlight. She traced the light higher up and counterclockwise to Peter's. "Nothing. It seems we are trapped." She slumped against the wall.

"No shit Sherlock, we are definitely trapped." Kyle snorted and fell back against the wall.

Peter shook his head. "No we're not. There's a way out of here." He gave Kyle his flashlight. "Hold this, I think I know what to do. Just gotta find a way…a place." Peter rubbed his hand on the wall. From above his head, down slowly to the floor, he moved his hand on the wall. The light shined on a crease in the cement, one of four on the surrounding wall. He traced a finger down the seam. Nothing. Still nothing seemed to work.

"Your rubbing the wall got us nowhere, dude. Anymore bright ideas?" Kyle sat and tapped the flashlight on the floor.

Peter growled at Kyle. "Shut up. Just shut up. Before I forget you saved our lives and I wipe my fist across your face."

Kyle waved the flashlight across the floor. "Sticks and stones, dude, sticks and stones," he chuckled.

Peter's eyes followed the light to a small circular insignia embedded in the middle of the rounded room. He got down on his knees as his hand heated up. His fingers stroked the raised red scar on his hand. With a gulp and a silent prayer, he placed his hand on the design carved in the floor.

Angel walked over. "Pete, what are you doing?"

"I don't know, but it's gotta work." Nothing, he felt nothing. He looked up into the dark and chanted, "C'mon, please, please, please." Prickling fine needles pierced his skin, and the now familiar rush of adrenaline pulsated around his scar.

Click. The cylinder-shaped wall was moving.

Kyle scrambled over to them. "Shit! What the hell did you do?"

Every muscle in Peter's body tensed as the needles withdrew and blood from his hand seeped into the creases of the emblem on the floor. He pulled his hand away and wiped the blood on his jean shorts.

Angel gasped. "Oh my God. Pete, what did you do? Why? How did you cut your hand?" She stepped back. "It looks like its absorbing it."

"It is." Peter stood. The wall moved clockwise, then counterclockwise as if it were a cipher on a lock. With a final click, the floor jerked and dropped another foot as the wall slid in place to reveal a door.

"Wow, impressive." Kyle heaved a sigh. "One thing for sure, never a dull moment with you."

Peter grinned and shook his head. "I warned you. Don't say I didn't." He was the first to walk through the door. His fingers slid down the thick cement wall in which the door was encased. As soon as he stepped across the threshold, several clicking noises vibrated throughout the cement hallway. Lights encased in the creases in the ceiling, lit up the small hallway that came to a dead end after a few doors. A large weapon, unlike any they'd ever seen, was encased in clear glass from ceiling to floor. It reminded Peter of a sword, but this sword...it was wicked. It had three circles on the end of its handle. It flared out with ridges on the bottom of the blade, but at the tip it was smooth.

"Damn, I am starting to think I'm loco," Peter mumbled.

Kyle clucked his teeth and walked around Peter several steps down the hall.

"Not crazy, we are all seeing this. And it's...wow, it's amazing." Angel rested a hand on Peter's lower back as Kyle walked around them.

Clicking noises thumped behind them. Swerving around, Angel ran at the door as it closed. But the cylinder in which they'd come in shifted and moved the door behind a block of cement in the bowed wall.

She balled her fist and hit the wall. "Guess we are here for a while."

Peter took a deep breath and stepped further into the hall. Various designs were etched in the walls. More maps of world, or rather pieces of it, were scattered.

"Before I take one more step, I have to know. How the hell did that just happen?" Kyle looked pointedly at Peter's angry face.

Peter shrugged. "Don't worry about it. Remember, don't ask no questions, just do what the hell I tell you or go your own way."

"Okay. I'll back off. For now." Kyle walked past Peter. "Since we are stuck here at least for tonight, I want to sleep—like now."

"I feel ya, I'm whipped too." Peter pointed to one of the four doors on each side of them. "We're taking the first room."

Angel's hand snagged Peter's arm. "You sure there's nothing in this place we should worry about."

He didn't feel in danger. Actually for the first time in a long time, Peter had to admit that he felt extremely safe. Although, he knew they couldn't hide out in this sanctuary for too long, he just had a feeling that here was where they needed to be for now. "Naw, it's good. It's safe here. No one here but us. We can look around after we take a snooze, 'cause I'm tired."

"Me too." Kyle waved back at them. He disappeared into the first room on the right.

Peter turned to Angel, the stale air of the enclosed sanctuary making him suppress a cough. "Look, tell me—do you feel bad here? Scared?"

She took a moment to think and peered just beyond him at the wall. "No. It's just…Pete, so much is happening. Too fast." Her hand rested on his chest. With weary eyes, she sighed. "What are we going to do now?"

"C'mon." He grabbed her hand and tugged Angel to the first room across from where Kyle disappeared. The metal door didn't have a knob. It was a muted gray to match the cement walls. He pushed it in.

"Don't you want to check this place out?" Angel asked, hesitantly going into the room turned around.

"Yeah, but right now, I want to be with you more. Alone."

The room had multiple plush throw rugs hanging from the wall like pictures. Scattered large pillows littered the floor on the edges of decorated rugs. Bookcases of ancient text lined the walls. Dust covered all the shelves made of metal, which were carved into two of the walls.

Peter briefly let go of her hand and pushed the door closed. He leaned against it with his legs bent. Feeling at ease with her, he tugged her into a hug, nestling her between his legs.

Angel broke down as their eyes met and tear after tear fell quietly down her face. "I'm sorry I'm being such a girl." She smiled through her tears and lifted a hand to wipe the stray streams away.

"I love it when you're a girl." Peter grabbed her hand before she could rub her tear-streaked face. He leaned in and kissed her tears. Releasing her hands, he pulled her in and gently touched his lips to hers. And his heartbeat kicked up a notch when her hands snaked around his neck. She was the only one to do this, to accept him, to want him this deeply, just as much as he wanted her. God, he hoped it was real—that it would last. That once he'd told her everything, she'd still feel the same about him.

Angel sighed as Peter snatched her ball cap off. He tossed it on the floor then dragged his hand down her white bandana and tight skull-cap she used to conceal her hair. Her dark tresses fell around her shoulders. Peter sank his fingers into its thickness of her hair. Then he groaned as he dipped inside her mouth to deepen the kiss.

He felt elated to finally see her exposed and flicked at the hem of her baggy T-shirt before shimming them up over her shoulders. Briefly, he broke off their kiss to toss her shirt on the floor.

Peter moved her slightly away. Taking several deep breaths, he closed his eyes to regain some composure. "Angel," he stared at her lips, wanting her so bad it hurt. "We gotta stop—or I won't want to."

Her jaw dropped and she bit her bottom lip. "Stop…before you do what?"

Peter slid her gently away and put some space between them. He walked to the plush ottoman under the heavy rug decorating the wall and sat. "Don't play stupid." His eyes held hers.

Embarrassed, she twisted the hem of her shirt with her finger as she sat against the door. "I'm not playing stupid. What's with you? You run hot then but now you're acting cold."

He raked his hand through his dark curls, then down his face. "Crazy. Everything that's happened to me in the last month has been totally screwed up and insane. Now this dude Kyle is here and his ass is unstable. A drinker and dope-head who's full of shit."

Angel pulled her hair to the side and started to braid it. "Yeah, but he did save us, you know. That means something because he didn't have to do it. He could've run."

"Don't braid it. I want to see it loose like that." He smiled when she shyly removed her hand from her braid. He got up and stretched. "Look, I get that he saved us. I get that I don't have a bad vibe about him, personally—but the dude is doing stuff that will get us hemmed up by the cops if he's with us." He waved a hand at the door. "He doesn't really give a damn about us, just himself. I don't know why the hell he is taggin' us."

Her eyebrow crinkled and she stood as she took off the last of her baggy T-shirts to reveal a formfitting exercise top.

Peter's mouth watered. "Damn, you're beautiful."

Angel's eyes widened at his penetrating stare. "You too," she whispered.

"Sorry I'm edgy, but I don't know if I can stay here without kickin' his smart ass." He tightened his fist.

"Just ignore him. He's already a little bit afraid of you." She bent to pick up her shirts. Slinging them over her shoulder, she snatched up a few of the large pillows resting against the wall.

He snorted. "Right, ignore the jerk who thinks he's doing us a favor by being a pain in my ass." Peter picked up several pillows and tossed them in the middle of the floor next to Angel.

"First we have to figure out how to leave here, then we can see where Kyle wants to go." She folded her shirts and put them on a nearby plushy cushioned bench next to the bookshelf.

Peter got a rug off the wall. He tossed it on the floor and straightened it out with his foot. "I don't think the nut knows where he is going. He's probably just as dead as we are if we don't figure out what or who is after us."

Angel dug in her bag for a dark bandana then used it to wipe down some of the books she could reach. "You think his father was a member of the Decretum Venia like my father was?"

"I hope, but who knows—only he does. And I don't know whether he's telling the truth or not since the guy's story changed more than once. Besides, just 'cause somebody belongs to something don't mean you can trust him. Lots of times I heard peeps say they were 'Christians' or religious like that shit is supposed to make them trustworthy—or better than anybody else."

Angel gave Peter an odd look. "Why do you say that like you're angry? I figured since you grew up in a church orphanage you would be okay with that."

"Naw, I ain't. Plenty of times when I snuck out of the orphanage I saw people with crosses on their necks pass Hanna and her father by like they were trash. Hell, Shyan told me she was a 'good Christian girl' but wanted to have sex with me the first day we met. And don't let me get started on some of the kids from various other religions that came into the orphanage."

"So, why are you judging them if you don't want to be judged?" Angel pulled out a book and went over to the rug by Peter's feet to prop up on one of the overstuffed pillows.

He pulled off his shirt and tossed it across the room to land on his backpack. "I ain't judging, just observing and commenting." He relaxed on the pillow beside her.

They lay there quiet for a moment. Peter stared at the ceiling and took a deep breath. Visions of Hanna dying in his arms caused a slice of guilt to blaze down his chest and his eyes shuttered closed.

"So did you…you know, have sex with her?" Angel swallowed as she lifted her book to cover her eyes.

His eyes flew opened and he plucked the book out of her hand. "Why do you want to know? What will it prove?"

She sat up on her elbows. "Nothing, I'm just curious."

Peter's traced her full lower lip with his thumb, and then kissed her. Before she could kiss him back he tilted away to look at her. "Curiosity killed the cat, got Pandora to open the box, and sometimes…it hurts everyone."

Angel worried her lower lip with her teeth as if she wanted to say more.

"Let's leave the past in the past." He bought her into his arms as he settled back on the pillows. "The only thing I care about is what I do with you."

She lightly touched his brown chest, her small pale finger tracing the ridge of his breastbone. "Do you want to do it…with me?"

He smiled and laid his hand on hers. "Yeah, but not for a long time. I don't want to mess this up with you, Angel. I want what we have to be right. Nothing in my life has been—ever. But this, what I feel for you, I don't want to screw it up."

"It's not going to get screwed up. I'm not Shyan. I've never been with anyone else—and don't want to."

He let out a long breath. "That's what scares me. Maybe," he released her hand and put it on his forehead, "you may want to try out somebody else since I'm the first guy you've been with like this. Or, you could be attracted to somebody who looks like…Kyle."

She sat up. "Why would you think that? Don't you know me at all? You think…you think…I'd like Kyle because he's white like me?"

He shrugged away from her and sat up with his knees bent. "You said it—I didn't."

Angel pointed at him. Her lips thinned out in a frown as she growled under her breath. "Don't you put that on me, Pete." She cursed him out in Spanish, *"Es estúpido centrada en uno mismo,"* and grabbed a pillow. She kept mumbling as she laid at the foot of the rug, turning her back to him.

Chapter 30

Angel wasn't talking to him. And he deserved it. He stayed still for a moment and the lights, embedded in the creases of the ceiling, dimmed. His eyebrows lifted as he stared at the lights until he gathered the courage to apologize. He didn't blame her—she'd busted him. Yeah she was white and he was…other, dark-skinned, unruly curled hair like his father. Although Shyan was mixed, her skin was tan and people didn't stare at them when they were out together. But even now, when they went out and Angel looked like a young boy, peeps checked them out like they didn't fit in. It didn't bother him, too much—he guessed. Well, maybe a little if he was honest, it ticked him off. And he did notice how uncomfortable it made her, whether she wanted to admit to it or not.

And Kyle…he didn't want the dude to figure out Angel was really Angelique. If that happened, he knew the prick would try her. Peter knew the type—they showed up in the orphanage and at the clubs he frequented all the time. They thought they were God's gift to women. Truth was, he didn't have a problem talking to girls, even getting the ones he wanted. The problem always cropped up when it came to him having to 'fess up about where he lived, having no parents, no car and no damn money. Usually he'd lie to them just to get in their pants. Just to feel like—fake like someone cared. Funny how things changed. Now he had money, he did have a car, but no home and no one—not even Pastor Finn. At least at the orphanage he had a semblance of a family, a father figure in Pastor Finn.

He sighed and sat up. Peter hesitantly touched Angel's shoulder. She jerked away. Peter swallowed as he heard the distinct echo of sniffles.

"Leave me alone." She moved further away. "If you think I would pick Kyle or anyone because of their color, then maybe…maybe this won't work with us."

"Angel…I'm sorry. I—" His fist tightened.

She huffed. "You may be sorry, but you meant what you said, Pete. That…you can't take back. You basically think I'm shallow and don't know my own feelings. Like I don't know who I'm in…*like* with, and that color, someone's skin actually makes a difference when it comes to what I feel inside." Angel rolled onto her stomach, her head turned away from him. "But that just means you don't know me at all. And if you felt that way about me, why would you even want to be with me? I guess I'm just convenient." She shrugged. "Just here."

"Naw Angel, it ain't like that."

With a snort, she punched her pillow. "I don't want to talk anymore. Goodnight Peter."

His eyes shuttered closed. The stab of pain in his heart was familiar but more painful than ever before. He blew it, but damn if he knew how to make her feel better. Peter didn't sleep, couldn't until he heard her soft steady breathing. When she was in a deep sleep, he moved beside her, laid his head on the oversized pillow and snuggled her into his arms. If this was all he could get for now—he'd take it. Just to touch her while she slept gave him comfort and he hoped would keep his nightmares at bay.

***

Someone was calling his name. *Mother*—his mother. From a distance in the darkened recesses of his mind her voice whispered and drew nearer with each utterance of his name. Then all of a sudden she yelled, "*He knows your name. Run!*"

Peter rocketed up. Angel rolled over and mumbled under her breath before tucking her legs into a ball. He studied Angel's sleeping form. His blood was pumping from the effects of his nightmare. He'd been running towards his mother's voice, the emptiness of loneliness like a weight on his shoulders. But even in his dreams he couldn't get his parents back.

The watch on his wrist beeped to alert him that morning was approaching. His stomach growled and he figured he better get up, sleep was slipping from him for another night. Peter slowly stood and took one last glance at Angel before he went to his bag to rummage around for a protein bar. He put one in his pocket and stuffed another in his mouth.

Angel didn't know she gave him a bit of hope. Just the fact that she stayed in the room with him instead of leaving to find Kyle or moving off the rug to sleep alone let him know he had some time to figure out how to convince her that she misunderstood.

The door creaked. Peter sprinted across the room to stand in the opening crack of the doorway. He braced his foot against the door and forced his shoulder through to stop Kyle from opening it.

"What do you want?" Peter asked, the scowl on his face raw with his mistrust.

Kyle grinned. "You and your boyfriend..."

"Shut up!" Peter grabbed Kyle's shirt. "Your ass is one second from kicked," he gritted.

"Promises, promises." He quirked up an eyebrow. "You got food?"

Peter narrowed his eyes. "You weren't slipping in my room for food."

He smirked. "Okay, I admit, I was curious." Kyle tried peeking over Peter's shoulder.

Pushing Kyle's chest, Peter squeezed out of the door and closed it behind him. "Here, this should shut you up." Peter pulled a protein bar out of his back pocket.

Kyle took it and ripped it open with his teeth. "It's smashed, did you sit on this, dude?" He eyed it suspiciously before taking a bite.

"No fool." Peter went toward the opened door that Kyle came from. "What's the other room like?"

"Can't explain it. It's something you have to see for yourself." Kyle turned, expecting Peter to follow.

Peter tugged at his door to make sure it was closed before trailing behind Kyle, who disappeared into the room ahead. When he crossed the threshold his mouth dropped open. The walls were made of a clear glass layer with strange weapons of all sizes and variations suspended between what appeared to be a cement back wall and a thick glass overlay. There were so many weapons crammed together in almost an artful display on the walls that he couldn't stop himself from walking forward to trace one.

A jeweled pitchfork-shaped knife, with rubies and emeralds encrusted on its metal handle, caught his eye. In its center there was a ruby that glimmered as the ceiling lights hit it. Peter's finger traced across the flat glass casing that separated him from the wicked tool. He could have sworn the emerald glowed brighter.

"Told you it was something you had to see." Kyle stepped in front of him and leaned on the wall. "Freakin' beautiful." His arms folded as he looked up on the opposite wall.

Peter pivoted, taking in the odd differences in the weaponry. Some looked ancient, yet others looked futuristic like they were snatched from a sci-fi movie. Guns with pointed barrels, shields with pointed curved knives in their corners. The oddest thing of all was that these weapons looked as though they were made for giants, men well over nine feet tall.

"Is it me or do these look like," Peter shook his head, "maybe they weren't made for men—*human* men?"

Kyle crossed his arm and scratched his chin. "Could be that this is just art. Realistically, no man on earth could actually use this stuff much less carry it around. Those weapons look like they weigh a ton." Kyle laughed. "And don't let me find out you are a space geek, into aliens and bullshit like that."

"No, I don't believe in aliens." Peter sighed before sitting on the thick sturdy wooden bench of many that lined the walls. For a moment he wondered where Kyle had slept until he spied a small, ripped blanket next to Kyle's backpack that was propped up against the opposite wall.

Kyle was staring at the shield on the wall. His eyes widened. "I'll be damned."

"Say what?" Peter looked at him confused. "What's with you?"

Kyle pointed at the shield, its silver and gold front had intricate lines of artful lines speckled with diamonds, and a crest in the middle made out of blood red rubies. It had three connected circles with crosses and a triangle. The outer edges of the circles were looped with an oval that had a bar protruding from its middle and closed by a smaller circle.

"The *Decretum Venia's* crest. A symbol of the Order of Grace my father babbled on about most of my life." He stood up on his toes and traced the crest with his finger.

"So your father was a member of the order? How? What do you know about it?"

Kyle exhaled an angry breath. "Yeah, that's all he talked about. The bastard." His lips bowed up. "He didn't care about my mother or me." Kyle kept his back turned to Peter as his fist tightened. He hit against the wall. "I was tainted, spoiled, dirty—since my mother wasn't selected from the order to be his wife. It came a time when he wanted nothing to do with either of us. Especially me, since I reminded him of her."

"I thought you said your father went against his parents to marry her. Seems like that must've meant he loved her."

"No, it meant he didn't want her to have his firstborn son without being married to him. She was pregnant with me, so he married her. The woman his parents chose for him refused to marry someone that had a child out of wedlock. And his beliefs—his place in the order—didn't allow him to abort me, and his chances for having a purebred son born of the blessings from the *Decretum Venia* were now an impossibility."

"Damn, I thought it sucked to not have parents. Seems to me, it sucked to have yours."

Kyle's rueful smile faded and he nodded. "Yeah, it did. My father was an asshole who beat up my mother, ignored her and got all preachy on us about what the *Decretum Venia* expected of him, and how we were sent from the devil to punish and torture him because his child was supposed to be chosen to protect the sanctuary."

Peter stood and stretched. "He told you about the sanctuaries? What did he say?"

"Yeah, the man told me a lot. He didn't teach it, just spat it at me as if I wasn't worthy to—" Kyle wiped his hand down his face. "Besides, once we survived that crazy elevator ride, I knew you must be of the blood."

"What do you mean?"

"Something happened to you." Kyle's eyes ran down Peter's frame. "You have the power to unlock places like this. How, I don't know exactly, but I do know that not everyone can do it."

"What are you gettin' at, man?" Peter stepped to him.

"While you were sleeping, I've been remembering." Kyle pivoted away. "This, this place is a sanctuary. The sanctuaries are what the *Decretum Venia* was created to protect. No one member knows where they all are, but the children born into the order can ascend—gain awareness—before they are no longer under the protection of the Creator when they turn eighteen. Not only that, there are certain sanctuaries that are left unseen. No one is known to have found them. Some of the lesser protected places are used to teach the young and are rather exposed."

"I'm confused, can you explain what ascend is. And what kind of protection?" Peter rested his hands on his hip.

"*Decretum Venia* has been around since the beginning of time. They are protectors of the word, the ancient holy word. It's not a religion; it's the core artifact regarding the basis of all religions. What you believe about God, angels, humans, demons all originate from the teachings from blood born members of the *Decretum Venia* who were sworn to disseminate that knowledge in whatever forms and as many forms possible."

"How'd you find out about them—the internet?" Peter strolled over to study one of the guns embedded in the wall.

"No, this stuff will never find its way on the net. Pieces of the information might, but never in one place that makes it too obvious. You'd have to know what you're looking for. The members are sworn to secrecy. I learned from my father—and he from his. Then when we turn eighteen, the chosen who accept their call to the *Decretum Venia*, research in upper level sanctuaries." He observed Peter for a moment. "Did your father teach you any of this?"

Peter shrugged. "Don't remember. He spent more time playing with me and just—being a good father." He frowned a bit. "But now that I think about it, he had started teaching me Latin, symbols and stuff like that, from the time I was little. He died when I was around ten. After that, the place I was raised was like a school. They taught us about the *Decretum Venia* but never mentioned the name of it. We just learned small bits about it—and me even less since I thought school was just damn boring."

"Well, at least your dad wasn't a sick bastard like mine was."

"So what about your mom, did she know about his beliefs?"

Kyle snorted. "If she did, it wasn't something she cared about since she thought she was in love with him when she got pregnant with me. Hell, I think she still loved him even after she found out he was cheating on her—time and time again. The day she found him with his secretary, she got in the accident, and my life went steadily to shit from then on."

"So what's your deal, Kyle? Why do you really want to hang with us?" Peter's eyebrow lifted. "And why does your story keep changing."

"I'm starting to trust you, I guess. Don't we all hold something back?" Kyle stared at him, his face rigid. "Because I haven't got nowhere else to go."

"That so?" Peter's eyebrow lifted.

"Besides, I had no idea how I was going to find the sanctuary my father kept talking about. Now though—I believe it. All he said…it's true."

Peter and Kyle were silent for a moment, each caught up in their own thoughts as they sauntered around on opposite sides of the room.

"What about enemies? Do you know why that cop helped us? Who he was talking about that was after us?"

Kyle pursed his lips then made a smacking sound. "Sort of. Since I didn't get along with my father, I did some snooping around in his stuff. He had all kinds of books, letters and notes he kept under a floorboard in his office at home."

"How'd you know it was there? You spied on him like you did on me and Angel?"

Kyle rolled his eyes. "What I did to find out more about my father started as an accident. I had gone to talk to him one night. You know, I wanted to clear the air between us. Mom was high as shit off some prescription drug, and I wanted—I hoped—that him and I could have a relationship. I went to tell him how Mom threatened me to sell drugs."

"Damn, that sucks." Peter slumped down on a bench.

"What sucked was that when I went to his office I saw him on the floor next to his desk putting his documents inside with a book." Kyle rubbed his eyes with his thumb and forefinger. "But I stepped back and waited. Later, I asked him about the order, told him about Mom and he accused me of being a child of Extraho of Obscurum—his curse for going against his family's wishes." He shook his head. "I didn't know what that meant, but I damned sure figured I should find out. After that, I bought and sold my mother's drugs, but I also searched around for this Extraho of Obscurum, which means, *Dragon of Darkness*."

Peter was confused.

"Extraho of Obscurum is the enemy to the Order of Grace? How'd you find out about them?" Angel asked.

They both turned at the sound of her voice.

Kyle chuckled. "He's awake."

Peter looked cautiously at Angel, trying to gauge if she had forgiven him. "Hey, Angel."

"Peter." She nodded stiffly. "So, Kyle, what do you know of the Extraho of Obscurum? My father talked about them only once when he was teaching me about the order." Angel glanced around the room, her mouth dropping slightly in surprise.

"They are in every crime organization and law enforcement agency, and those bastards are filthy, freakin' rich and twisted."

"How d'you know? Find out about them and what they were into?" Peter's eyes narrowed.

"The drugs, selling the drugs you hear things, especially being a white kid selling them at a preppy school who had kids of both secret organizations attending. When I started selling the drugs, kids that were from Extraho of Obscurum assumed I was associated with their ancestry. I kept my mouth shut and let the fools do all the talking. And let me tell you—even the kids made my skin crawl. What the hell they are teaching them is sick beyond anything your freakin' nightmares. Lots of them kids had scars and bruises from the rituals their parents put them through. Some of them never returned back to the school after a 'happening', as they called it."

Angel dropped to her knees. "Whoa! Am I hearing you say what I think I'm hearing? You went to school with these kids? Descendents of

187

both organizations?" She shook her head from side to side. "I was hidden from those kinds of places. My father and mother were both in the Order of Grace and told me those schools were no longer safe for us."

Kyle lifted an eyebrow. "I figured something was up since the numbers of kids from the Order of Grace seemed to slim out over the years. Only kids like me—ones who had parents who didn't want to pass the history on, were too stupid to run."

Peter humphed. "So uh, since your parents went missing and you were in this school playin' both sides like a *Benedict Arnold*, what the hell set things off to make you want to run instead of call the cops when your parents went missing?" Peter couldn't read this kid. He still wasn't on board with trusting him no matter how much he came clean in his story.

"My parents weren't missing before I left the school." Kyle tensed. "I slipped and told one of my clients who my father was. Then that prick went home and researched things about my father. A few days later, my clients, kids I'd been selling to for over a year, tried to kill me. I hid out a few days, then figured I'd go home and tell my dad. I thought at least then he'd help me, but when I got home…" He raked a trembling hand through his hair. "Shit! Blood, so much blood….everywhere, like the freaks decorated the place with it. I had to get out of there so I stole my neighbor's beat-up old junk car and drove to my cousin's house where I crashed for a few weeks before I met you," his voice broke.

Angel's eyebrows frowned with concern and she went over to pat Kyle on the back. "I'm sorry, Kyle. I know how you feel. My parents died the same way."

Peter's fist clenched closed as he watched Angel console Kyle. Jealousy poured through his veins like acid. His hand throbbed in answer to his anger. He took a calming breath and stood. "Now what? Where do you want us to drop you after we get out of here?"

Kyle collected himself, his eyes still watery from his fight with tears. "I was hoping, if you'd have me, I could stay with you. This place," he waved his hands as he pivoted around, "is what I've dreamed of. It's what my father didn't think I was worthy to see but someone who counts—the Creator of all—put me here, led me to you two, so it's got to mean something. It's got to mean this is where I belong, even though by all accounts, I shouldn't be here."

Chapter 31

Gavin went to greet the others. Members of the Extraho of Obscurum had started to arrive for the bonding ceremony. His master would finally be able to live within his body. The psychic Lucien found would become the channel to seal the act. Angelica Ramirez's blood would be pumped into his body to give the master the power to break through the barriers placed over the hidden sanctuaries of the *Decretum Venia*. Peter Saint's blood would be used to unlock the secrets found in the clues revealed by his ancestors. All was foretold and bargained with the death of many others in order to gain this knowledge from the master. Unfortunately, they've only ever been able to find one of those places—the property that had cost him many of Lucien's men.

"Everything is coming into place," Gavin murmured as the first of his guests crossed the threshold to great him with a nod.

"Gavin! Gavin Steele, you are most honored to be the one to lead us to our long awaited victory." Devlin Nash smiled then kneeled at Gavin's feet before kissing his shoe.

Gavin waited for the butler to help Devlin to his feet. His mentor after his father's passing had that hungry look in his eyes. He had the appearance of someone who knew they could never wield the power, but received a small satisfaction just from basking in the glow of it. "Do you have the channel?"

Gavin's lip curled up. "That and more. Lucien will drop her off before he attends to the rest of the pieces needed for the final ceremony."

The other men and women repeated Devlin's welcome, then each were helped up by the butler and led to their rooms. The last guest was the current guest of honor, Gavin's psychic channel, "Sarah!" Gavin widened his arms, and a rare smiled creased his handsome features as he grasped the startled woman's hands. "Lucien. We were getting worried you'd lost your way." He lifted an eyebrow at his brother who stood behind Sarah with a forced grin.

"Gavin, why don't you have Charles get Sarah settled in while we speak briefly?"

Sarah regained her composure and glanced back at Lucien, who leaned in and kissed her on the lips, whispering endearments to her.

"I'll see you later?" she asked. Her eyes were filled with eager adoration.

"You bet on it, I wouldn't miss your work for all the world, gorgeous." He kissed her forehead once more before placing her in Charles' capable hands.

"Gavin, thanks for the warm welcome, you have a lovely home," Sarah said, smiling back at him before regaining her stride to follow the butler.

Gavin's fake smile fell. "What is it, Lucien? Good news it better be."

"Brother, can we go in your office please?" Lucien's forced smile dropped and he led the way to Gavin's office.

Gavin noticed Lucien didn't glance at the large wood framed doorway, ornate antique furniture that gave the office an estate feel, instead he slid smoothly into the oversized leather chair facing the dark wood desk. Gavin sat behind the desk, his hands bracing each side of his slightly higher chair, then leaned forward as another butler closed the door. "Speak."

"My men had them. Two of them. They'd dumped the car with the tags from the property. One of our paid guys got a message to look out and he happened to be working the carnival in Georgia. He followed them and was about to bring them in," Lucien licked his lips, "but another kid, the third one to join up with them, hit him over the head. One of our cops got word they were on the run. To look for three boys in a car leaving the area. He called in with the tags, but the idiot let them go."

"Did he?" Gavin said as he rested his chin on his balled fist.

Lucien swallowed. "He's been dealt with and buried just outside town. But the helicopter I sent spotted them and made a call to our guys nearby."

"And…" Gavin leisurely reached in his drawer for one of his knives he kept encased within. He pulled it out and placed it on the desk between him and Lucien.

"There was a car chase and they," Lucien's eyes slipped to the knife, "got away. But the helicopter was on them. They drove off-road, into the woods, and the guy…he said, it was like the woods ate them. First they could see the car. Hell, they even said the kids parked it and walked to some gravesite. But then…nothing, the woods closed up and they saw nothing."

"That so?" Gavin's eyes moved from Lucien's stricken gaze to the knife. "So what must you do to clean this up for me, Lucien? Will you have the elders waiting for the final bloodletting? We can accommodate them, of course, for as long as possible. But I will not be so patient with each passing day until the final ceremony can be done. Because of your mistake—I will only be able to complete the first part of the ceremony."

Lucien reached for the knife, then held the handle firmly as he unbuttoned his shirt with the other hand. "No, I will see to it that they are found. All three of them. And with the description the cop gave us, it's clear the other boy is one we've been looking for. Kyle Fenhaven, a mixed breed, but it is believed his blood will still be useful." He tightened his fingers around the edge of the desk. "My men are watching where they pulled off the road and the copter is on lookout in the area. They won't get far. If they resurface—we'll know it."

Gavin's gaze fell to the litter of scars on Lucien's chest. He lifted his eyes to stare at Lucien dispassionately while his brother sliced through his skin to make his penance.

Gavin reached in his drawer to pull out a handkerchief. "Brother." He handed it to Lucien, who casually took it to stop his bleeding. "You will fix this."

"You have my word Gavin, or my head on your mantel of prizes. I will succeed."

Chapter 32

Peter and the others spent the day reading while eating the last of their food. Peter grimaced as he dug deeper into his backpack to pull out a box of Pop-Tarts. They couldn't hang out here much longer.

Angel came into the room to get something out of her bag. "There's a shower in the last room on the right. Kyle's there now, do you want to go next?"

He watched her awhile as she snatched out another T-shirt. "Angel, can we talk…please?"

She stood with her back to his, and pushed her shoulders back before turning around to face him. "For what Peter? I got your apology. It's accepted, but now I don't know if I want to be with you like before."

Peter closed the door. Then he leaned against it. "Why not? I told you…or tried to tell you, that I don't care about the race thing. But I thought it made you feel a bit off when we were out and peeps were looking at us strange, even though we looked like to guys just hangin' out together."

She crossed her arms over her chest. "Did your bullhead stop to think that's why I was uncomfortable? That every minute I'm trying to act like a boy, I'm self-conscious I'll be found out? Don't you get that? Or is it that you are the one who is uncomfortable enough to notice what you *think* people are thinking about us?"

His shoulder's fell. "Maybe, maybe you are a lil' right about that. But it's more of an insecurity about how it made you feel than how I felt about it." Peter reached out to touch her shoulder. She stepped back out of reach. His hand fell. "I'm just jealous, awright? I don't want you to leave me for Kyle…or anyone else. I'm no good for you and I know it, but I can't walk away. I'll fight for you Angel…my Angel." He raked his hand through his curls so he wouldn't tick her off further and pull her into his arms for a kiss.

She frowned and threw the T-shirt over her shoulder. "I know you're jealous, but I also know I trust you, Peter, and it has nothing to do with all the girls *you've* been with, your sleeping around with them or your old hook-ups. It has to do with the way I feel about you after I got to know you. I know you a lot more than you think, but until I know you can really trust that I'm not going to float from one guy to the next, then this is not going to work."

He rubbed his fingers against his thumbs trying to convince himself that pulling her too him and just kissing her was the totally wrong thing to do. "God Angel, don't do this to us. Just give me time—us time to get used to this. A chance, just one more chance, *please.*"

Angel's eyes watered. With shaking hands she reached out to him and took a step forward into his arms. "Pete, I-I shouldn't give in this easy."

Relief flooded him and he snuggled her tightly to him. Lifting her up to his full 6ft 3inch frame, his kissed her. Sliding into the depths of her warm mouth, he felt unworthy of her forgiveness. Deep inside he knew he'd always want her only for himself. That having Kyle and other guys around would set him on edge. But now he'd take whatever she gave him. He'd try.

Easing her down against his body, he pulled back from their kiss. "Angel, thank you. I won't throw this chance away." He lifted her chin to look her in the eye. "I love you."

A surprised burst of enlightenment glowed on her face. "Pete." She stood on her toes. "I love you too!"Angel pulled him down to kiss him once more.

He tensed, the door creaked and he pulled back. Turning around just before Kyle opened the door, he jammed his hands in his back pocket.

"What's up man? Door closed, means knock!"

Kyle leaned against the doorframe. "Door locked means knock in my book." He looked from Peter to Angel. "What you looking guilty about, dude? Been talking about me behind my back again?"

Peter tried to relax before he approached Kyle. "What do you want anyway?"

"Came to tell you that I finished my shower, it's all yours." His eyebrow lifted.

Angel reached for her towel and clutched her stuff as she walked past Kyle and uttered, "Thanks, Kyle."

They watched Angel scurry down the hall. "You find anything in the books here?"

Kyle scratched his chin. "Yes and no. C'mon, let me show you what I was studying today. It's in the room called the *Cocoon of Knowledge*."

"Cocoon of Knowledge. How'd you know?"

"Dear old Dad, spat out it was where he studied. A reminder that I would never know what it meant to be enlightened."

"Sorry for bringing up your issues, man. I know I don't want to remember mine."

"Not your fault I got so much shit in my trunk," Kyle threw back at him as they went into the room opposite the bathing room.

The room had ceiling-high bookshelves and was about four times larger than the other rooms. It smelled of old books and dust. Eight long metal tables sat in the middle of the room; large wood benches were on each side. Books were propped on various tables as though someone was reading through them at random. Peter figured Kyle and Angel had been studying in here while he was perusing the books in his room.

"So what'd you find?" He ran a hand on the dusty table. "Most of the books in my room are geography books. They trace back to maps before Jesus, and some even before that. Also, star charts, the movements of all of them."

"Hmm." Kyle's hand trailed across the books lining the wall. Dust kicked up and left a finger-track behind him. "These books here are all on the history of the Order of Grace." He pointed to the opposite wall where the books were all black and red. The bold writing reminded him of...blood. "Those are all on the Extraho of Obscurum. Zee enemy." Kyle ended his fake French accent with a dry laugh and an exaggerated bow.

Peter frowned. "What about them? Show me what you found."

Angel entered looking refreshed and well hidden in a clean T-shirt. "Kyle found the juicy parts. He has a talent for speed reading ancient text."

"You can say that. Sometimes those internet tools help, besides I took Latin in that prep school. Boooooring. As well as Hebrew, French, Greek...need I say more?"

Peter moved his head slowly moved side to side. "Man, you're a real piece of..."

Kyle held up a finger. "Don't say it, 'cause...it's true."

Angel laughed. "Glad you two are bonding. Now can we get to business? Kyle, show him what we found."

They followed Kyle to the two opened books sitting side by side on the middle table. One book from the Extraho of Obscurum historical collection and another from the Order of Grace's collection were layered on each other. Several others from each collection were stacked on each side.

"Here, and....yep, right here." Kyle pointed to each text, one was written in Latin while the other in Greek. "They both make reference to the blood of the children aligned with the Order of Grace. It says, 'there is power in their blood, before the final year of the crossover to impose their free will'. That's from the Order of Grace, historical reference number 7638, which seems to be before Jesus' time. Now, there in the

Extraho of Obscurum book, dated a little later, it says, 'steal the blood of the young, unveil the stronghold of thy enemy', which would indicate that there is a reason we—the kids of the *Decretum Venia*—would be hunted and killed."

Peter stepped back from the books. "Whoa! That... Shit! That answers a lot." Flashes of Hanna's blood on his hand, her fingers, the change in him, the warnings from his mother, everything not only pointed to the fact that his parents were definitely pure blood *Decretum Venia*, but that, for some unforeseen reason, he was being protected by the order. "When did they start to hide the kids in the Order of Grace?"

Kyle smirked. "You knew I'd search for that, didn't you?" He put up a finger and walked to a nearby table, then waved them over. "Right here. The members of *Decretum Venia* integrated themselves within places the Extraho of Obscurum were known to frequent, their business, schools, and living places, in order to keep an eye on any sign that their purpose was revealed. See, the members, descendents of the Extraho of Obscurum, didn't know about the Sanctuaries or Strongholds. Well, they never knew where they existed, or even if they truly did. But one big, freakin' mistake was made. Two men from each order were friends, they'd grown up together, loved archeology, and all that stuff. Anyway, they went on a dig together. They touched a talisman, one that had the same symbol on it you saw on the sword in the other room. When they touched it at the same time, the descendent of the Extraho of Obscurum was given enlightenment like that of the descendents of the Order of Grace of various sanctuaries."

"I get that. I read briefly about it at another place. But it only mentioned the act of them touching it. Nothing more, just that they did and something was revealed. Did you find out more?"

"I found it in the books of the Extraho of Obscurum," Angel piped in. "They want our blood. The blood of the children, because they can use it to find out our secrets, to break into the Sanctuaries that hold our knowledge. But the Strongholds, they hold the relics, artifacts, and power of the Order of Grace. Not even adult members of the order know where the Strongholds are, but they are the main thing that we are all called to protect."

Kyle put his foot up on the bench. "Now what? We don't know where it is or could be. But it's obvious that the Stronghold is what we need to get to. What we need to protect."

"Let's think on it. We're out of food, so we have to get out of here in the morning." Peter already knew the answer. They would go to the Stronghold. He also knew, deep in his blood, that he would be the one to lead them there.

Chapter 33

Today would be Gavin's last day disconnected from the master. After the bonding ceremony he would no longer have to use a sacrificial connection to know what the master desired of him. He would *become* the master.

Gavin stood in front of the platform. The other high-ranking members of Extraho of Obscurum were chanting behind him. The dark night was lit only by the moon and the blazing fires on the poles that surrounded their gifts. Sarah was one. The man they'd filled with the blood of their enemy was the other. They'd drained the man dry. Pieces of his flesh lay in sacred serving platters in front of each high priest. Some of the man's blood was encased within Gavin's safe, kept frozen for later use, and the remainder of it was shared with those around him in preparation for the ceremony.

Sarah sat with legs crossed, hands outstretched, moving to an invisible beat in time with the chanting of the others. She'd thought she was being worshipped, that the psychic power she wielded would punish those who killed the man she'd thought trusted her.

Gavin couldn't help his grin as his mouth salivated with the knowledge of what was to come. It never surprised him when it came to the nature of men and women. Power, greed and the self-absorbed satisfaction in being adored always allowed him the access to manipulate such pawns to his purpose. He'd told Sarah she was to them a goddess—one to be worshiped and adored for her gift. Something Gavin himself wished he could possess. She sat there, eating up his and Lucien's words as Lucien whispered endearments of encouragements in her ear. She'd bought the bait hook, line, and sinker, and was here being offered up to the master.

The smell of the sea, the crashing of the waves, the chanting of the pure blood devotees, all called forth the power of the master and his minions. Like crabs rising from the sand, demons of darkness lifted from the ground like living shadows. They hovered with their upper torsos jutting out of the earth waiting for the master to arrive, their black-shadowed humanlike figures luminous in the moonlit sky. It was as though they'd shaped themselves as a mockery of the bodies they wished to consume. Eyes of blood red were void of pupils and stared at their master's new vessel—Gavin.

The torch flames rose higher as Lucien took his place before Sarah, their gift to the dragon. The sacred knife Lucien had tucked within his black pants was hidden from her view.

Sarah's body began to shake; the winds around them thickened. It twisted and turned around the psychic. Her hair was ripped out of the band that held it from her face as her spine arched. Sarah's eyes flew open, only the whites showing as they rolled back in her head.

Lucien rose, lifted the sacred knife and pierced her heart. Light poured out of her body, from her eyes, nose, and mouth, followed by a dark, thick moving cloud. The light from her soul was being ridden by the darkness of the masters from the spirit world to the present.

Gavin rose and cried out the words. "I am yours, master. Fill your vessel. It is time!"

The light of Sarah's soul blew up into a million pieces as the darkness funneled towards Gavin, piercing his eyes and mouth, pushing his screams downward within him. His entire body felt as though it was ablaze, as if his very soul was being sucked into the dark abyss to trade places with the once-imprisoned demon he'd called master. He was suffocating on putrid air. Hooks pierced his body as the elders yanked him with hooked ropes by his skin to the platform as the darkness com-pletely consumed him. It solidified the bonding that made him one with the demon who'd called to him from the beginning of his life. The demon his father and his ancestors had promised him to from the beginning of time. The demon and he were one at that moment. A smile slipped to his face as wicked laughter filled the night.

It had begun.

Chapter 34

Peter's mother had come to him again that night. This time was worse than the others. Her warning was insistent, repetitive and pleading. Something had changed. Somehow the stakes had risen. He needed to find this Stronghold in order to get the answers he needed.

He sat up in bed and smoothed Angel's hair back before landing a soft kiss on her lips. She didn't budge, and he was glad. He didn't want to explain this anxious feeling he had, or his now-glowing red scar on his hand. Its raised edges throbbed, and the movement of the blood within felt like his hand had a mind of its own. What, he didn't know, but he got up and left the room.

Peter's first stop was Kyle's room. He eased open the door and realized the dufus snored. The low rumble filled the room. With one last look, he pivoted around and went to the Cocoon of Knowledge. The room seemed to come alive for him. On the back wall hung a long, frayed rug with symbols of the Order of Grace mixed in with a rose tree of thorns. He rubbed his hand downward over it.

Nothing. No sign of what to do. Just above the rug was a carved out design similar to the one in the floor of the elevator-like cylinder they'd arrived in. He picked up a nearby bench and pushed it under the rug. Taking a deep breath, he stepped up on makeshift stool. He rubbed his fingers against his thumb before reaching up. The rug fell to the floor, and he jumped back.

Quickly, he steadied himself on the teetering bench. Peter stretched and slapped his hand on the rounded inlay. The piercing needles stung as they siphoned blood from his hand. It was sad that now it was something he was getting used to. He heard several clicks. The ground shook. His breath caught in his throat as one of the walls tilted inward. The panel slid up and into place on the ceiling of a tiny cinder blocked room. A golden pedestal was embedded into the floor. The pedestal shook and slid forward to stop in front of him. On its flat surface, a raised metal emblem of the Order of Grace, bore protruding points—curved metal pieces that looked like they were on fire from within.

Peter jumped from the bench. The emblem called to him. He closed his eyes, aiming his palm at the protruding spikes.

"Stop!" Angel shrieked from the doorway.

Peter grunted as his hand was pierced by the sharp edges, just missing bone. Blood ran down the sides of the rounded emblem and disappeared as the emblem sank within the platform. A hologram appeared. It wouldn't let go of his hand as the needles felt like they curved at the tip within his skin.

"Ahhhhhhhh!" He tried to jerk his hand away. Within a second, the needles retracted. It felt like his hand was on fire.

A floating word and map coordinates appeared above the base.

His chest was heaving. The scar on his hand seemed to seal closed on its own, but his eyes never left the hologram. He reached his shaking hands forward.

Angel ran to him. Her hands worked quickly to tear off a piece of her oversized shirt and wrap around his hand. "God, what have you done?" she choked out.

"I don't know. Do you know what that says?"

Angel tightened the last knot around his hand and her eyes danced over the image. She gasped and put a hand up to her mouth. Taking a step back she said, "Stronghold. It's in Greek. Those…" she lifted a finger, "are the coordinates." Peter put his hand through the hologram. The image dissipated. Then the podium slid back behind the wall.

"What the hell is going on?" Kyle came in the room, rubbing his eyes. "What did you do? This place is wrecked."

Pete grinned at him. "The Stronghold, I know where it is. And I know how to get out of here."

"Pete, are you sure that's what we should do? What if we're still being followed?" Angel asked.

Kyle chuckled. "Yeah right. Like who the hell could find us trapped underground surrounded by cement?"

Angel looked concerned. "I don't know. I…guess you're right."

Peter shrugged. "We don't have a choice. They'll try to track us no matter what. If we get to the Stronghold, it may have answers. Answers that will help us fight them back and win." He started toward the door.

Angel tugged him back. "Win against the devil? His demons? Because you do know that those worshippers, who are blood-tied to the Extraho of Obscurum, are led by an evil you and I couldn't even comprehend."

Kyle strolled closer, he glanced at Peter's hand and confusion marred his expression for a moment. "How else are we going to live? This is life or death—our lives or death. Those sick bastards want to drain us of our blood. Don't you get that? I know I'm not willing to roll over and let them stick me."

"Me either. It's not gonna happen. If I can get answers and a way to beat them, I'm gonna do it. We have to meet Rosa. After we go to the Stronghold and get some answers, we have to let the others in the order know."

Angel sighed. "So when are we going?"

Peter stormed into the hall. "Now. We go now."

Chapter 35

They rushed into the room they'd shared. Peter closed the door and hurried on to his backpack. They worked silently packing their things.

"Peter?"

He looked up from his bag. "Yeah?"

"Are you really sure about this?" Angel asked in her feminine voice.

"More sure of this than anything. We gotta take the fight to them. I'm freakin' tired of running. I've been on the run for as long as I can remember. We are stronger than those sick bastards. We can change things. Save everyone."

She toyed with the edge of her shirt. "But what if that's what they want us to do? What if they—the evil ones—are trying to get us to reveal where the Stronghold is? We could make things worse for us. That place is sacred and meant to never be found. A Stronghold is like a place you protect."

Peter shook his head. "Naw, Hanna started this. She gave me this—Shit, I don't know if it's a curse or gift." He lifted his hand and snatched off the torn binding. "I know it's selfish, but I have to find out why me. What is th-this symbol on my hand? How to stop the killing, kidnapping, and the Dragon of Darkness."

"What if we can't stop them? They'll kill us all." She took off her hat and scarf. Sighing with worry, she started to braid her hair.

Peter put on his backpack went to her. Lifting Angel's chin, he softly touched her lips with his. The familiar tingling sensation teased his gut and he deepened the kiss. Her braiding forgotten, she whimpered and pushed further into the kiss.

Grudgingly, he pulled away. "I want this. You. I want to have a normal relationship with just you and me. Not one where we're running and you have to hide how beautiful you are behind baggy shirts, and hats covering your hair." He wiped a hand down his face and took a step back from her. "I want…I want to be... I want to protect you, to be the guy you say I am."

A tear slid down her face, she kissed him. "You already are. I'm just afraid for us." She hugged him tightly. "I've seen them, I know how evil they are, Pete. They…they love killing. And they seem like they are on a mission, like they'll never stop until they find us."

"That may be, but this time, we're gonna flip the script. We'll go to the Stronghold to find out how to stop them, and I'll go to Gavin Steele myself to end this, if I have to. Your parents ran from him and warned you about him for a reason. I got a feeling there's more to the man than we think. He killed your parents and he's after you."

"You're right, they did say he was well connected. My mother seemed afraid of him."

"Naw, he's a lot deeper in this shit than you or I know. I feel it, I just know it. Like it's a whisper in the back of my mind. I don't doubt that creep is the cause of this." He pulled her to him, his hand buried in her hair.

The door creaked open. "Whoa!" Kyle hit the door with his fist. "I knew something was off with you two."

Angel and Peter jumped apart. Peter swore as his angry gaze landed on Kyle's smirk.

"A girl. I knew it. You didn't look the type to float the other—"

"Shut the freak up, Kyle." Peter moved Angel aside, grabbed Kyle by the shirt, then rammed him against the door. "She has to hide the fact that she's a girl. They are lookin' for her!"

Kyle smacked his teeth and shook his head. "Not anymore. The cop ratted us out as three dudes, not two guys and a girl."

Peter dropped him. "So what you sayin'?"

"I'm saying that we'd be better off with her looking like a girl. At first glance—we won't be what they are looking for."

"I don't know, Kyle, my father was very specific about me dressing like a boy to protect myself. The reason for it I don't know, but it's kept me hidden all this time." She twisted her fingers in her hand and bit her lip.

Peter picked up his backpack and put it on. "Kyle's got a point. Besides, I'll protect you."

Kyle bowed. "Me too, my lady." His fake English accent and waving hand bought a grin to Angel's face.

"You are silly." Angel laughed.

"Either that or one stack short and riding the loony bus." Peter bent and picked up Angel's cap. "I'm wearing this now. Enjoy lookin' like a girl since me and smartass got your back."

Angel grinned and pulled the two loose shirts she had on over her head. "I can't say I'm not liking the idea."

They headed out of the room and down the hall to the bowed out wall that hid the elevator.

"So, uh, are you going to do that blood-letting thing you do?" Kyle leaned against the wall and waited for Peter.

Peter looked him over, and wondered if he was the only one who could do it. "You know, why don't you and Angel do it first?"

Kyle shook his head and waved his hand from side to side. "No way. If we do it, there may be a booby trap and we'll all die here before we even get going."

With a snort, Peter pulled on his baseball cap. "Didn't think you had it in ya to do it. 'Sides, how do you know?"

"I read, dude. Do you? It's fundamental." Kyle pointed to the hall. "All kinds of warnings were found in those books. I'm not chancing it. Nope, no way in hell I'm letting some wall bleed me."

Peter eyed him up and down. "Sure you don't got nothin' ta hide?"

"We all have something to hide, but I'm not letting that thing up there stick me, and possibly poison me, to prove I'm on your team. Me saving your big, dumb butt should be proof enough."

Angel stepped up between them. "Wimps. I'll try it." She walked past Peter, stood on her toes and smacked her hand on the circle. Cringing, her eyes closed as she fought to stifle a yell. The needles popped back into place within the wall.

"Angel! Angel!" Peter moved to catch her when she collapsed and slid to the floor. He patted her face.

Kyle wrapped a bandana he'd gotten out of her bag around her hand. "You think maybe…it poisoned her?" Kyle queried Peter, worry etched in his features.

"God, I hope not," his voice cracked.

Angel groaned. "Pete." Her head moved side to side. "That was stupid." She sat up and put her hand on her head. "I feel dizzy, but," she squeezed her injured hand, "I'll be okay."

"What happened?" Kyle asked sheepishly.

"It hurt—bad." Angel released a whimper. "The needles went deep. Like to the bone. It sucked some of my blood out. Then instead of pulling blood out, it was pushing something in. Whatever it was made me feel dizzy."

"That never happened to me." Peter raised his hand, the angry red brand.

"How? What happened to your hand, exactly?" Kyle asked.

Peter sighed at Kyle's pointed look. "It's a long story, but someone died and gave this to me. Truth is, I don't know what it is."

"Maybe it's a gift. It might get us into the Stronghold." Kyle lifted his hands and pivoted around. "It got us here dude, and that's a pretty freaking amazing gift." Kyle pulled at Peter's hand, traced the palm with his finger then uttered, "Wish I had it."

Angel whispered. "I think I know what this is…the purification process. I studied it in the books. It was foretold that there is generation of the order that will have to go through the purification process. I think we are part of that generation, " she frowned, "which may be why the dragon wants us so badly. And now, we just started it."

"Humph, so what does that mean?" Kyle asked.

"I don't know, but the generation that goes through the purification process is the one to get the anointing of great gifts. Gifts beyond what the current members could ever imagine. No one's ever recorded what happens after it, but that the anointing is for protection of the host."

Kyle walked up to the rounded emblem. "Well, then, it's my turn." He slapped his hand on it. He held still while the pins pricked his skin. "Ouch." He waited. "Nothing. I don't feel a damn thing." He slid his hand down the wall.

"Maybe it's different for each person." Angel stood up feeling refreshed.

Kyle snorted. "I don't feel different or even dizzy. Nothing happened most likely because I'm not full blood. My mother was nothing to the order and my father was kicked out." He hit his fist on the wall. "I don't care about this shit anymore. I am what I am. And it ain't part of this stupid ass order."

Peter pushed Kyle against the wall. "Get your head straight! You sure you're with us? Is your mind made up with who you are following— or is what your spaced-out dad said true?"

Kyle punched him.

Peter's jaw cracked to the side as blood trickled down his lip. He licked it and grinned. "Just what I've been waitin' for." Peter grabbed him by the shirt and jabbed Kyle in the nose.

"Stop it! Now!" Angel yelled, and wedged herself between them.

Peter pushed her back to duck Kyle's blow and elbowed him in the stomach. Damn, it felt good to hit him. Peter smiled. Kyle growled and charged Peter's stomach. They fell back with Kyle on top. Peter pulled Kyle's shirt and punched up. Adrenaline poured through him, and he was itching to land another blow.

Angel pulled Kyle off of Peter and took his place on Peter's stomach, blocking Peter's hit meant for Kyle.

"Stop! Gah! You two are being stupid."

Kyle was groaning and rolling around on the floor holding his nose. Peter was heaving up air with his fist at his eyes. "Damn. I'm sorry Angel."

She slid off him and grabbed his hand. "You both are forgiven, if you can keep your hands off of each other and save it for the real enemies."

Peter sucked on his swollen lip to stop the bleeding. He limped over to Kyle and stuck out his hand to help him up. Kyle and he stared each other down for a moment before Kyle's hand reached for his.

"Sorry man, that was a raw remark about your dad. Just guess I was mad mine wasn't around that long."

"It's alright."

"Can we get out of here now?" Angel put on her backpack.

"Yeah, I'm good and damn ready." Peter slammed his hand on the emblem.

Chapter 36

It was still dark. Peter realized the place looked like it had when they first parked. They made their way from the tomb.

Awed, Peter muttered, "The trees moved back." The tall trees were spread out and their car had bird droppings on its rusty exterior. The creaking sound and clicks behind them confirmed the tomb was back underground. They stood there for a while and just stared at the small gravestone that had been a doorway to their safe place.

"Now what?" Angel asked.

"We get the hell out of here and fast. Head south to the Stronghold and then meet Rosa at Pastor Finn's place."

"Who's Pastor Finn?" Kyle asked.

They threw their bags in the backseat beside Angel.

"Our contact for the Order of Grace. And…well, Pastor Finn is the closest thing to a father I've had the last few years."

Kyle eyed Peter as he slid in the driver's seat and held out his hand for the keys. "Why don't I drive this time, dude?"

"Naw, I experienced what you called driving, and I just want to be ready in case trouble hits us on the main road."

Kyle stood at the driver's side door with his arms crossed. "It's my car and I'm tired of playing nice, so your ass is going to ride shotgun. Kay?"

Peter growled, but conceded before moving over to the passenger's side. "Feelin' a little salty? You better not get us caught, bro."

"I won't." Kyle gunned the engine and they took off.

"Try the main road, Rt. 95 South. Take it straight until we get to the Glades."

Angel sat up. "The swamp? What the heck is in the swamp?"

"Don't know, I just know that's where we're headin'." Peter bit a thumbnail, thinking they could drive straight. But he wanted to ditch the car since he figured the guys after them would be searching for this one.

Peter released a silent breath, relieved when they hit the main highway without incident or followers.

"Seems like we are clear. The slimeballs cut clear since they couldn't find us." Kyle grinned. Relief flooded his features and broke their edgy silence.

"Yeah, but, we still need to ditch the ride. I don't want no one followin' us where we gotta go."

"I still don't know about that, Pete. We could be leading them to something we aren't supposed to let them know about. Remember, Rosa said the barn was the only one of the properties to ever get into their hands. Maybe that was because they didn't know where these places were."

Kyle stepped up the speed and Peter watched the thick lines of trees pass by. Cars going the opposite direction were like a stream of lights that flashed and lulled Peter into an uneasy calm.

"We don't have a choice. There's not another Sanctuary around. We can stop for the night and scope out a car to snatch to replace this one. I have some tags we can switch off with."

Kyle's eyebrow rose. "Clean tags?"

"You know it."

Angel cleared her throat. "What's with the helicopter search lights?" She blinked. "You don't think that's them looking for us, do you?"

Kyle chuckled. "No way. Only the cops or hospitals have that kind of clout. Those creeps wouldn't want to bring that much attention to themselves. They've been a secret society for centuries, flying in the skies with a searchlight would bring them too much press."

"Hmm, if you say so." Angel sounded doubtful, but sat back in her seat quietly watching the lights twisting through the darkness of the night in search of something.

Peter watched her, and felt a tingling on the back of his neck. But squashed it down and faced the front window. *We don't have a choice, us or them—and I'm tired or running.*

They rode for a few hours and the dawn of daylight teased the sky with red streaks.

"Gas is needed—like now. There are a few motels off that exit too. They probably will take cash." Kyle drove off the highway.

"This should be cool, we're only a couple of hours from the spot." Peter played with the portable navigation system Kyle had stuck up on the window.

"You act like you've never seen one of those things before." Kyle turned the car into a gas station with a cheesy motel attached.

"I've seen them when I searched the internet, but never got to touch one. Pastor Finn had been a cop and the man knew every street in the city by heart. When he took me out a few times with him to get food or test his repairs to his cars, I'd asked him why he didn't use them."

"Seems like you were just a bit shy of a priest in training." Kyle chuckled.

Peter laughed too. "Naw, it wasn't that bad. But we were safe there, even though at times…" he reflected a moment where he'd stared out of the main room and had wanted to run away, "I wished for my old life back."

Snorting, Kyle's hands clenched the wheel tighter. "Even I sometimes do too."

"You guys finally getting along now?" Angel leaned up in her seat and ruffled both their heads. "Maybe now we can concentrate on the plan instead of beating each other up."

Peter watched the road, thankful for only a small splattering of cars as they pulled into one of the older motels several miles off the main highway. Kyle parked out of easy sight and they sat in the car staring at the blinking neon light.

"I don't know, a seedy motel in the middle of the South? Uh-um, man, you know I'd stick out." Peter looked in the side view mirror at Angel, whose eyebrow lifted.

"Hey, me too. No way they'd give me a room without looking me up and down." He tossed his head in Angel's direction. "But a girl. One looking helpless. They'd help her out."

Peter grinned. "Yeah, I think you're right."

"Girl here! You could at least act like I'm in the car with you, stupi-does," she huffed.

"The accent's slipping. You may want to watch that when you go in and get us a room." Kyle chuckled.

She stuck her hand between them. "Money. Hand over enough for the room and to pay them to keep quiet."

Kyle rolled his eyes. "Somebody's been watching way too many movies."

Peter reached in his pocket and handed her three hundred dollars. "Only offer them extra money if they give you a hard time. If you pay it up too soon, they gonna think you've got somethin' to hide."

"Gotcha." She crumbled the money in her pocket and hopped out the car.

They watched her walk across the parking lot to the main door.

"So, uh, did you meet her dressed as a dude? Or after you two got to-gether?"

Peter cut his eyes at him, irritated. "What do you think?" He adjusted the chair and leaned back, studying the passing cars. "I thought she was a young kid when I first saw her. Then she followed me and tried to lift some cash from me."

"Isn't that what the girls always go after? The cash." He laughed.

Peter joined in. "Yeah, I guess. So what's your deal? You leave a hottie at home?"

Kyle shook his head. "Nope. I hit and go. Never had time or the inclination to keep one around. Girls were just too damned nosey. Soon as they asked me questions like, 'Are your parents rich?' or 'How do you have so much cash?' I ghost on them and moved on."

"So you's a playa?" Peter smirked. "Funny, you don't seem the type."

"I don't wear a sign, but I don't have a problem getting my share."

"As long as we clear that your eyes stay off what's mine. And, Angel, she's mine."

"That so? Well, let's hope your pretty lady don't change her mind. If she does, all is fair in love—and war." He winked at Peter.

"You just don't know how bad I wanna punch that stupid-ass grin off your face."

"Yeah, I do. That's why I'm doing it." Kyle slapped Peter's shoulder. "Here she comes."

Something was different about Kyle. He may not have felt anything when his hand was pricked by the emblem, but Kyle was actually starting to change. But how, Peter didn't know.

Angel hurried to the car. She snatched the door open and climbed in. "It was easy. They didn't ask any questions and just took the bill in cash. Since I had more money, I asked for adjoining rooms where there wasn't anyone on either side of us."

Peter knocked on the side of the car. "Good. We stay here tonight, but before light, we snatch one of these cars and keep headin' south."

Chapter 37

Lucien hit the top of the table. "Don't cross me! Follow that damn car and bring me those kids now."

The line went fuzzy. "Sir, it's only me and Jake. Don't you want us to tail them until we have back-up?"

"No, use your damn guns and bring them down. They're just kids!" He leaned forward and clenched his fists. Fear of his brother had kept his easily heated temper controlled most of the time. But that fear was nothing compared to what Gavin had become—a demon host.

"Okay boss, consider it done."

The air in the room changed. Lucian tensed. Willing each muscle in his body to relax, he slowly pivoted around.

Gavin walked in, wiping his hands on a towel then dabbing smudged blood off the side his face. "Your men giving you trouble?"

Lucien put a calm jovial smile on his face. "No. They just needed encouragement."

"I see." Gavin raked over Lucien's features for a moment. "You know, your brother can tell when you're lying."

Lucien blinked. He new this was Gavin's body, but something had changed. Something deep within. The eyes looking back at him were blue, but now ringed with a thin gold line. Gavin's demon master had taken over his body—sharing it with Gavin. "Master," Lucien bowed his head, "I did not know it was you."

Gavin smiled back at him, the look a mockery of Gavin's sly grin now was laced with something, deeply and utterly evil.

Lucien shivered.

"Don't be afraid. You'll learn the difference between us. Gavin's gift will be used to build the Transfero of Lux Lucis that my kind will use to gain entrance to our enemy's gates. But you Lucien, will be our servant. It is important that you not fail. If you are successful in serving us, you too will be a host."

Lucien fell to his knees. "Anything, I'll do anything." Deep inside, terror at letting one of darkness share his soul teased the back of his mind. But memories of what his defiance against the inevitable had gotten him forced him to fill his consciousness with the soothing numbness that had helped him survive as Gavin's brother all these years.

Gavin reached down and lifted Lucien's face at the chin. "I know, but will you have the strength or the loyalty of your subjects to do it all? Will you be strong enough to carry one of us within you?"

"Master. Gavin knows I'm capable."

"Indeed he does. Now, you may sit. We have much to discuss." Gavin went to the fireplace and sat gracefully. Watchful like a tigress hunting a meal, he waited for Lucien to compose himself.

Lucien sat across from him and waited.

"The children you seek, they have to be found before their eighteenth birthdays. There blood will lose its potency if we do not bleed them by then."

"I understand. It was what Gavin and I discovered when we first experimented with them."

Gavin's tongue slivering out over his lip as Lucien squirmed. "Yes, I know. We manipulated one of their kind. Hanna was special. A strong channel, she was so acute to the spirit world that we didn't need a human to use her—*possess* her. But we pushed her too hard. Her mind was weak and, instead of gaining control of that vessel, we pushed her to death and the others protected her—*blessed* her," he spat. "But this Peter Saints, he was the last one her soul touched before slipping from us. His blood is the most potent, since it mingled with hers. We believe he, and only he, at this time, has the ability to gain us the knowledge to overcome the others of their kind. By all means, if you capture them, he must be with them."

"Then I will get him, master." Lucien gulped.

Gavin lifted his finger and smiled as the nail grew, extending into a sharpened point. He slid it down Lucien's face. "I know. You have no choice. I could do unspeakable harm to you if you do not succeed."

Lucien closed his eyes against the pain, deeper than any cut Gavin had given him in the past; this small scratch seemed to cut away at his soul.

Chapter 38

Peter shut the door. His mouth watered when Angel sashayed into their room. Ignoring the yellow wallpapered walls, the skimpy queen-sized bed and the brown carpet, his stomach flurried with anticipation of her kiss. He heard a click and the adjoining door opened up with Kyle humming some stupid slow song.

"Sorry to be blocking your love fest, but do you have some soda?"

"Man, you really are tickin' me off." Peter snatched his bag from the floor and tossed a Gatorade to Kyle's smirking form.

"Hum, need extra strength for anything special?" Kyle leaned on the doorframe.

Angel giggled. "Kyle, stop playing with him. You know he's cranky."

He winked at Angel. "Yeah." Kyle nodded at Peter. "He is. Maybe you can fix that." With a chuckle he closed the door.

Peter leaned on the door and locked it. "We gotta find that nut his own girl."

"Really?" She put a hand on her hip and spun around before flopping back on the bed. "You actually want Kyle happy?"

Peter stalked slowly toward her. A low growl slipped from him as she giggled and rolled away to push the button on the wall above the bed. The bed started to shake. "Girl, come here!" He laughed and dove on the bed.

"Catch me!" She tickled him under the arm and rolled out of reach before he could grab her. "You want to make Kyle happy…" She teased in a sing-song voice then reached over to pull his hair.

"Naw, I want him to leave us alone." Peter chuckled then grabbed Angel's feet before she slipped off the bed. He gave her ankle a strong tug then reached out for her arm to pull her on top of him.

She smiled. "So you caught me? You know I let you do that, don't you?"

"Yeah, sure you did." Peter held her firmly against him. Her heart beat rapidly next to his. He swallowed. His chest felt as though it swelled to meet hers. They stared at each other for a moment. He choked on the love he saw reflected in her eyes. No one had ever looked at him like that, and he was high on it. Addicted. Taking a slow breath, his hands traveled slowly down her back to rest just above the swell of her hips.

"Pete," she said breathlessly, "make me forget." Her eyes watered.

He wished he could forget too, he needed her so bad. His hands shook as he snuggled her closer to him. Leaning up, he gently touched her lips to his. "I love you, Angel." Then he placed a hand into her dark tresses and deepened their kiss. Butterflies filled his chest. He groaned, moving his head from side to side as his mouth devoured her sweetness.

With a nip to her lower lip, he pushed his hip over and braced her while he rolled on top. He pulled away to look down at her, hunger glowing in his eyes.

She framed his face with her hands. "I love you. So much, I feel like I'm on fire when you touch me," she whispered. "I feel like I can live through anything with you. As long as you are with me."

"Me too. I've never felt this way for anyone. No one, but you." He leaned down and nipped on her lower lip then trailed soft kisses down her chin to her neck. He bit softly at the base of her neck. "You taste so good, I could eat you," he growled with a chuckle. Peter nipped the lobe of her ear, and slipped his hand just under the hem of her shirt. "Angel." He looked up at her pleading silently for her permission.

Angel took his hand as he pushed up; gently she kissed the puckered scar and pulled back. His eyes shifted close. Barely, he held onto his control as he felt her kiss the tips of his fingers.

"God, girl, you make me crazy hungry for you."

With a sigh, she placed his hand on her face and slowly trailed it down the swell of her breast to the edge of her shirt. "Anything, Pete, I'd do anything for you. If only we could be safe. I want us to be safe."

"I'll make it happen." Peter held his hand there to steady his racing heart, then licked his lips. "Girl, I feel like...you make me feel like I mean something. Like I'm worth your love. Like I can do anything." He let out a silent breath and kissed her, his tongue tickling the outline of her lips. His hand gradually moved upward, pushing her shirt up just under her chest.

"Pete, I believe in you...in us."

He looked at her and knew she meant it. He slid downward and kissed her stomach. Trailing kisses to her belly button, he tickled her with the tip of his nose.

She giggled. "That tickles."

"You like that?" He nipped at the soft spot just above her belly button. Then jumped at the persistent knock on the door, and the click of the button on the wall as the bed stopped shaking. "I'm gonna kill him," he mumbled.

"Hey guys! I'm going to the restaurant. Want anything?"

Peter groaned and slid Angel off him. "See!" He waved his hand at the door. "I told you the butthole needs a distraction. He's just trying to piss me off."

"True, but I am hungry." She sucked in her lower lip. The appearance of anxious discomfort fluttered over her face.

His gut wrenched, he wanted her so much. Like right that moment, but he knew mixing things up with making love to her wasn't something he should do right now. He didn't even have any condoms, so it was a no-go for now anyway. The last thing he wanted was to complicate their already muffed up situation by making her pregnant. Not to mention, if he was reading her right, she'd changed her mind about taking things further. He raked a hand through is hair and got off the bed.

"We're comin'. Wait for us downstairs."

Angel stood and pulled her shirt over her hips and smiled teasingly at the mumbling Peter. "You know, he's just lonely. He needs friends, just like we do."

Peter threw up a wave. "Whatever." His hand rummaged through his bag. He stuffed his money, ID, and gun into a smaller backpack, then headed to the door. He couldn't bring himself to look at her again, he was so damned needy for her touch. This was bad; his feelings for her were consuming him, almost to the point of an addiction. He knew from experience if he pushed a girl too far, she'd run away. And he'd never forgive himself if he caused her to run from him. He wouldn't survive it. He'd barely survived getting his heart ripped out by Shyan—but Angel would burn it beyond repair.

Angel touched his shoulder; he flinched. "Pete." She cleared her throat. "I, we…,"

He tilted his chin to look at her, his hand resting on the knob, his muscles tensed. "We were moving too fast, Angel. With all the shit we have to deal with right now, going all the way with you now would be damn stupid." His other hand slid down his face. "Let's just cool it off, 'kay? It's best for both of us right now if we do."

Her hand trembled on his shoulder before she pulled it away. "Yeah, I got it. Loud, and, clear."

Peter yanked opened the door and stormed out. He squeezed his eyelids against the pain in his chest, and tightened his hand into a fist. He'd hurt her—pushed her away again. But damn, messing this up with her would mean he'd lose her forever. She probably thought he was mad at her about stopping. But all of it was too much to deal with, the visions, her love, his growing obsession and need for her. What the hell was wrong with him? He'd been in love before—at least close, but this thing with Angel was stronger. Something had changed, and it wasn't just the way he felt about her. It was as if now, he couldn't live without her. The thought of pushing her away, made him feel like he was being ripped apart.

Kyle met him at the foot of the steps. He held his hand up to stop Peter. "Dude, what the hell is going on with you?" His eyebrows lifted. "You look like you're pissed. Did I interrupt something—"

Peter's hand grabbed Kyle's shirt. He held it tight, closed his eyes and took several calming breaths. "You did." He released Kyle's shirt with a push. "Thanks." Then he walked past Kyle while rubbing his hands together. He felt like every nerve in his body was on edge. He stopped his retreat to hop a little on the balls of his feet.

"No, you didn't …you know?" Kyle stood beside him.

"Naw, fool I ain't stupid. We didn't even have protection, and I don't want no babies."

Kyle pivoted in front of him. "What is it? Something else wrong?"

Peter swallowed and licked his lips. "You can say that. Man, I'm edgy, like…like I don't know, like I'm ready to beat the crap out of something. Like if I would've made love to Angel—I could've hurt her. I can't freakin' explain it."

"I can," Kyle stated solemnly. "I feel something too."

"What the hell do you feel?" Peter stuffed his itching hands in the pockets of his jean shorts.

"Like something bad is going to happen. Dude, the stinking hairs on my neck feel like they're lifting. That's why I kept bugging you two. I didn't want to be alone."

Peter smirked. "I did peg you to be a bit of a chump."

Kyle laughed. "Yeah, right."

They both looked up at Angel who ran down the stairs. Her hair pulled back into a ponytail and her T-shirt exposing her firm arms and tiny waist.

"I'll never get used to looking at her this way." Kyle slapped him on the back.

"Me either. Just don't get too caught up, I'll have to kick your ass if you touch her."

"I know, you keep reminding me." Kyle chuckled.

Angel came up to them, her eyes never leaving Peter's. She played with the loose strap on her backpack that she had slung over one shoulder. "You guys ready to eat?"

Peter stepped up and enveloped her close to him. He touched his lips to hers. He said, "Sorry baby," then hugged her before turning around and grabbing her hand.

She tugged his hand, brought it up to her lips and kissed it.

"I'm starving, but no one seems to care." Kyle elbowed her arm.

"Kyle, you are such an attention hog." She elbowed him back.

"I hate to disappoint you, but the only place close by I scoped out that had food and supplies was Walmart." He pointed on the opposite side of the gas station. "They have an all-night sub shop inside."

Peter's stomach growled. "How'd you know?"

"Dang, Dude, your stomach growl that loud all the time?" Kyle peeked behind them at their car parked in the corner of the lot, a distance away from their rooms. "While you two were getting all heated up, I was using my binoculars to check out the place. I think I stared at that Walmart for like a half an hour, then some lady came out with a sub and soda."

"You got money for supplies?" Peter said.

"No, but you do." Kyle tilted his gaze to Pete's backpack.

Peter dug in his pocket and handed Kyle some cash. "What kinda supplies you talkin' about?"

"We need a computer, a cellphone, and knives—weapons."

Angel smacked her teeth. "Peter said no cell phones, and I think he's right."

Kyle sighed. "We need them, dude. We can get a pay 'n go phone, and with a computer I can hack into someone else's line. Scramble the signals so we can't be found. With a computer I can find out some dirt on this Gavin dude you told us about Angel."

Peter hopped up on the curb at the entrance of Walmart. "I get that. You're right, man. Since we ain't runnin' no more, it's time for us to get the tools to start tracking them down."

Chapter 39

Peter stretched and sipped his soda while he tapped his fingers on the small table in the back corner of the Subway shop in the front of the Walmart. He drowned out the other's conversation and watched the few cashiers working that night joke with each other while cleaning around their registers.

It couldn't be helped—this vibe he had that something was odd. That he was on the edge of a cliff about to be pushed off. His eyes slid closed, Hanna's face floated around in his thoughts, but her face wasn't like he'd seen it before. It wasn't dirty or crusted with dried saliva; it was clean, pale and beautiful. Even while alive he'd seen that innocence in her. The thing that made him stop and help her in the first place. The fact that even while she was starving, she still smiled in a childlike manner way younger than her years.

He rubbed his eyes, mentally calling out to her. *Why me Hanna?*

"Earth to Pete?" Angel reached over and put her hand on his tapping finger.

Peter shook his head, stretched his hand out and held hers within his. "I'm good. Just thinkin' 'bout stuff."

Kyle snapped his fingers at Peter. "So, you didn't just hear the intelligent plan I had? You flipped me off to daydream?" Kyle placed the shopping bag on the table. "This here is all we need to turn the tables on those bastards." He patted the bag.

Peter lifted an eyebrow. "Yeah, that sounds real freakin' intelligent. Rubbin' a bag like it's gonna fix this mess we're in." He sighed. "Did you come up with a how?"

"Humph. Had you been listening instead of dazing out on us, you would've heard all the gory details. But since you didn't. Oh well." Kyle sucked his tooth and wrapped the handle of the bag around his hand.

"Man go on and spill. You got my full attention now." Peter jabbed Kyle's hand with his finger.

"If you insist." Kyle broke out with a grin. "You lucky it's so good I don't mind telling you again."

With a smack of his teeth, Peter balled up a napkin and tossed it at him. "Speak, fool."

"Okay, okay…impatience." Kyle waved his hand. "With the computer equipment, the GPS, and some hack tools," he winked, "I can find the bastards. Figure out who's in the organization, the ties and the guy Angel mentioned—this Gavin Steele, I can tap into his company's database."

"Really? Then you are stupid." Peter smacked the table with the heated palm of his hand. "I can't believe you have that type of skill, man. You think that company and the Dragons of Darkness will make it easy for anyone to check them out?" He shook his head. "Naw, I don't see how it'll work."

Kyle frowned. "Oh, ye of little faith. You have no idea what skills I have. But I'll save the good stuff for later." He winked.

Angel poked Kyle's forearm. "That guy's staring at us." Her eyes slid to the side.

Peter leaned back and cut a glance at the man standing in line, fidgeting with his wallet like he was trying to decide what to order. The guy didn't seem like he was staring them down, but he figured they shouldn't take any chances. "Let's move." He stood up.

They followed beside him as he made his way to the front door of the store. Peter spied the guy and caught him staring at them oddly. A tingle snaked up his neck and he grabbed Angel's hand before tugging her behind him.

"We have to leave here by the morning." Peter shook his head. "I got a feelin' our time is up. Somebody's gonna catch on to us."

Kyle caught up and slid in rhythm beside him. "You're right. But I know these dudes. Went to school with them. Hell, even stole some of their secrets, only at the time I was too stupid to investigate it further. But now, I have a reason to. Now, I get to turn the tables on them and bring down the scum for that matter."

"Humph. Slow your roll, Kyle. I didn't realize you were holding back all that hostility behind your dumb-ass jokes and imitation suave show." Peter slapped him on the back. "I'm startin' to like you more and more each day, man."

Angel rolled her eyes. "Can you guys stop your bro-mance and pay attention to our surroundings?" She elbowed Kyle. "Look, there are more cars here."

Kyle pivoted and then tapped Peter on the shoulder. "I only see two more cars. Doesn't seem like anything to worry about. This place is a dive, but I'm sure it gets some business."

She hesitated. "I guess, but those are really nice cars. Why would anyone that could afford cars like those want to sleep in the roach motel?"

"Good catch. Let's go to the room and get things started," his head tilted toward Kyle's, "Sherlock Kyle's investigation."

Peter stopped at the stairs leading up to the room and pushed Angel ahead while holding out a hand to Kyle. She looked back at him and he nodded. "Go on up. I'll follow in a sec."

Kyle waited until Angel jogged up the stairs and jogged across the open gated walkway to slip into their room. He tilted his chin at Kyle. "So what's up?"

"You still have that eerie feeling?" Kyle's eyes looked heavy with a tinge of wildness in them.

Peter recognized the fear in Kyle's gaze, because deep in his stomach he felt it too. "Yep, looks like it's gonna be a long night. We have to get some answers. If we don't, I know Angel's life is definitely in danger. And you and me too if something happens to her."

"I got that. Since they have her name," Kyle peeked up at the door Angel had gone into, "and I'm sure they are looking for me too, we're probably more a danger to you than you are to us."

Peter waved him off. "Not true. Their spies got all our names. Now, they know you got someone else with ya, my ass is as good as dead too if we don't turn this shit around."

"True." Kyle swallowed. "Uh, dude, how you feel about me bunking with you two tonight?" He shrugged and kicked a rock while tightening his hand around the bag. "I know you and your girl might want some time alone, but I really need your help figuring stuff out about this Gavin dude."

Peter smirked. "Yeah, right. You look spooked man, and I wouldn't dog ya out like that." He scratched his scarred palm and stuffed his hand in his pocket. "Just give me about 30 minutes to straighten things out with Angel. You know, talk to her about what happened earlier tonight."

Kyle's face broke out in a grin. "You mean slinking your way out of the dog house?"

Peter nodded. "You picked up on that, huh?"

"Yeah. She only touched you a few times tonight, and that lovey look was replaced with a pissed off glare. Couldn't miss it if I was sitting a mile away."

Peter tapped Kyle's shoulder with his fist. "Thanks for pointin' that out for me, bro. Thanks a freakin' lot." He jogged up the steps to his room, with Kyle behind him. He and Kyle stood at their doors.

Kyle winked at him. "Thirty minutes dude, and I'm knocking."

Peter nodded and opened the door.

Chapter 40

Angel was sitting on the bed searching through her bag. She glanced at Peter when he entered, and held his gaze briefly before digging back in her pack.

"Hey?" He leaned back against the door. "You mad?"

She nailed him with a tormented gaze. "Yes. No, I don't know." With a sigh, her face fell into her hands.

An ache settled in his chest and he went to her, knelt and pulled her hands from her face. "Look at me." His thumb smeared the tears that streaked her cheek. "I'm no good at this, ya' know." He leaned in and kissed her then rested his forehead against hers. "For as long as I can remember, I was trapped in the eye of a tornado."

Her hands came up, surrounded his neck and Angel rested her head in the crook of his neck. Peter reached around her and slowly rubbed her back. "The one time I was happy, when I was a kid, was when I remember how my parents loved me. Even that was snatched away from me. But Pastor Finn, he tried, I guess in his own cracked up way, to give me a bit of a home. The fact is, even that wasn't the best. That doesn't compare to what…what I feel," his voice hitched, "for you." He squeezed her close to his chest. "But all that shit, everything that's happened to me, it made me feel numb. That is, until now. Now, I know that I can change things. That I can be something to someone and matter because of it."

"I'm sorry you didn't have anyone. Sometimes, I wish I didn't know how good it could be to be loved. I remember how my parents always told me they loved me." She sniffed. "I had friends too. I used to make friends easy. And I got to see so many places. I never felt lonely, till they were taken from me."

"Humph. It's like we are both screwed up. But I'm going to get this right between us. I don't want to rush."

Angel kissed him. His heart swelled. He held his lips closed to hers, his hand under her chin then pulled back.

Her eyes widened as she sat back on the bed. "Pete, me either. Part of me was mad at you for reading me wrong. I-I wasn't ready to have sex. But I wanted to get closer to you." She crossed her arms. "But you put me in the same category as all the other girls you dated. Girls you probably did go all the way with. You acted like just because I asked about having sex, and because I let you touch me…kiss me that it automatically meant I wanted to go all the way. When I'm ready—and I don't know when that will be, I hope you'll wait for me."

Peter bit his lip. "Damn. I'm stupid. And sorry, because I was wrong. But that's not all. Earlier tonight, I felt like I was pumped up…like I had a burst of energy that got hotter the closer I got to you. I almost couldn't stop myself from kissing you. From," he stood up and raked his hand through his hair, "from wantin' more…wantin' it all from you. But I want you to know I'll wait."

"I wanted it too, felt on edge too. But I wasn't ready for more." She pointed to her head. "At least not here. I just don't want you to act like I'm like the rest of those girls, because they will never…ever, love you the way I love you, Pete." She hugged him.

Kyle burst through the door. "Sleepover! I got everything we need to turn the tables on these bastards."

Peter held Angel while she wiped her face clean. "Man, your timing freakin' sucks."

Kyle set his bags down and pulled out the laptop. "Yeah, tell me something I don't already know." He quickly went about setting up the equipment. Then he tossed cell phones to Peter and Angel.

"I told you we can be traced by the phones." Peter unwrapped his arm from Angel.

"Not these. These are now high-tech, top secret cellies. I hacked them to have encrypted untraceable signals. Also, I put some souped-up search tools on the systems so you put in phrases, words and it'll do all the matching of related and hidden links into system. It's like a personal hack script. I got it from my home stash of hack tools, all conveniently located in my personal cloud." He pointed to his forehead and tapped it with his forefinger. "Totally freakin' brilliant." He winked at Peter and waved his hand at another bag.

Peter bent to pat around in the bag, frowning he stood, almost dropping it. "Where the hell you get this shit? Explosives, freakin' knives, guns?"

Kyle shrugged then plugged the computer into the wall. He leaned back and cracked his knuckles. "I've been dragging it around all this time. Brought it from home. It's my dad's stash. He was really into this stuff. I took it with me when I left. Figured, he'd want me to have it."

Peter fiddled with the cellphone. "You been plannin' a war for a long time man."

"That's because I knew about it for a lot longer than you did, dude. At least the one against me."

Angel sat cross-legged on the floor between them. She reached out for the laptop Kyle gave her and started research. "We all are going to have to search these guys out if we want to find out everything we can about them."

Peter went to the desk and picked up the notebook laptop Kyle slid to him. Opened it up and pecked at the keys. "What are we lookin' for? You got ideas on where to start?"

Angel raised her finger. "Gavin Steele, CEO of Steele Industries. Then we should probably look at his family tree. The business has been around in different forms for centuries. My father mentioned that Steele Industries was really good at recreating itself." She bit her nail. "Oh, and he also said that the Steele family had money, old money. You know like for generations and generations." Her fingers flew over the keyboard.

"Crime too. Those snake-asses are involved in all sorts of underground crime rings. The kids at the school I went to were the major drug dealers there, and those kids got some high quality stuff. And on top of that, they had the school security in their pockets to push it. That's why when I started trying to sell my stuff, they offered to recruit me."

Peter's eyebrow lifted. His old doubts about Kyle's loyalties came up to tease him and his question came out deep. "So did they? Recruit you?"

Kyle stopped typing and cut his eyes at Peter. "No. That's when all shit hit the fan and the massacre of my parents happened." He jabbed two fingers at Peter. "You my friend, have serious trust issues."

"And you don't?" Peter's hand flipped up. "Besides, 'You my friend have serious lying issues'. You lie like a rug." He snickered. "We all are screwed up."

"Speak for yourself. I know I'm not claiming to be crazy. I have a strong grasp on reality. What we've been through is real."

Angel added, "Yeah, real, like what…*hell* on earth." She let out a squeal and covered her mouth. "You'll never believe this. Gavin's family started Steele Industries as we know it, about three generations ago, like in the early 1900's."

"What else are they into?" Peter asked.

Her fingers trailed the small screen. "Architecture, energy, mining of precious gems. But there are other families too that have a lasting business relationship with the Steele family. They have all married into the Steele family at one generation or another."

Peter looked at his screen. His Google combined its search with Kyle's hack software, and the results taunted him with something he couldn't believe he was seeing. "I got somethin' too. I searched on the artifact I saw in the book at Rosa's place. There's a list, one that's pieced together from other sources, all of them have the symbol of the Dragon that we researched at the sanctuary. I searched for anything with that symbol and saw a pattern. Something they put on their calls, email, messages to the masses. It's in Latin. The Latin word for hunt, *venari*. And that word was meant for—the children of the *Decretum Venia*. They've been hunting and killing us for centuries. Until now," his eyes slid down to the screen, "the word had changed from kill to *capture*."

Kyle bought his fist up to his chin. "Yeah, I can see that. I got pages on one of their other companies. Bio-genetics research is one that seemed odd. Not to mention all the crime organizations that dip into the gun trade, kid sex trade, mafia, stock companies and international products."

"What gives with the bio-genetics research?" Peter asked.

Angel's stricken looked traveled from Peter's eyes to his hand. "I think I know what they are researching."

"How?" Kyle asked.

"I overheard things my father talked about with my mother late at night when they thought I was sleep. Now that I know how Peter got us into the sanctuaries, it makes me wonder if that research company I remember by name is actually one of the owners my father said had the last name, Crow."

"So what's up with this Crow guy?" Peter asked.

"He's one of the key people in the Extraho of Obscurum. My dad," Angel hesitated, thinking. "My dad said he was pure evil. That he was doing research for Steele Industries. When he was telling my mother, his voice lowered, but I heard him say the research was dangerous to the purpose of the *Decretum Venia*. Fear was in his voice, I could even hear it tremor when he begged my mother to join him on the run. He told her they would drain the children—his child," her hand rested on her neck "of every drop of their blood to find out the secrets of the order. That was the first time we ran."

"Damn." Peter sat down next to her and wrapped his arm around her shoulder. "That means that if they catch Angel, or even you Kyle, they plan on draining you." His eyebrow crimped. "But for what?"

Kyle stood. "Okay, I'm going way out on a limb here. But if they own a research center where they research blood. And the sanctuaries are protected based on blood or DNA pulled from someone who is a descendant of *Decretum VeniaDecretum Venia* then all they have to do is transplant our blood to a host in order to trick the protective security to these sanctuaries. And now that we know that in addition to there being sanctuaries— safe houses for someone of the order to hide out—the sanctuaries are nothing compared to what we may find in a Stronghold."

Peter jumped up and started pacing. "They want somethin', somethin' big. Breakin' into the sanctuaries will help them find it. The stronghold. But I have a feelin' it's even more than that."

"Well…" Angel pushed herself up and sat on the edge of the bed. She pounded the keys on her computer, "with what happened to Pete to change him or 'activate' him I don't think that has happened in like forever."

"I remember reading one of the books on the *Decretum Venia* that they knew of a generation," Kyle's knees came up. "a generation that would be more than protectors of the sanctuaries and the history of the Creator. That there would be a time when pure bloods would be anointed as the time for war came near. These kids would be powerful. Have gifts beyond the comprehension of men. But I didn't understand exactly what that meant." His bit his finger. "I get it now. It said the anointed ones had to be younger than eighteen. They would be activated through the blessed blood of another, or by an active agent within one of the sanctuaries."

Angel let out an audible gasp. "Pete, then maybe Hanna...You think she was blessed? Maybe, it's her blood that changed you. That activated you."

Realization dawned in Peter's chest and in his soul. He knew it deep within. The dreams, Hanna's words, his vision of his mother. Everything was coming together. "It could be true. But if it is, then that means that they will never stop searchin' for us. This could be more than we can deal with on our own. We have to warn the others. Pastor Finn and Rosa need to know. Like now. Ugh!" His hand burned, hotter than ever before. As if it was confirming his worst fear. "And if this is it, than the hell on Earth we've been livin' has gotten worse—much worse."

Kyle's stare collided with Peter's. "You thinking what I'm thinking, dude?"

"I'm thinkin' we need to get the hell outta here as soon as possible. Kyle and I will have to find another car to jack."

"I don't know about you, dude, but I'm tired as all get-out."

"Me too, Pete. Can we sneak in just a few hours then leave?"

He sighed and nodded at Kyle. "You are not sleepin' in this bed with us. But the floor is yours if you want it."

"I've slept in worst places. Besides, my hack virus is searching while we zonk out." He grinned and unrolled his sleeping bag.

Chapter 41

Peter woke first. He felt like crap, but got up anyway. Angel's sleeping form caused a lopsided smile to break out on his face. She'd wrapped cozily around him while she slept. Like she felt safe with him. He'd be lying to himself if he tried to fake that it didn't make him feel like he could do anything.

He grabbed an energy drink off the nightstand and stuffed a protein bar in his mouth as he realized daybreak was upon them and peeking through the ratty curtains. Tracing his hand down the curve of Angel's cheek, he leaned over and whispered, "Wake up, babe."

"I heard that—and I'm not your babe." Kyle threw a balled up sock at Peter's head.

"Man, shut up! You're sick, ya' know that?"

Kyle hopped up. "Yeah, I know."

Angel awoke and slipped off the bed. "I'm first to the bathroom."

"I'll use the one in my room." Kyle headed to the door. "But I'll be back in 10 min, so don't get too comfortable."

Peter threw his other protein bar at the back of Kyle's head.

Kyle ducked through the door. "You missed!"

He went to the bathroom door. "Hey Angel, I just wanna wash up. You okay with me sharing the bathroom with you?"

She giggled. "Sure. If you promise to behave yourself and stay on the other side of the curtain and not peek."

"I ain't gonna lie and say it will be easy. But I'll be good...*today*." Peter chuckled and snatched off his shirt. After he washed, he changed clothes. He'd just finished zipping his pants when the shower stopped.

His eyes slid over to the shower and spied Angel peeking from the curtain. "I thought you said no peekin'."

Her full lip quirked up. "I said you couldn't peek." She winked at him.

He shook his head. "Girl, you bad. And I like it."

"Hey! Kyle's back. Are you decent?" Kyle pushed opened the bathroom door.

Angel screamed and hid back behind the curtain.

"Kyle," Peter hissed.

"I know, I know…my timing sucks." Kyle moved out of Peter's way and closed the door. "But I think we should skip out."

"Gotcha. Let's get this stuff packed up."

They started cleaning the room. Kyle put the computer equipment in a rollaway duffle bag, then stood up and stretched.

Angel came out of the bathroom, her hair in waves around her shapely form over her T-shirt.

"Dude, I can't believe I thought she was a guy." Kyle whistled.

"Me either."

Angel cleared her throat. "Uh, I'm standing right here." Her eyes traveled to her bags and she stomped her feet while stuffing her hands in her jean pockets. "Crap! I left my ID in the car. I'll be right back and then finish packing this stuff while you and Kyle find us another car."

Kyle reached in his pocket and gave her the keys. She opened the front door without looking back.

Peter caught up with her and snagged her arm. "Be quick about it 'kay?" Peter leaned down and kissed lightly on the lips. He held her hand and looked down into the parking lot. "There's another car out there that wasn't here earlier. Be careful."

While they waited for her to get her ID out of the car they made haste in packing.

Peter stretched and looked at all the packed bags. "Man, we got a lot of stuff. About two bags each now." He peeked at his watch, frowning he nailed Kyle with a fear filled gaze. A tingling sensation of danger crept up his neck. "Where the hell is Angel?"

"Don't know. I'll go check while you bring the stuff to the door." Kyle stuffed a gun in his belt.

Peter grabbed his and did the same. Then picked up a pocketknife they'd scooped up at the store earlier and put it in his back pocket. No way was he letting Kyle be the only one check on her.

Peter slowly opened the door, and searched the parking lot. *Nothing. Where is she?* A muffled scream squeaked beneath him. Horror gripped him, and he clinched his teeth at the scene below. A large man was holding Angel's arms back. He was struggling to force her into a black sedan. She front kicked another tall man in black jeans who was trying to subdue her.

Kyle was wrestling with a guy for his gun. And another man came up behind him with a pistol pointed at his head.

Peter took a deep breath, a calming one. And he spied a hammer at his foot. Picking it up by its worn handle, his eyes narrowed as he aimed for the head of the man with the gun. His fingers tightened for a brief moment before he swung it at the assailant. It sailed through the air. With a loud crack, the hammer hit its mark. The guy fell forward onto Kyle's back. The other guy under Kyle elbowed Kyle upward into his chin.

His heart pounding, Peter raced down the steps. A yelp escaped from the guy holding Angel. She lost a shoe and it hit her assailant in the eye. Angrily, the attacker in front of her grabbed her foot and twisted it around.

Peter jumped over the railing onto the back of the guy at her foot. The guy twisted around, knocking Peter off balance. Then he punched Peter in the stomach. Air rushed out of Peter's lungs. His eyes watered against the shot of pain as he staggered back. Growling deep in his throat, Peter grabbed the man by his shirt, jerked him forward and landed a blow with his knee to the guy's nose. Blood spurted from the guy's face. Peter two-pieced the guy. His assailant stumbled back. The attacker recovered to jab Peter in the stomach. Peter's stomach clenched against the ache and he elbowed the guy in the chest. The man landed another punch to Peter's chest. Peter lunged forward, grabbed the guy by the neck, and wrapped his arm tightly around the attacker to force him facedown to the ground.

"C'mon Rick! Get his ass in the car!" yelled the brute holding Angel.

Peter slackened his hold on his opponent and reared up to charge at the open door of the car.

Angel's cries increased until the man at the door punched her one final time. The guy hopped in the car, and closed the door.

"No!" Peter dove for the car as it sped away. A piercing knife of fire from a bullet barreled through his back and out his shoulder. He screamed but didn't know if it was from his loss of Angel or the pain. Gunshots exchanged behind him. Bright lights flared in front of him as another shot hit him in the shoulder. He fell to the ground.

"Shit! Oh…shit," Kyle's shaky voice swore behind him. "We've got to go!"

Peter's eyes were heavy. Too heavy. His chest hurt. *Angel. Oh, God, Angel. I couldn't save her.*

"I know, dude. Those bastards got her. Let me get you in the car. I'll get us out of here."

He felt Kyle drag and half carry him to a car then push him in. Lights flashed in front of him as tears blurred his vision. Nausea taunted his stomach and with trembling hands he held onto the door as he purged.

"Angel! I'll save you," Peter's voice cracked. He dragged his forearm against his lips. He couldn't stop the tears running down his face if he tried. The ache was too great. Losing Angel felt like his heart was ripped out.

Peter listened while Kyle opened the trunk and threw stuff in. Back and forth he went until Peter heard a curse as the trunk closed. He wanted to move, to help, to go to Angel, but his body felt so weak. His shirt was warm and sticky from his blood. He groaned, and sobbed while chanting Angel's name like a prayer.

Kyle shook him. "Dude, you have to tell me where the Stronghold is. It's the only place we can go that's safe."

"We gotta…get…Angel," he answered hoarsely.

"I know, but you can't do shit in this condition. You'll die and give them what they want." Kyle wrapped a hand around Peter's forearm. "Trust me dude, *trust me*, I will get her. But I have to make sure you are alive first."

With a grunt, Peter leaned forward, blinked so he could see a bit straighter and gritted his teeth as he put in the coordinates to the Stronghold. Their portable GPS confirmed the location, and Kyle pulled off.

"Cops…,they comin' for us," Peter muttered.

Kyle gunned the engine. "Probably, but because we were in the back of a deserted motel, doubtful they'll get there anytime soon. Especially, since those sick freaks tried to capture us. The freakin' owner wasn't nowhere to be found. I bet they paid his slimy ass off to get a chance at us."

Peter's head fell back on the headrest. "Gotta find her."

"We are, and those dragon followers left their cell phones and laptops in here. When we get to a place I can stop off, I'll encrypt the phones and get all the messages. We'll find her. And when we do, I'm blowing some shit up."

Peter couldn't help the broken chuckle that seeped from his lips. He was started to like the way Kyle was thinking.

Chapter 42

Peter felt like he was being held down by sandbags. They'd stopped several times along the highway and some rocky roads to use the bathroom. Kyle swore several times while working on one of the laptops and checking under the car.

"Kyle." His voice came out in a raspy whisper.

"I guess we are almost there, dude. But you sure this is right?" Kyle sounded confused.

His eyes burned, but Peter opened them anyway. He forced free a breath as he braced his feet against the floor to sit up for a better look. "What the…" Peter coughed. Squeezing his eyes against tears of pain, he pushed his aching body up, and then ran his fingers across the tightly woven cloth around his stomach and shoulder.

"You slept through me putting that on you."

Peter let out a grunt, his throat hurt to bad to talk. But his eyes traveled the expanse in front of them. A swamp. Trees, taller than Peter had ever seen sprung up from the murky green waters. Dusting of green splotches scattered the top, and high grass peeked up along the edges of the massive swamplands. The place looked like no one had traveled there in centuries.

"Ugh." Dizziness hit him. He put his hand to his head.

"Dude! Figure it out. We are in the middle of a freakin' swamp and I don't see anything in our future but being gator bait."

Peter put his hand up to his head. It throbbed, but he had to force himself to think clearly—to remember what he'd seen at the last sanctuary. He closed his eyes briefly, forcing himself to concentrate.

"Here drink this to get your head together." Kyle handed him a big bottle of Monster energy drink.

Peter gulped it down. "Tree, the top of the Stronghold had," he coughed, "a tree."

Kyle looked at him like he'd lost his mind but then nodded slowly. "Yeah, right, a tree." He tapped the windshield that showed over a thousand trees scattered in front of them, their sunken trunks submerged in the waters. "Well, looks like you have lots to chose from." A thump against the car made Kyle jump.

Peter pushed the button to roll down his window, and swallowed his fear. Another thump, harder this time, sounded as the car moved. The water rippled beneath his window just before a white-bodied alligator's jaws broke the surface. "Shit!" He jerked back into Kyle's shoulder. A stab of pain reawakened in his shoulder as a reminder of his injuries.

Kyle lifted up from his feet to peek over Peter's shoulder. "What! What is it?"

"White, a white alligator!"

"Seriously? Damn, never seen one of them before. Is it still there?"

Peter leaned over cautiously. The water was now calm. "I don't know, man."

With a sigh, Kyle reached into the backseat and grabbed his backpack. "You still have your gun?"

"Yeah." Peter swallowed back a wave of nausea. "I'll know the tree when I see it." He concentrated, prayed and stared at the expanse of trees ahead. His eyes traveled back and forth. Most all of the trees were over a 120 feet tall. But one tree was only about half the size of the others. It appeared to stand in the middle of them as if it was being protected—or purposefully hidden.

"So? You got it?" Kyle shuffled around in the front seat.

"I think so, but I don't think this one is gonna be easy."

"No joke? I feel like that too. Especially, since that was a rare albino alligator that hit our car, like it was warning us."

Peter nodded. "It was. I have a bad feelin' 'bout this." In answer, the car's tire was bumped again, then again from the other side.

Kyle stared at him with panic barely suppressed on his face before he gulped. "You want me to go first?" His gaze slid down to the pink tinged wrappings he made from Peter's T-shirts. "You're bloody. Won't that make predators see you as a beacon of food in their starving pit of water?"

"Last I checked, gators don't smell. They don't have to." He reached in the back and grabbed an umbrella.

With a sigh, Kyle went beneath his seat and picked up a hammer. Holding it firmly he joked, "Remember this?" He pulled a small back-pack from under the seat. "I put your bag under your seat for you."

Peter winced against the ache in his side. His fingers grasped the backpack and draped it over his arm. He grunted, slowly opened the door, and slipped his foot into the warm swamp water. The tip of his shoe tested the water as it sloshed his shin, causing his pant leg to sway against him. He gritted his teeth, tightened his hold on the strap of his backpack, and then put his other arm through.

The car door moved behind him. Doubts about this tickled his neck in a final warning of sorts. Even though he and Kyle had been through a lot, sometimes he still had his suspicions about the kid. The guy was definite-ly a liar, but taking him to the Stronghold couldn't be helped. He had to save Angel, even if it meant Kyle's eventual betrayal.

"Dude, you forgot to close your door. I know it's not your car, but it's all we got and we might need to keep it in one piece."

"Stop cryin' I'm tryin' to concentrate!" Peter spat, his eyes following the moving indent in the water. The one coming straight at them. Twitch-ing itches of fear crept up his back. His leg locked and he leaned forward to test the deepening ground in front of him.

A slight splash disturbed the quiet. Then another and another.

"No! There's more of them." Kyle pointed to the edge of the swamp. Alligators, small and large, were breaking through the grass, unhurried in their progress. He stepped toward Peter. "Ugh!" Kyle fell face-first into the water. His head swung back and he struggled. "Hole, sinking. I'm…" he sputtered, "sinking!"

Peter forgot his pain. He lunged for Kyle's hand. "Stop fightin', you'll sink faster!" He leaned forward, pointing the tip of his umbrella in Kyle's direction.

He coughed, then froze. Slowly, he grabbed the tip of the umbrella. "Got it." Kyle tugged, pulling himself out of the sinkhole to step on firm ground.

A breath of relief escaped Peter. "C'mon."

"Ugh!" Kyle jumped and he yanked the leech slivering up his thigh. "Yuck." He threw it.

Peter shook his head, turning away. He spied the tree up ahead and felt Kyle move quickly. Behind him, water sprayed and splashed. He stumbled, the tip of an alligator tail slapped back, knocking him forward and causing him to lose grip of the umbrella.

"Yah!" Kyle cried.

Peter righted his stance. Then he pivoted as the alligator reared its head above water. He grunted, and tapped its nose. Peter wrapped his hands on the sides of its closed mouth. For a moment, it stilled, its eyes studying Peter's. Then it twisted. Peter lost hold of it. The beast stepped back with its open jaws, and lunged for him.

"No!" Kyle yelled, coming from the side, he swung the hammer. Its sharp base stuck in the neck of the alligator. A hissing sound escaped the wound as the beast slid beneath the waters.

Peter's chest heaved, and he relaxed. A sharp sting pierced his neck. He was jerked back. "Oww!" Tears dripped from his eyes. Peter struggled against the gators tugging. His head swung back, connected with the firm edge of the alligator's nose, and all went bright white then black.

Drowning, he was drowning. *Mommy! Mommy! Help*...Visions of his mother's reassuring smile looking back at him jarred him. A ghostly memory of her dragging him by his arm, deep in the water fluttered. She drew him close and pushed her breath through his lips before tugging at him again. Then she was thrusting him up toward the sun.

Coughing racked his aching chest. He sprang up out of the water but was jerked back once again by the alligators teeth clenched tightly through his backpack. Angry and determined, "Angel," he murmured. Peter flipped around. He slid his leg over the alligator's back. He growled, straddled the alligator's back and held its mouth shut.

"Kyle!" Peter pulled back the alligator's head. Kyle's shot rang through the air. Multiple bullets followed. Peter held the struggling alligator firm until it struggled no more.

Their eyes held. Gulping, Peter slid off the beast with a shiver. The thing was over fifteen feet long. It could have killed him—heck, tried to kill him. "The tree!" Peter sprinted through the deepening water. His eyes never left the small tree with water moccasins around it. The tall thick trees closed in around it.

"Freakin' snakes, Peter! Pythons, I swear it. They're in the water," Kyle shrieked, fear evident in his voice.

Peter kept running, praying Kyle was behind him. He released a staggered breath. Finally, he stood in front of the tree. Except for its height, it looked like all the others. Kyle's scream jarred his thoughts. He spun around. Kyle stood frozen, staring at the copper colored snake slithering into the water. Behind it, still and watchful waited the twenty-foot albino alligator he'd spied earlier. He'd known it by its ruby red eyes.

Kyle snapped out of his daze. The large snake's mouth expanded and commenced sucking in the head of one of the smaller alligators. It thrashed about but a moment before it appeared to be lulled into a drugged submission.

"Peter! Hurry up!"

His hand trembled. He frantically felt around on the tree's trunk. Kyle's command snapped him out of his shock at the scene behind him. He couldn't lose focus. He had to find this. This was the answer to save Angel, to save them all. He fingers scratched at the algae and dirt on the tree. Just above his fingers he saw a faint glow.

"Hurry up! The white gator's coming!"

"Shut up," Peter growled. His muscles tensed. With a yell, he slammed his heated hand on the faintly glowing symbol covered in green moss. His palm connected. The stick of three small needles incited his chant, "C'mon, come on!" He prayed it was their way in.

"Oh, my, GOD!" Kyle whispered.

Water at his hips sloshed. It began to recede, lower. And lower. In trepidation, he turned. His jaw dropped at the sight. The water in the swamp appeared to be draining—being sucked in through the crevices of the swamp floor, while the alligators stood around them, frozen. None were as long as the albino alligator that appeared to stare at him with a semblance of respect. Dead pythons, more than Peter could have imagined, lay in the water twitching at the stubby legs of many of the alligators.

The gators stood there. The tree trunk glowed. Peter watched as every bit of moisture was absorbed into the ground. The once-muddy bottom of the swamp became a cracked blackened land. The face-off ended and the alligators moved as if they were trained to surround them in protection. They trampled their thick muscled bodies of their python attackers. Their proud and deadly forms stood several yards in a perfectly formed semi-circle around Peter and Kyle, like statues ready for war.

A creak vibrated behind them. They pivoted when the tree trunk cracked open to reveal a metal cylinder. Peter slapped his palm on the symbol of three intertwined circles, and the front of the cylinder slid within the lower depths of the trunk. They stepped inside, neither had words to explain what happened and resolutely leaned against the back wall of the elevator. A clear paneled wall rose up from the floor to close them in. Within minutes, the ground moistened and water spurted up from the cracks. The alligators stood ramrod still while water sloshed around them, filling up the once dried land and climbing up the clear door until it reached Peter's hip. A faint beeping sound startled them and Peter looked around for another symbol.

"It's up there, on the ceiling." Kyle pointed.

"How am I supposed to reach that?"

"You can stand on my shoulders." Kyle bent for Peter.

Peter braced himself, the sharp pain in his shoulder reminding him of his purpose. He steadied himself and reached to place his hand on the raised symbol on the ceiling. This time the familiar prick didn't come. A wet substance teased his heated opened palm and the lit symbol shined brighter before they heard a series of clicking.

He jumped off Kyle's shoulders and the elevator began to descend. "Angel. How are we gonna find her?" Peter's staggered voice came out quietly.

"I don't know exactly. But I brought my laptop. And I'm loving my waterproof backpack right now." Kyle's eyes slid to Peter's soaked backpack and he smirked. "Maybe you should've invested in one."

Peter rolled his eyes. "No computerized stuff to worry about. What I got when me and Angel was on the road was good enough."

"Why is that? Most kids have a cell phone, pager, iPod...something."

"Pastor Finn didn't buy any for us. He told us not to have them because the dangerous people that our parents were hiding us from could use them to find us. We did have some use of computers. He had soft-ware that would automatically wipe off any trace of our surfing and if we tried to create a Facebook or Google page, it would block us out."

"Whoa, that's wicked. So you grew up sheltered."

He snorted. "Sheltered? From what...death? Murder? Bad people? Naw, I wasn't sheltered. But now that I think on it, I was protected. First by my parents, then by Pastor Finn." He cut a glance at Kyle, briefly sizing him up.

The elevator came to a stop. They both peeked at each other with matching expressions of doubt.

"This is it? The Stronghold?" Kyle whispered.

The sound of hissing air came from below. The air between the clear elevator door and the metal wall seemed to deplete when they merged into one. The door opened and they stepped out.

Peter's lips tightened. His hand rubbed his shoulder wound. He looked up at the domed ceiling made of silver with an inlayed gold map of the old world. Surrounding the map was black colored metal with tiny lights that resembled major star patterns. Where the ceiling met the lower wall was a band of glass.

Another glass encasement at the base of the dome practically glowed. Dark waters that resembled the swamp water above were being sucked through unseen vents. Several fish flapped at the base of the encased wall before descending beneath the window. Sturdy metal of silver and inlays of gold framed the place. The entire room was made of it.

"What now?"

Peter shook his head. "I don't know. I don't know."

Chapter 43

Peter closed his eyes and took a deep breath, trying to concentrate. This Stronghold was a place of great importance to someone. But to him, he only hoped it held the answers to why they were being dogged down. He stared at the lit signals on the ceiling. They throbbed like the pain in his body, like the burn on his hand. Without warning they stopped. Then they shined brighter before a line of light burst from their center to connect them.

"It's arming things. At least that's what it looks like." Kyle's voice hitched.

"Why would it arm those places now?" Peter raised his hand and flexed it. He willed the mark on his hand to show him something, anything that would make it easier to find Angel. Tendrils of ghostly smoke slivered from the center of his palm, replicating the map of the sanctuaries displayed to him at Rosa's barn.

"Whoa! What the h—" Kyle stepped back. "How'd you?"

"Shut up, I'm tryin' to concentrate." His heart beat faster. He recognized the sanctuaries. They were similar to the ones in the ceiling. "If these are the sanctuaries." He pointed upward with his other hand. *Those, are Strongholds*.

"What are those places?" Kyle pointed before Peter closed his hand. "What makes this place so special?"

"Nothing. I don't know," Peter lied. "Whatever it is...it's somethin' to protect. Somethin' those bastards who stole Angel want."

"Makes sense, since they couldn't get in this place without out blood anyway." Kyle slowly spun around. "But don't worry about finding Angel. When you were sleep I disabled the tracking device that was in their car. And guess what?"

"What?" Peter clenched his hand and searched the metal walls for clues. The zigzagged inlayed lines of blue light on one wall drew him closer.

"I know where she is, where the other mother-sucker took her."

Every muscle in Peter's body tensed. "How far?"

"You wouldn't believe me if I told you."

Peter slid off his soaked backpack. "Try me."

"No more than a hundred miles up the road. On the swanky beach side where all the rich and famous live."

"Gotta hand it to you. You're good." Peter rubbed his hand down on the wall where on the side that appeared to pulsate. A swirled up pale blue light disappeared into the wall when his hand rubbed across it.

"I knew it all the time. You always were a doubter," Kyle winked at him.

"Whatever. Just shut—" Before he finished, he dropped his jaw slightly. The wall sunk in where the drumming lights once shone. Several clicks sounded around the room. The wall pushed backwards like a beating heart to reveal more and more of a hidden hall that reminded Peter of a subway tunnel encased in silver.

"This is freakin' unreal." Kyle slapped Peter on his back. "I thought my dad was full of dog crap."

Peter winced at the sudden slicing pain on his shoulder. "C'mon, maybe there are answers in here." Peter waved a hand at Kyle. His shoulder twitched again. But he gritted his teeth through the ache. His eyes planted on the smooth wall at the end of the tunnel.

Kyle came up beside him. "You all right? There's blood coming through the bandage."

"Oh, like you really care." Peter's lip tilted up. And faked a scowl then forced a grin. "I'm cool."

"I like the grin, dude. You know you're one of my best buds."

"That right? Even after I kicked your—" Peter didn't finish, but couldn't deny the settle warnings in his gut at Kyle's duplicity.

"Don't even say it. I kicked yours first."

Peter shook his head and reached for the wall that separated him from the unknown. The encased symbol of three circles with an angel underneath beckoned him.

He shuttered his eyes closed. Peter heard Kyle take a step back and mumble, "We must be crazy…" as his hand flattened on the middle circle.

The foot of the angelic figure opened. A robotic hand extended. Peter let out a gasp when it took hold of his hand. He struggled against it, but the thing held him firm. It appeared to split and another smaller robotic arm extended from it to force his mouth open. The two pronged metal fingers slipped inside and swiped under his tongue while the other arm held his scarred hand in place. A thick needle extended and drew blood from him.

"Ugh," Peter gagged. His eyes watered from the pain. The needle retracted and its finger traced the symbol on Peter's hand.

"What, the…!" A cracking sounded behind them. "A wall! It's closing us in," Kyle yelled.

Peter was released and the robotic arms collapsed into the door. An infrared light filled the small boxed-in space and scanned their bodies. Then a voice sounded. "Welcome, *populus*."

"Host? It's saying it in Latin. Why is it calling us a host? L-like symbiotic host from some freakin' twisted space flick?" Kyle murmured.

"Don't know." Peter's hand came up to his shoulder to brace it as the doorway opened. He choked on the lump in his throat. Then blinked away the errant tears.

A book, about a foot thick, encased in gold, was suspended in the middle of the room. Light from an unknown source seemed to come from the book. The light radiated from it reached from the unbelievably high ceiling to the floor. The book hung about six feet off the ground, immobile. Peter felt a tug, a calling. His steps felt heavy with lead. But he took one step. Then another. And another. Angel's life depended on it.

Just one more step.

Kyle's hand jutted forward to stop him. "I don't know about this. Something, God… Something is telling me we need to leave this alone."

Peter yanked his hand away. "I can't. There's this thing in me that's making me feel like if I leave, I'd die. Angel will die." His voice cracked, "Every cell in my body wants to touch that book."

"Peter…I just got a bad feeling about this." Kyle took hold of Peter's shirt and yanked.

"Let go! My blood is on fire for that thing!" His mouth watered, his hand itched, his feet had a mind of its own. Peter pushed Kyle backward.

Kyle flew across the floor like a rag doll. His body hit the wall. "Ugh! No!"

Peter ran to the book, slid to a stop just in front of it. His eyes shut as the feeling of blissful peace filled him. The euphoria of finally being, *home.*

Light—blinding light—clouded his vision. Pain, like every bone in his body was simultaneously breaking, caused him to scream. His blood, so hot, burning as it pulsed through his veins. It felt as though his soul was being snatched out of his body. Then the initial shock of pain ebbed as if he was being carried away from his twisted and broken flesh.

Chapter 44

Peter groaned. His eyes were closed and the darkness relaxed him further. Exhaustion taunted him, and he just wanted to stay asleep.

"Luke 23!"

Peter was shoved. Hard.

"Luke! Awaken, we must move. Now!"

He opened his eyes. God. The nightmare wasn't over. A man, with piercing green eyes, long jet-black hair, and a cleft in his chin was studying him from six inches away.

"My name is Peter," he coughed, "Peter Saints." He looked down at his body and realized it wasn't his. Thick legs moved back and forth at his command. The hand that rubbed down his chest was three times larger than his own—and it was fair-skinned. He pulled at the blond strands that hung over his eyes, and scrambled back with a yelp.

"By the Creator's Holy Grace, ye wish ye were a saint. But ye ain't nothing but an angel with no wings, and a soft head." The man knocked on Peter's head with his knuckles. Then he lifted Peter and put an arm under his.

"No, man, I'm Peter." He thrashed about against him.

The giant guy held him tighter. "Yeah, yeah, and I'm Jaakan, the Creator's most favored one. Ha ha!"

"Seriously, let me go!" Peter fell away and stumbled. His body felt awkward, larger than before. His eyes focused finally. He blinked two or three times but the image before him didn't leave.

He was surrounded by men, and a woman, who looked like giants compared to the scattering of people just beyond the circle of massive sized men and women around him. The smell, like burning cinders engulfed him, and he coughed, dropping to his knee. The darkness of night held a fog that teased the moon, and Peter's eyes burned from the heaviness in the air. The scattering of giants, in the midst of grown men and women that only came up as high as these enormously muscled creatures rib cages made him take a step back. Terror caused his muscles to clench.

The woman stepped forward. Her blue eyes seemed to inspect him "Something's wrong with him." She lifted Peter's chin. "Maybe a head injury?" The curl of her long blonde hair teased his shoulder.

She reminded him of Hanna. But his eyes had to be lying to him. Because this would be Hanna as a grown woman—a giant. The dry cracked ground, burnt trees, and a wall of black moving smoke with thundering fire that sparked within it stood behind her. It made Peter wonder if this nightmare had put him in hell. The barrier in front of them seemed to span from the ground up to the heavens. He gulped.

"Ah, he's fine. We have to move before the demons are upon us." The man's booming voice vibrated in Peter's ear.

A warrior's yell that pierced the night, "They already are." The woman turned toward the war call.

The tall man who held onto Peter bent and lifted him. "Luke 23. I hope ye still 'ave your wits about ye. I have to protect the Creator's precious ones and can't look after ye." He thrust a sword at Peter that he'd pulled off his back. Then whispered, "Remember, slice them at the neck. They've stolen our technology and their armor is stronger than ever. Don't say Michael 2's never done nothing for ye."

The huge man ran off shouting a battle cry. The silver necklace around the guy's neck sparked before it appeared to spew metal from within it. In a flash his lower body was encased in beveled silver that shimmered as he moved like diamonds.

Peter stood there, his hand clutching the handle of the sword. Another man, one of the much shorter ones, came up to him. Peter's body jerked when he realized that he was *looking* down at a grown man. He guessed the man was at least 6 ft 5 inches tall.

"My blessed one, we have to go before the attackers from the south follow." The man reached out. "Luke 23, I don't believe you are well. But we need you to fight, or we'll never save Jaakan. We're too close to pull back. Too many already gone."

Peter nodded. He figured it was no use trying to make them understand that he wasn't this Luke 23 person they kept calling him. But he'd fight, 'cause truth was, he wanted to hurt something right now.

He lifted his sword, roared, and felt power fill him with each step. The other giants, male and female that he'd seen earlier were being consumed by a herd of demon invaders. His arm froze and he nearly gagged when his eyes landed on their attackers. Demons, he guessed, but the truth was—demons he'd seen didn't look half as sinister as these creatures.

They all looked so different, yet just as evil. Some were taller than the others. Their faces red masses of burned skin, with curved horns that met over their heads. There were holes where their eyes should be. They wielded huge swords with their oversized arms that were covered in spotty pieces of rotting flesh. A copper-like metal framed their shoulders then crisscrossed over portions of their distorted chests. Some of them didn't have legs but huge snake bottoms covered in copper around their hips. Their faces were void of eyeballs, and exposed bones that looked almost human were filled in with muscle beneath.

The sharp stab of a sword sliced down Peter's bare back. His spine curved. His sword whipped around. He swallowed his terror when his eyes collided with his attacker.

"Die! You angel of light," she spat.

Her face was framed by red colored bones that formed into one large horn and a broken jagged horned crown. At the base of its head wiggled red, hissing snakes with tongues of fire. Her copper colored armor jutted from her shoulder and multiple linked chains covered her bra made of human skeleton heads.

Peter sliced his sword down and cut across her muscle-packed stomach. With a grunt, he swung again into her broad scaled hips.

"Yah!" Her pointed snake tail whipped around. Then stabbed him through the side of his stomach.

"Ugh." Peter blinked against tears. His breath was knocked out of him. He was lifted high into the air. Anger and the determination to win fueled the adrenaline rush that poured through him. "You ugly...." Peter threw his sword at her exposed neck, severing her head. The blade cut clear through. He expelled the breath he'd been holding. Then he was yanked from side to side by her twitching tail.

"Get Luke! He's fallen. Take him to *Haven*," someone yelled in the distance.

Exhaustion consumed him, and the fighting noises behind him seemed to fade away. His head bounced as the tail finally stopped thrashing him. Unconsciousness claimed him once again.

Chapter 45

Lucien couldn't keep his eyes off the girl. She was beautiful like her name, *Angel*.

Angel didn't cry. Her eyelids twitched. The pale skin on her face was marred with bruises and dried blood. But she wouldn't look at *him*— Gavin. Lucien figured it was because, like himself, the girl would have nightmares of Gavin tormenting her for the rest of her life.

"Lucien! We need the gathering." Gavin's caressed her cheek then forced her mouth opened before stuffing a rag deep within. He leaned in, "This is so you won't scream—and trust me, you'll want to by the time we are finished with you."

The girl, Angel opened her eyes. Narrowed them at Lucien and kicked against the flat concrete platform they'd placed her on. "Go…back…to…'ell," she forced past the gag.

"Been there, and it is home. You will talk. I know something has changed about you." Gavin sniffed around her. "I smell it."

Lucien came closer. "It is set, they'll be here tonight. There will be ten portal psychics for your ceremony."

Gavin lips curled up in a sick grin. "Don't believe for a moment that you are not to be punished."

"Master, my men died trying to get the other two with her." Lucien dropped to his knees, pleading with his eyes at the mimic of Gavin.

"She is nothing, just part of the puzzle. But Peter Saints, he's a des-cendent of the first one—the ancestor who revealed this secret to my kind from the first. Something in him, and from him alone, can unlock this mystery. This secret I know the one she calls God is hiding from us."

"The boy will come for her." Lucien's eyes danced over the strug-gling Angel. "He fought my men trying to save her. And I bet when he comes, he'll have more of the answers you seek, my master. Because he'll want to find a way to defeat us."

Gavin bent, nose to nose with Lucien. "You better hope it happens before the ceremony on the morrow, or you will be sacrificed with the psychics. And trust me, where they go will be much worse than anything I could ever do to you here on this plane you call Earth. There—it's my domain and I am very creative with my methods of torture."

Lucien's head dropped. He bit his tongue so hard blood dribbled from his lips. But he stayed steady while sweat beaded on his forehead.

"Humph." Gavin sniffed the air. "Blood and sweat." He reached forward and forced Lucien's mouth open to swipe inside. "Yes, blood."

Lucien forced back a gag, tears rolled from his eyes. The feeling was there again. It felt like this demon-Gavin's hand burnt deeper than the back of his tongue, the thing was burning at his spirit.

It grinned. "Tsk, tsk—and I thought Gavin trained you." He straightened. His eyes turned to slits as he looked hungrily at Lucien. Then he pivoted smoothly before walking out of the room. Lucien didn't move until his legs were numb. He gulped, took a deep breath then stood.

Angel slapped her legs down harder. Her eyes never left Lucien's face. He wondered if she could see it, a slight softness in him. She was probably wondering that maybe, just maybe he'd help her. And some small part of him, the part he'd hidden from Gavin, wanted too. Somberly, Lucien walked toward her.

"You know he'll kill me if he knew I was doing this. But that *thing* is not my brother." Lucien ran a hand down her face lovingly. "You're too beautiful for the likes of that demon walker, anyway. He's probably eating away at my brother's soul while he roams around in his body like he belongs there." He ran a hand down his face.

She didn't move. Didn't blink. He could tell from the stricken expression on Angel's face that her heart beat fast in her chest. Lucien couldn't help staring at her, because he knew he was scaring her just as much as Gavin—or something that looked like Gavin.

Whatever happened to Gavin had changed him from what Lucien had remembered him to be. Who was he kidding, the Gavin he knew seemed wicked, but this new Gavin—he was beyond evil. Lucien hoped he was a little bit different than what his brother and his twisted father had wanted him to become.

She mumbled into the cloth, and tilted her head up to get his attention.

Lucien placed a hand on the gag at her mouth. A tear fell from his eye as his hand trembled on her lips. "I can't let you go. Truth is, you wouldn't be safe with me if I took you. The urges," his chin pointed at the door, "that Gavin and my father put in me." He let out a tortured yell. "I'd want to hurt you. But now, those feelings are silent. The hunger to hurt someone like they hurt me is buried." He tugged out the scarf and he put his hand to her lips. "Shhh."

"Please," Angel whispered. Her eyes watered and her hands trembled from the rush of relief at Lucien giving her some reprieve.

"He'll hear you. Your kind is not safe. We all…are doomed." Lucien's hand slid from her mouth. His finger came up to his lip. "Shhh. Shhh." Then he turned, leaving her with her fears.

Chapter 46

"Ahhhhhh!" Peter's entire body was drenched in sweat. He was shivering on the hard, dry dirt beneath him.

"Luke 23! Calm down, I can't heal you if you fight it," the woman, who reminded him of Hanna, yelled at him. She forced his shoulders down with her firm hands.

"Ye have ta pray over 'em. It be the only way now. That demon poisoned him." The huge warrior with the green eyes put a hand on Peter's forehead. "He did nae activate his armor. Nae his sword or shield. I gave 'em mine 'oping he'd know what to do. It was as if, he did nae know how."

She sighed. "You're right, but before we chance it we need to draw out some of his DNA to put into the humans that will be left behind after this war is over. Just in case." She leaned in closer. "In case he doesn't make it."

"The Creator of All wouldna take 'em now when we need 'em to record our moment of victory, I don't think."

Her needle pierced Peter's arm while Michael 2, held it steady. "If he leaves us, he'd want one of the Saints to have his gift. They all are worthy, but their baby's soul is the most innocent. Little Joel Saints will grow and Luke 23's DNA will bond to him. I pray it will be able to hide deep within the boy so our enemies will never find out our secret."

"Wh-what are you doing?" Peter forced out. Numbing fire pounded through his body. The most frustrating part of it all was that he couldn't move his legs, the big dumb ones on this strange body he was in.

She smiled at him, an innocent one like Hanna did. He blinked, knowing he had to be seeing things.

"PATER noster, qui es in caelis, sanctificetur nomen tuum," she whispered almost in a sing-song fashion.

Peter's vision grew cloudy just as he realized she was saying the Lord's prayer in Latin.

***

Yeah, he was going certifiably crazy. Now he was standing, "Whoa!" on what appeared to be clear blue water in a world where the sky was dark. The moon was so bright it looked like he could reach out and touch it.

Peter lifted up his brown hand—the one Hanna had marked—and saw the symbol sinking deep into his skin. He frowned.

"It's still there," a deep voice called.

A breath caught in Peter's throat. "You? Who are? Where am I?" He coughed. "Am I dead?"

The giant angel stood in front of him. Wings gloriously formed sprung out to the sides of a chest that had to be over seven feet wide and a frame well over ten feet of pure muscle. "No, you're not dead. You are too important."

Peter forced his tensed muscles to relax. "I'm dreaming."

"Negative. This is real. And I brought you here—out of the book of our secrets before it's too late. The book you touched made you experience a time and place that I recorded, locked and thought was hidden *forever.*"

"What secrets? Why…" Peter ran a hand down his face. "Why is this happening to me?"

"What? You've done this! You have been deceived by an evil of which you can't begin to comprehend. That evil one has started another war. But this time our Creator will not sacrifice his angels to fight it. You should've never sought out the Strongholds. Their locations were well hidden from all—and for a good reason."

Peter lifted his foot off the calm water, it felt like silk at his feet. He crossed his arms and tried to hold on to a semblance of calm. "I don't understand. I didn't start a war? There's thousands of wars going on now as we speak. How could I start any?" Peter waved a hand. "Man, I am crazy."

"The body you were just in, the war you just experienced—you experienced it through ME!" Luke 23 hit his fist to his chest. "My bloodline sealed the book you opened. Michael 2's line created the weapons we used to fight them. Gabriel 19's bloodline created the technology to protect humankind's future by taking our DNA and fusing it with humans in case this happened."

"Nephilim? Are you sayin' I'm some half human-half angel man?"

Luke 23 stepped closer. "No. Not exactly. Let me explain. Millions of years ago, a man—a human, created a device that transported his human body into the heavenly plane. That device can even give demons the ability to transport themselves to the heavenly realm while wrapped in the bodies of their human counterparts. Angels—those of us that hadn't been part of the fallen who'd followed Lucifer near the beginning of time, were jealous of how our Creator treated the human that appeared."

"Sounds a lot like the last group of angels that got kicked out of heaven." Peter snorted.

"No, this was different. We still loved our Creator and would never want to hurt Him or a being from his hand. But He was dissatisfied with us for our actions. He cast us out of the heavenly realm, stripped us of our wings to show us that man's journey on Earth was so much harder than our servitude to man. Man's journey on Earth was to test—to prove themselves worthy of the gift of everlasting life. We Angels—already had that gift."

"Oh, I get it. He threw you out of heaven to teach you a lesson. You were ungrateful." Peter smirked.

"That wasn't all. He allowed Lucifer and his demons to rise and take true flesh and blood form. But they had to cloak themselves in human flesh in order to pass through the protected plane, or casum, that separated them from the Creator of All. They knew that the Creator of All would never turn a human away. But during this war, they were able to roam on Earth. They raped, killed and massacred everything in their reach. That's how the Nephilim came to be." He sighed.

"So the Nephilim are born between humans and the demons that raped them?" Peter crossed his arms and rubbed them with his hands.

"They were once Angels, and after the Creator of All found that they used their beauty to seduce the woman or gain trust from the males, He turned them into creatures that showed their true nature. They impregnated the woman, in the attempt to taint humans, and to build an army bonded to their insidious cause. Those Nephilim, are the only ones able to hear the voices from their demon ancestors."

"What happened to the demons after they knocked up all those women?"

"The Creator of All removed their bodily forms, and cast them to the astral region called hell. Although they can manifest to hurt those of your kind or to provoke humans to do their will, they can never walk Earth in their own true flesh. We, the angels of the Creator of All, would never defile a human by lying with them. We just fused the part of our DNA that had our strongest traits with that of the humans we served who were most favored by the Creator."

"So those demons I fought in your body, they were once angels that followed Lucifer? And when ya'll hit the scene, the Creator of all allowed them to return to Earth in physical fleshy form and the first things they wanted to kill was—you?"

"That and more. Since we were earthbound, we could be killed forever, and we would have to prove our love of our Creator and loyalty to man in order to regain our everlasting life and role as angels of the Creator of All once more." He sighed, looking ashamed. "Our Creator also returned the human, Jaakan, to Earth, but one of the demons kidnapped him before we could protect him. They took him and created a barrier which none of us could breach. Every one of us that tried to go through the Wall Of Ash never returned."

Peter swallowed. "So did I...Was I the cause of your death back there?"

Luke 23 stepped forward and gently rested his hand on Peter's shoulder. "I didn't die. You never caused anyone's death Peter. The evil one has purposely killed everyone you've loved to manipulate you into giving away the knowledge found in your blood—the only key to the books I recorded. For over a million years this had remained hidden. I recorded every instance of that thousand-year war. And now my son, he knows about it."

"Thanks for tryin' to make me feel better. I'm startin' to feel like death follows me."

"No, the demon by the name of Balaal does. He's one of the elite demon warriors. They are planning to recreate history. And they want to use our creation to do it—the children of the ones we served."

"How can they recreate it? We knew they wanted our blood. But the Order is keeping most of the kids hidden."

"It's more than your blood. The demons can't walk the Earth any longer in their own flesh. You will see them, but others cannot. Only in extreme cases can they physically manifest themselves—and only a few of them are strong enough to do it. They must find human hosts in order to infiltrate the heavenly plane with whatever machine they build to get them there. Not only that, but they need your bloodline to open up the history of that war to figure out what went wrong—and to find the source of our weaponry which helped us win that massacre and save the human they kidnapped. Those weapons can help you eradicate them in their tracks."

"Are you going to stop it?"

His lips thinned. "We are forbidden to. You, my son, and the others we helped create from our DNA, will have to fight this. The Order of Grace comes from a long line of humans that we were sworn to protect during the devastation of the war. Those humans served us, just as much as we have done them over the centuries. They've made the Creator most proud."

"No…no." Peter shook his head. "I'm not what He wants. I can't save the world, everythin' I touch…everyone, is dead. Don't you get it? I just don't think I got it in me to believe in nothin' not even—myself."

"You can, but the Creator won't force you. It's your choice." Luke 23 released him. "What is it you choose? To fight, to become the warrior you were fashioned to be—or to sit back, and let someone else endure the pain—the lesson meant only for you?"

"Lesson? My pain!" Peter's fist rose. "Every breath I take has been painful from the day my parents were snatched from me." Tears slid down his face. His fist went to his eyes and he let out a broken sob. "I-I'm nothin', not even a speck worth what you are asking me to do."

Luke 23 pulled Peter closely into a hug. "You are a warrior. Through your suffering you have found strength. He's chosen you already, molded you for this—and he'll give you every victory. All you have to do is reach for it. Take it, and claim it as your own."

Peter took in a ragged breath. His eyes tightened. "I do."

Chapter 47

"Peter…oh God, let him wake up," Kyle's broken voice whispered.

Wind rushed through Peter's mouth. He gulped air as if coming from the depths of a sea. Peter heard staggered sobs. But he felt like his body was inflating with a power of which he couldn't explain. Lightning shocks trembled through his muscles, his brain, and his hands. The palm with Hanna's symbol pulsated, a reminder that something had changed. It no longer burned but seemed to be an exit to the flow of the essence that filled him.

"Please be alive." Kyle slapped Peter's face. "Wake up, you butt! Don't freakin' leave me here to save her by myself. Angel's your girlfriend."

"Yeah." Peter's hand grabbed Kyle's wrist. His eyes popped opened. "And if you slap me one more time, I'm gonna slap you back."

"Thank God!" Kyle's eyes rolled when Peter released him. With a sigh, he slouched. Unkempt spikes of Kyle's hair stuck out in multiple angles. His flushed face appeared both shocked and relieved.

Peter jumped up off the floor, invigorated. He let out a roar. "Let's do this."

Kyle got up. "Ugh, yeah." He hesitantly pumped his fist in the air while looking at Peter like he'd lost his mind. "Look, I don't know about you, but I just saw you lifted about 20 ft in the air. Your body bowed in an unnatural position." He scratched the back of his head vigorously before he stuck his shaking hand in his pocket. "It looked like bones were moving and shifting in your body. And I swear you must have grown a foot plus added about 20lbs of muscles. But what freaked me out the most was you sprouted wings—like," Kyle took a step back, "a bird, then they withered up, dried and were ripped off your back in a bloody fashion before they disappeared." Kyle pointed at him, "And dude, you were like that for over an hour. Hovering in the air like you were being held up by an invisible string. Then you healed. And get this…" he frowned, "Your hand never left the book. Not once. Then you dropped, hit the ground and bounced. And the book—disappeared. Gone. Poof." He snapped his fingers. "For awhile you laid there still. Like you were dead. Not one breath of freakin' air. I did CPR, beat you silly, kicked you and begged God to wake you up." He grimaced, "then you awake like nothing happened. But now…" Kyle eyeballed Peter's frame. "You have definitely changed. *Comprende*?"

Peter slowly moved his head up and down. "Gotcha. I won't hurt you." He grinned. "A lot happened. I'll explain it on the way to get to Angel. Just be prepared, it's a crazy story." Pivoting around, he ran to the door. He rubbed a hand down it and it opened.

"How'd you know to do that?" Kyle followed.

"I don't know. It's like a part of me has been here before. What do you know about Angel's location and how fast can we get there?"

They picked up their bags and headed to the elevator.

"I know the exact location—which house she's at. Also, I hacked into their security system—the one the scum left in the car we stole. Now it's like our own surveillance device and I have a feed set up to a free spot on the internet I can link into using my phone."

Peter opened the elevator just as the tanks on the walls started to fill up with water from the swamp above. The doors closed. He swung his damp backpack on. "Dang, you are good."

"Hey, private school teaches kids geek skills. I just perfected it. Had to protect my side business since I didn't have no gang to back me up. Just charm and brains saved my butt many days."

The elevator opened and their feet pressed into the dry ground while they made their way past the statuesque alligator. Peter stopped in front of the albino gator. Its head bowed to him while it moved out of the way of their trail to the car.

"Whoa, what was up with that?" Kyle asked and jogged to the door.

"He knows my blood." Peter opened his door, tossed his backpack on the floor and hopped in. "Kick it. Let's save my girl and kill us some demons."

***

After straight driving and one stop for gas, they pulled off the main highway. They continued down a well-kept paved private road.

Peter's hand gripped the wheel, not just in anger, but partially because he was seriously spooked. The things he'd seen since they left the swamp had him jumpy. He'd swear he was going loco again. But something in his heart told him that the dark, ghostly images of demons he'd seen hanging around some of the people at the gas station, then at the rest areas were a real as they could get.

The short, cropped bushes gave him some comfort, because at least the shadows with red eyes weren't looking at him. Challenging him to admit they were real.

"So, I have a lock on them. I just looked at the video feed in the car that took Angel. They gave a hand signal pass code to get into the gates. You have to say, 'I'm here to see the Master of the house.' And move your hand like this." Kyle put his hand between Peter and the windshield. "Also, just for extra precaution, I hacked into their security systems to repeat vids so we shouldn't be caught."

Peter swerved the car a bit. "What was that? Put your hand down man, you messin' with my driving."

Kyle stared at him. "I'm not the one messing with you. You've been acting like a reject from the psyche ward since we left the swamp."

"Shut up, I told you the deal." Peter recalled Kyle's jaw dropping when he told him about the war. About his travel through slipping arrays of time and space. But he respected the guy for at least listening to the entire crazy playback.

"I sent a distress call to the Order of Grace on the encrypted email address you found for Pastor Finn. They've got Gavin Steele's address and all the info we gathered on him and more. But I didn't tell them about you or…uh, your hallucination-slash-time traveling." Kyle shut the small computer notebook and slid it under the seat. "But from what you told me, I still don't get they way you acted at the gas station back there. Dude, for a black guy, you turned freakin' white as a ghost when that man came up to you and asked for some spare cash."

Peter swallowed. "You didn't see what I saw…" He shook his head.

"Go on, spill it. I'm used to hearing crazy talk. Remember, I grew up around this stuff."

"A demon was on that man, its…its fire orange tongue was licking him." Peter's eyes closed. He tried to physically force out the image by gripping the steering wheel tighter and shaking it. "And when the guy put out his hand to me, the thing stopped licking the man and looked at me. Then its mouth opened three times its size and roared at me."

"Whoa! I didn't see that. Nothing. But maybe it realized you could see it."

He nodded. "It knew I could. Then the thing pulled on the guy and that's when he started to run from me."

"Yeah, that's when I got the clue something was a little off with you. But dude, this is serious."

They both fell quiet when they came up to the twenty-foot Iron Gate. The guard waved at them.

"Remember what I said, dude. Say the words with the hand signal."

"Got it." Peter rolled down the window. He worked his hands in the symbol Kyle showed him. "I'm here to see the Master of the house."

The guard eyed them suspiciously and leaned forward to peer over at Kyle. "Your business here?"

"To work, sir," Peter replied, working at his proper speech and diction.

"Humph. Go to the back lot behind the smaller house. Park it there. The butler is directing people to their jobs."

Peter nodded and pulled away slowly.

"So uh, did he have a demon on him?" Kyle whispered.

"Stop whispering like one's in here with us."

"Well, did he?"

Peter almost pushed the breaks, temporarily spooked by the amount of people heading to the back lot. "Naw, he didn't."

Kyle drummed his fingers on the dashboard. "Then maybe he's on our side."

"What makes you think that?"

"The Order of Grace sends in transcenders that can go either way. The dark ones can't figure them out. Something in their spiritual DNA makes them unreadable to psychics and spirit talkers."

"Well, from what I see up ahead, I pray we got a lot more of them here on our side, because if not—we're in some deep water."

Chapter 48

Peter had never seen evil this close and personal before. And his eyes didn't lie. It was here in this place, in full effect. Demons were draped on the people like jackets. Peter had to figure out how to get Angel and Kyle out here safe.

"Do you know where Angel is?" he asked Kyle. His fingers drummed on the steering wheel.

"Duh. I wouldn't bring you here if I didn't. I rigged all the cameras here, dude, and let me tell you, it's some sick crap going on in this party. My cams picked up stuff worse then any horror flick, chop flick or my freakin' nightmares. All I got to say is, at least Angel is not where the other people this guy Gavin had his hands on."

Peter tried not to ogle directly at anyone when he drove past the small crowds waiting for a parking space. He drove to a break in a trail of planted trees on the side of the house. "I'm looking for a place we can make a quick getaway."

"Uh, there." Kyle pointed. "Sorry dude, I forgot to tell you. I've been scoping this place out for the same thing, and that spot over there is our way out. And thank God that's it's not gated. It's like a service road for large deliveries or something." He cleared his throat. "I started looking for an escape route when I saw where this dude keeps the dismembered parts of his victims."

Peter fought against a shiver. *Was Kyle for real? This guy…I'm not gonna think about it. Angel, I'm here to save her.* "Where is she and how can we get in?"

"Again, I keep telling you that I'm the plan, man. Remember growling at me when I made you stop at Home Depot?"

Peter parked the car behind the bushes. The tires rolled onto the mulched ground between a tree and a line of bushes. "And, your point is?"

"I got us uniforms that some of the workers had on. These work jumpers will get us close to her. They have her outside now, she's tied down to some alter in this conveniently cleared part of the beach. There's a small guest house there."

"No one's with her?"

"Uh, I didn't say that. Mr. Gavin Steele and two other guards are there waiting for us to kick their sorry asses," he snickered. Kyle reached in his backpack and pulled out two taser guns. "Here, let's try not to have any bloodshed. Tasers will knock these dudes out, but will keep us out of jail if they try to slip a flip on us and say we broke in."

Peter smirked. "You tryin' to sound street like me, white boy?"

"Ya' know it, my bro." Kyle slapped fists with him.

"You corny man, real corny." He twisted in his seat while Kyle climbed in the back. Then he tugged on the tan work jumper. "You ready?"

"As ever, dude." Kyle opened the door and climbed. "It's clear, but it looks like we have to get past a guard at that crossover by those trees over there to get to the beach."

Peter didn't like a thing he was seeing. Demons were all around him. The hairs on his arms froze up at the thought of what he would have to do to save Angel. But Luke 23 had promised him, the victory would be his, he only had to fight the battle to get it. Angel was worth more than anything on Earth to him, she was his heart.

Peter's hand tightened on the taser gun that fit snug in his hand. Kyle followed close by. They made their way through the firmly packed decorative bushes to the garden walkway. The main house had an elaborate garden on the back with pebbled walkways. Lights were tucked in the crevices where landscaped plants hugged the curvy trails. Chinese paper lamps hung from the palm trees that led to the beach.

The moon hung in the sky, taunted by moving clouds that cast an orange ghostly glow upon it. They'd passed by a woman, tall compared to most and she stepped out of their path briefly.

"Where are you going, boys?" she asked, her voice deep, almost masculine.

Peter stopped just past her, his head low, the hairs on his neck in attention. "We have to get ready for the …uh, festivities." He cleared his throat.

Kyle's shoulder bumped his. "Yeah, is there something we can help you with?"

Peter refused to turn and look at her. He hid his eyes from the glimpse of the demon that had its legs wrapped around her waist while its eyes were half closed, its head on her neck. When he'd walked past, he smelled the sulfur. The demon's body resembled tightly sculptured ash with slit eyes of flames.

"That's the wrong way. The help is to report to the main house for duties. The beach guest house is off limits until the event."

He slid the taser into his pocket. "We were already assigned the garden."

"Well then, get to it," she said.

Peter relaxed, not waiting for her footsteps to get softer before he hurried on.

Kyle yanked at Peter's sleeve. "What's wrong with you? She's gone, but you're acting spooked."

"I am." Peter started down the path again. "That woman had a demon wrapped around her waist licking on her neck like she was candy."

"What did it look like, because I didn't see anything except a woman who looked like a vampire who got their fangs pulled out." Kyle snickered.

"It ain't funny, man. This is serious. I think those things can sense I can see them and I don't know what'll happen if they notice." But he was sure he'd find out soon enough. He neared the path leading down to the beach, and the man at the arched entrance stood at a quarter mile distance from the smaller house where he believed Angel was being held.

"Wait a minute." Kyle elbowed him. "You've got to pull it together. If we're not cool and quiet we'll bring the other guards down on us. Right now it seems most of the people are at the main house. Or, considering what I've watched on the vids I taped, the prep place for the slaughter."

Peter thinned his lips, his eyes never leaving the large muscled Conan-looking guard standing up ahead at the beach entrance. "Who are they plannin' on slaughtering? I thought you said they just wanted us for our blood."

"Yeah, well lucky us, because from the jumbled conversations I was able to pick up—they plan on slicing open some psychics they are using for this ceremony tonight."

"It's all right. I'm pulling it together—got to for my girl. I'm getting her out of here. This is just takin' some time to get used to."

"You need to do it at now since the so-called festivities start in a few hours. I timed this ride perfectly and I don't care what happened to you in that place, there's no way we can make it out of here without keeping it quiet."

"I got it. I'm ready. Let's do it." Peter loosened up, but the burning on his palm didn't recede. Trying to act nonchalant, he walked up to the guard.

The man crossed his arms, sized them up. "Aren't you supposed to be at the house?"

Kyle spoke up. "They sent us down here to get things ready."

They guy tilted his head, looking over Kyle's shoulder. "Nathen, who the hell sent these guys down here? Master Gavin said no one could pass unless they have news about the others."

Peter tilted his chin slightly in the direction of the guy who'd sneaked up behind them.

"I don't know, but I'm not going nowhere near Master Gavin. He's in a bad mood and anybody that bothered him ends up," the guy cleared his throat, "incapacitated."

"Umm," the guard answered. "Go on," he nodded at Peter and Kyle. "Stay clear of Master Gavin, and the guest star for the mass joining ceremony tonight, if you know what's good for you."

The guy behind them asked the guard, "You want me to cover for you? They said you might need a bathroom break or something?"

Peter went around the guard and Kyle came up beside him. "That was close, but you had him by about three inches. I swear it looked like you got taller."

"Don't think so, I've always been tall."

"If you say so. But I'm six-foot tall, you had me by about an inch the other day—but now, I'm looking up to you. That's not natural." Kyle cleared his throat.

"I'm not natural, now shut up. We're gettin' close." Peter didn't have time to look at the beach. It had been years since he'd been to one—much less play on it.

The smaller beach house stood proudly out of the sand. Its decorative curved roof gave it the appearance of a beach hideaway. The white stucco sides melted into an elaborate porch with curved steps onto the sand. It was devoid of windows on the sides, which made Peter curious as to why someone would build a beach house and not have an abundance of windows.

Peter only had eyes for the sick-o that was talking to some guy on his knees. He'd assumed Master Gavin was the tall blond guy who was on the porch looking down at another blond man who was on his knees practically kissing the Master's feet. They got up and went inside without sparing a glance in Peter's direction.

Kyle adjusted the service belt he had around his waist. "That's the dude who's behind all of this. The tall one is Gavin Steele. I think the one on his knees is his brother. I've seen their pictures all over the internet. One of the maids that had to clean up the mess under the house said Lucien was just as sick as his older brother."

"I can see that. The one bending down has two demons on him. But the one standing—" he stopped and swallowed—"that guy has the demon inside him."

They neared the steps, hesitating just a moment. The dark wood door was a contrast to the pale outer walls of the home and the whitewashed surface of the porch that was decorated with inlays of rocks and sanded shells.

Peter's hands quivered. He fought to keep his mind straight— focused. God, he had to do this for Angel but what he knew of these demons since being in Luke 23's body still scared him to death. He'd never backed down from a fight before, but this—this was much more than anything he ever thought he could overcome. Resolved, he reached out for the doorknob. Worms of heat pumped through his blood to end in a throbbing mass at his scared palm. He flexed it, then moved closer.

"I've got my weapons ready," Kyle whispered, "and your back covered."

Peter turned the knob slowly and gave the door a little push. It opened quietly. He waved Kyle in behind him. The interior was a contrast of darkness with dimmed lights, black and brown striped decorated wallpaper. A large framed picture of a dragon being crushed in the hands of a demon greeted them in the archway leading to a door beyond the outer room of black leather furniture. The demon in the picture looked innocent compared to the ones of Peter's nightmares. It was red with the typical horns and angry expression held by most pictures that depicted them as monsters.

"Where would they keep her?" Peter whispered, struggling to control the pulsating sensations in his body. Every cell in him told him to open that door. But he wanted to be sure.

"The door, I think. I wasn't able to get my vids in here. The security system was dead in this place I guess since it's not connected to the main house."

"Cool. C'mon then." Peter opened the door, and the dark met them. The lights were off on the steps. He went down several steps when the hairs on his neck rose.

"Hurry," Kyle whispered.

Peter's eyes narrowed. The guy named Lucien was at the top of the stairs with another man, and they were rushing at Kyle's back. Peter grabbed Kyle by the front of his jumpsuit and dragged him with him down the stairs.

"Hey what the…" Kyle fought him.

Lucien pounced from the top step and landed on Kyle's back. Kyle's body shot forward, knocking Peter into the air. They rolled down several steps before bouncing on the carpeted floor of the cellar in the beach house.

Peter growled. "Kyle—get Angel!" He rolled over and punched Lucien in the face. The demons who had been attached to him earlier, extracted shadowed claws from Lucien's shoulders. Their lower bodies were hidden within the floor. Like mirror images, they pushed up out of the ground and rose from the ground like soot humanoids with the exception of their eyes. The sockets were empty except for the tendrils of smoke that seeped from them.

Lucien bolted up. He grabbed a handful of Peter's hair.

Peter fought against the pressure of Lucien's hands. His head titled to the side from the force. Peter slipped his hand in his pocket. Heart pounding, he pulled out the taser. Lucien landed an uppercut to his chin. It hurt, but Peter didn't ponder it. He jabbed downward and activated the taser gun.

"Ugh." Peter hopped off Lucien's convulsing body.

Lucien's legs and shoulders bucked from the force of the volts of electricity jolting his system. A gurgle rumbled deep in his chest, before his head fell limp to the side.

For good measure, Peter checked the guy for weapons and pulled out a gun he found on Lucien. He stuffed it in his back pocket.

Peter heard Kyle's struggles, but couldn't help him. The demons had spotted him and flew threw the air at him, their thick legs pumping as their clawed hands extended. Peter sidestepped one. The other sliced down the side of his face. But he tried to dodge it. The cut wasn't deep. Peter could swear he felt something release—wiggling inside him. Like the thing was slicing away chunks of his soul with his skin.

With a roar, he jumped to his feet. His burning palm seemed to have a life of its own. The scar within it rose, and slim, sharp pointed streams of bone-like knives shot from his palm. The demon in front of him was pierced with the shards. It was sliced at the neck, torso and leg. Each severed piece floated in the air, separated from the creature's body. With a resounding shriek, its mouth opened three times its original size and it disappeared with a pop.

Peter twisted around. Grabbed the demon poised ready to attack. Punched at it, and landed on the side of its face. It stumbled back. Peter's palm burned bright with white light illuminating from it. He placed his open hand on the face of the demon pushing it to the ground. In a flash, it disappeared.

Kyle jumped up. "My man's down. I heard a scream back there."

Angel's strangled scream jolted them to action. They ran through a hallway to the only door ahead of them. The hidden room at the end of a dark wood paneled hall's door was ajar. Gavin's tall form was holding Angel up in the air by her neck.

"Let. Her. Go!" Peter burst in. The demon within Gavin's sinister grin looked three-dimensional. The fiend moved its face while Gavin's remained immobile. It looked as though a transparent shadow was captured beneath Gavin's skin.

"Not until I bleed her dry and use her blood to tell your secrets," he answered. Its burning hollow eyes never left Angel's squirming form. "Peter! Don't. It's a trap." Angel tried to land a kick to Gavin's face.

"He can't trap us." Peter charged Gavin.

"I'll break her neck and take your blood, Peter Saints." Gavin laughed. "It's what I wanted from the beginning. But now I know why, descendent of the sacred scribe, Luke 23."

Peter's palm met Gavin's face head on. He bent his fingers forward and pulled from his stomach, trying to dislodge the demon from Gavin. "Jump Angel!"

Gavin's hold loosened on Angel. She fell to the floor. The rumble of multiple feet pounded from above. Peter wrestled to yank the demon from within Gavin and placed his foot on Gavin's. He had a hand on the front of the demon's face, the other at the back of its smooth head. Biting his tongue, Peter tugged once more. The ghostly form of the demon materialized into a solid mass of ash. Gavin's limp body thudded to the floor.

"Kyle, get her and run!" Peter screamed as the demon's large orange-tipped fingers wrapped around his neck.

"There are people upstairs! We'll be caught," Kyle yelled.

Angel jumped up. "C'mon, there's a side exit that's underground and leads to the garden. I've seen them come and go from there while I was here." Angel jolted towards Peter. "But we can't leave without Peter." Kyle held her back.

The thing was choking him. Tears gathered in his eyes. His chest hurt when Kyle and Angel's fright-filled faces approached the demon on top of him. "NO! Go now. Meet out…at…gate."

"I won't!" Angel cried, tears pouring down her face. "How can it be…What is that…he?"

Peter shook his head. The demon's fingers grew talons of fire. Peter's mouth opened to scream. It stabbed into Peter's stomach. "Go," he croaked. Then without warning, his body shook. Surge after surge of strength filled him. The wound inflicted by the demon's claws glowed bright. Its talons were expelled outward. Peter flipped over, renewed. His legs straddled the demon's black chest.

"You may have killed my feeder demons, but I can manifest in this form here on your *Earth*," it growled. "You will give me your blood." It licked the bloodstained talon that was forced from Peter's body.

"But you'll die trying." Peter punched the demon's thick neck. He snatched its sharpened finger out of its mouth. Then tore the talon out of it. The talon of fire burned out into a smudge of simmering embers. "I'm stronger now." He countered the upward jab from the demon's other hand with his arm. Peter pierced his fingers in its flamed-filled eye. "I'm not afraid now."

It growled. And then it jerked up to unseat Peter. "I've tasted it. The war, the power we once owned." Its fist hit Peter's side, knocking him over.

Peter quickly righted himself. He lifted his hand. It held a slight glow that traveled up his body. "Now, I'm angry."

It snickered, "I love anger," then pulled Peter up off his knees by his jumpsuit. Then it threw him across the room.

Peter's head bounced against the wall. Peter shook of his daze to right himself.

Footsteps came from behind him. "Oh my God!"

Peter heard a scuffle off to the side, but he only had eyes for the demon charging him. He pushed out his palm. Light from within it flooded the room in waves of energy so strong the room shook. The ground cracked. The demon was sucked closer and closer toward the chasm by some invisible force. Its arms flailed from side to side. It screamed and thrashed about against the invisible force.

"Go-back-to-hell!" Light came from Peter's mouth, eyes, hands and nose. Streams of energy poured into the demon and a thundering boom shook the room as it disappeared.

Peter fell against the wall, weakened and dizzy.

A hand reached for him, lifted and dragged him through the door behind a statue of a dragon. "Son, don't worry. We'll get you out of here. You are not alone."

Peter's vision cleared and he stumbled. He righted himself on the man who was about his height with dark hair and kind eyes. "I know I'm not. At least not anymore."

"Your friends are just outside the gates. Follow this hallway to the stairs. Then run—run until you get there. And tell the others the war has started." The man released him.

Before Peter could turn to get a look at his face, he disappeared in the gloom within the tunnel. With a sigh, he forced away the aches from his injuries and ran like his life depended on it.

The night sky, the cool breeze from the waves hit his face. Peter pumped his arms harder. Fire alarms went off in the distance. Buildings exploded; fire blazed the larger house. The smoke made him gag, but he kept running. Then he saw the car—Angel stood at the open door waving him closer.

He pushed himself harder, slid to a stop. Then he dragged her close with his arms and into a hungry kiss. "I love you. Thank God, you're okay."

"Today guys! Friend trying to live. Get in the car!"

Peter slid her beside him. Kyle hit the gas kicked up dirt as they sped off.

Chapter 49

They didn't say a word for miles. Peter just held Angel tightly in his arms. She clung to him as if he were her lifeline. He felt like she was his. Kyle however, hummed.

"Man, can you just cut on the radio and stop torturing us with your jacked up singing?" Peter smacked Kyle in the back of the head. "Besides, where'd you get this car anyway?"

"*Decretum Venia* hooked us up. The distress call I sent out activated all the field agents so they knew our location. They even had some moles on location." He shrugged. "I'd never been so happy to see help in my life. When we came out the tunnel, a guy was waiting for us. I almost peed my pants. But he had his hands up and told us he was assigned to protect us. He pointed us to a car and killed several guards to get us to safety."

Angel snuggled closer to Peter, but a small shiver wracked her body. "That guy, Lucien…Gavin's brother. He helped me, but still he's definitely in with the demon league, if you get my point. Gavin was possessed by one who talked about some machine that would transport demons in human bodies to the heavenly realm." She sighed, "And I have to know, how did you kill those…things. At first it looked like you were fighting a ghost, until you pulled that…that thing out of Gavin."

"Something happened to me on our way to get you."

Angel sniffed. "I know. I saw them shoot you." Her voice broke. "I thought they killed you—both of you."

Kyle chuckled. "You know I don't die, right? And I always have to save Peter's ass."

"Shut up big-head, before I pop you again." Peter smiled. "Anyway, before I was interrupted, something happened at the Stronghold that changed me. Physically and…mentally. Not only that, but now we have to go back to Pastor Finn's and warn the order. Once I opened that Stronghold and released the knowledge it tried to protect, an awareness of a war that the Creator of All erased from time was reactivated. A thousand-year war where the demons walked the Earth in their own flesh form, enslaved us humans, and fought the Angels of Light over a man's soul who'd beamed himself up to heaven. And for some reason, I can see them, feel them, fight them—but none of you can unless the demons are strong enough to pass over."

"Whoa!" Kyle pushed the car harder. "That's bad. We opened something the order tried to hide for what…centuries? We are so screwed. And you—what are you? Like a beacon to them or something? You bring them out? Expose them and piss them off?"

Angel sat up and slid her hand into Peter's. "We didn't have a choice, Kyle. Those guys got the first clue when the Order of Grace made the first mistake of unveiling an ancient artifact and having both a descendent of the *Order of Grace* and one of the Extraho of Obscurum or Dragons of Darkness at the same archeological dig. But that's not it, they were killing our parents and bleeding us dry in order to break into the places they found out about on their own. Who's to say they wouldn't have unveiled the secret themselves eventually by using our blood?"

"You're right." Peter leaned over and kissed her cheek. "But for me, saving you was all that mattered. I was willing to risk anything to do it."

"Me too." Kyle faked a sob.

Peter kicked his seat. "Just drive. Looks like the war has started, and the warriors," he pointed at Angel and Kyle, "have arrived." Then he leaned over and kissed Angel.

LM Preston's Other Books (Read Samples on following pages)

LM Preston, www.lmpreston.com

The Pack by LM Preston– Teen, blind, vigilante on a mission to save the missing kids on mars. Shamira is considered an outcast by most, but little do they know that she is on a mission. Kids on Mars are disappearing, but Shamira decides to use the criminals' most unlikely weapons against them—the very kids that they have captured. In order to succeed, she is forced to trust another, something she is afraid to do. However, Valens, her connection to the underworld of her enemy, proves to be a useful ally. Time is slipping, and so is her control on the power that resides within her. But in order to save her brother's life, she is willing to risk it all.

Bandits by LM Preston - Daniel's father has gotten himself killed and left another mess for Daniel to clean up. To save his world from destruction, he must fight off his father's killers while discovering a way to save his world. He wants to go it alone, but his cousin and his best friend's sister, Jade insists on tagging along. Jade is off limits to him, but she insist on changing his mind. He hasn't decided if loving her is worth the beating he'll get from her brother in order to have her. Retrieving the treasure is his only choice. But in order to get it, Daniel must choose to either walk in his father's footsteps or to re-invent himself into the one to save his world.

Wastelands – Bandits Series, by LM Preston – Daniel's doing the unthinkable. He's planning to break into a prison to prove to his dead father that he has changed, only problem is – he hasn't.

Flutter Of Luv by LM Preston - Dawn, the neighborhood tomboy, is happy to be her best friend's shadow. Acceptance comes from playing football after school with the guys on the block while hiding safely behind her glasses, braces, and boyish ways. But Tony moves in, becomes the star running back on her school's football team, and changes her world and her view of herself forever.

Explorer X-Beta by LM Preston - Barely escaping their captors, Aadi and Eirena are determined to save their dying friend. After their final confrontation with the species that tortured them, they've changed—unfortunately, not for the better. The changes caused by a terrible experiment force Aadi to accept the possibility that he may never be fit to go home, and that holding onto his sanity, or leading his friends to safety will end in failure and may rip his friendship with Eirena apart, forever. Time is slipping away and the possibility of losing his friend is not an option, but the foe that awaits them may be worse than the one they left.

Bandits by LM Preston (sample)

Daniel rolled over and punched his pillow. "Ugh! I give up," he muttered.

Sleep always eluded him and tonight was no different. Groomed as a thief and mercenary, his mind was ready to act. Most nights it was hard to shut off. He definitely wouldn't get any sleep tonight with the distant murmur of voices that filled his head and grew louder each second.

"Gambling night," he spat out. Daniel snatched the pillow from under his head and covered his face. It didn't help, the angry voices filtered through anyway. He just didn't get it. Every week it was the same thing. Fights over cheating, his father's outright refusal to take on any snatch jobs, and then the old man getting chewed out. He was sick of his father's screw-ups.

Daniel shook his head at the thought of another late night caused by his dad's weekly game with his friends. He let out a deep breath, threw the pillow aside, and sat up on his bed. "Serves him right," he sneered. "Been picking up his jobs for three years now, and I'm ready for my own territory anyway. I'm finished picking up his slack—I'm done doing it…TONIGHT." He wiped his hand down his face then punched down on the rumpled bed.

Remorse crept up his back. He squeezed his eyes shut and then opened them. Maybe, he should've picked up the load his father refused to get from Haden. His father's best friend and leader of the EBRA, was sick of his dad's refusal to do his job.

Daniel looked down at the snoring body of his cousin on the floor, and acknowledged that Faulk didn't have the same dirty blond hair, dimples, or gray eyes as he. No, Faulk was different. His mother's Asian features dominated Faulk's face instead. He shoved Faulk's leg out of his way so he could stand. With a crack of his neck, he stretched, and then scratched his bare chest.

"Faulk," he smirked, "your parents would kill you if they knew you were hiding out here. Hell, my father may kill me when I tell him I let you in." Daniel figured Faulk had the Pierce family's adventurous spirit. Proven fact, since Faulk dropped out of flight school two days before his graduation, only to land on Daniel's doorstep.

Faulk had showed up earlier that day with a sack of wrinkled clothes, his flight school uniform and a stupid grin. Daniel let him in, even though he hadn't seen Faulk in years. The first and last time he'd laid eyes on Faulk was four years ago when Uncle Kiev came to demand that his father change his criminal ways and come home to Earth. No way Uncle Kiev would get my old man to change. He'd never give up being a Zukar. His father had been with the Zukar, a faction of thieves on Merwin ever since he was a kid. Celebrated for his undisputable snatch jobs, his father had become a legend.

The voices in the front room grew louder with angry shouts and the muted sounds of laser fire pierced the air. Daniel's head jerked toward the door, his brow wrinkling. The tingling down his back confirmed this wasn't the typical weekly banter. He pulled his gun from beneath his pillow. Gripping the handle of the gun, he crept to the door, and pushed it open. He leaned against the door and tilted the gun up, prepared to shoot. Ready to attack, he was stopped by a call from his ten-year-old brother.

"Psst," Nickel whispered from his bedroom doorway across the hall.

Daniel turned his angry gaze on his younger brother, whose short, light brown hair stood on end. Nickel's gray eyes filled with concern on his rounded face as he shook his head at his brother's stupidity. He gestured in their coded sign language. "No, too many."

Daniel's mouth thinned. He raised his free hand to motion for his brother to stay put, and crept slowly along the wall leading to the front room. Whispered arguments had elevated into shouting. More laser fire went off, and a smoke bomb followed, filling the long hallway with thick smoke before Daniel could make his way down. Daniel held his breath and fought his way through. His eyes burned, and his lungs fought to breathe. He narrowed his eyes and felt around in front of him. With his gun at the ready, he frantically searched for his father in the dull, smoke-filled room.

"Humph! The bastards ran."

Coughs sounded behind him. Daniel knew his brother and cousin were not far behind. The roar of an engine lit the night. He ran toward the front door to pursue the men who fled, but he tripped forward, stumbling over a firm body. He used his free hand to brace himself before falling face first on the floor. The smoke started to dissipate out of the opened door and Daniel didn't have to look at the body to see whose it was. The punch of dread hit him dead in his chest when he pushed himself back off the slightly rounded stomach of his father's large form.

Daniel held back a sob and swallowed. "Keep Nickel back! Keep 'em back," he yelled. He sat back on his knees and forced his angry eyes to land on his father.

"No! Damn! Who-did-this?" His lips formed a scowl. Tears from the smoke and his grief fell slowly. Balling his fist, he punched down on his bent knees as grief and desolation caved in on him. Anger at his father— even dislike—didn't take away the fact that he loved the old man and wanted him there with them. "Arghhhhhh!" His fist tightened, "I never wanted this. I'll kill them. Why didn't you just yell for help? I would've saved you," his voice cracked. He raised his fists and pushed them against his eyes to stop his tears.

Daniel heard his brother cry behind him. "No, no... Dad! Please don't be dead. NO!" Nickel tried furiously to fight his way out of Faulk's firm grip.

Daniel's muscles tightened, and years of training as a thief re-minded him to shove those sappy feelings of regret down. "Don't let him go Faulk. Not yet." He quickly pulled himself together. His expression grave while he examined his father to see if he was breathing. Nothing, he's gone. The old man's ...gone.

With a grunt, he tilted his father's body for a better look, just to be sure. His eyes traveled over his dead father, up and down his back. The finality of his father's fate sat heavy in his gut. The laser left a hole clean through his father's leg, but it was the knife to his heart that ultimately caused his death. His father's body landed with an eerie, lifeless thump when Daniel released him. Daniel looked at his father's grayish-blond hair and the shocked expression of his death in his eyes, and screamed out. Anger at his father's killers—even at his father's carelessness choked up within him.

Nickel broke free of Faulk and ran into Daniel's back. He collapsed to his knees, laid his head on his father's stomach, and cried in loud, choking sobs.

Putting his sorrow aside, Daniel reached back to console his little brother.

"Daddy, no...no." Nickel cried and kneed the floor in anger. "Why, Daniel? WHY him? Our Dad?"

Faulk came and put his hand on Daniel's shoulder. "Daniel, I'm sorry man. I'm so sorry. Maybe...maybe I should call my parents."

Daniel stood up with a glare. "Don't," he forced out the words through gritted teeth. "Your parents don't know this place. They'd make things worse. Trust me—much worse." His mouth thinned as he watched his brother cry.

"You gotta be kidding me! Your father was murdered, right here," Faulk pointed to the floor. "Here, while we were in our beds, dude. Cold blooded with us in the house. Who's to say our asses aren't next?" Faulk yelled, and then pushed Daniel's chest.

Daniel grabbed Faulk's shirt, balled it up in his hand and slammed him against the wall. "You came here uninvited. You wanted to live here, but you don't…Look, you don't know the Zukar. Outsiders stay the hell out of our business. Don't try your Earth logic on this planet. I'll handle it." He jammed his index finger into Faulk's chest. "And by the way, the next time you push me, you best be ready for a beat down. Now go to my room and pack up my weapons—all of 'em. I'll take care of Nickel," Daniel forced out, trying to hold onto his anger at Faulk's misplaced judgment. He pushed Faulk into the wall in disgust, and then let him go with a jerk, releasing his wrinkled shirt.

Daniel turned away from Faulk, and then bent down to touch his brother's trembling shoulder. "He's gone, Nick, but don't worry. I'll take care of you. You know I will."

Nickel turned to Daniel and hugged him. He sniffled and wiped the tears from his eyes. "I know you will. I'll take care of you too. Dad wanted me to."

Nickel gathered his composure and forced a determined expression on his face. "Are we going to the trove? We gotta get to Dad's stuff before they do. Someone wanted to know where his trove was, but he wouldn't tell them." Nickel pulled on Daniel's arm and whispered. "He told me a secret. Said if anything happened to him, I had to get his journal."

Daniel's eyebrow arched up. "His journal? Dad kept a diary, like a girl?" He groaned. "I knew the old man was turning soft."

Nickel frowned, working up a fierce appearance on his face. "No he wasn't! Dad wasn't soft. He was fierce and strong. He could still kick your butt, and you know it." He glared at Daniel angrily, still upset by the loss of his father, but he didn't hold the glare long. "Anyways, Dad never got a chance to tell me where he put the journal. Some bastard killed him tonight, before he could."

"We gotta get out of here. You search for the journal if it's so important, and I'll get my gear." Daniel grabbed Nickel by the arm to force him down the hallway so he couldn't go back over to where their father had fallen.

Nickel pulled away. "Okay. I'll look in the lower rooms. That's where he was when I last saw him. He might have had it there," Nickel said before running off.

"Faulk!" Daniel called while he ran down the hall to his room.

His cousin was fervently packing various weapons into their packs. "Yeah? This stuff is ready to go. Anything else?" Faulk took a quick glance around the room.

Daniel pointed to his closet. "Go into the safe in the floor of my closet. Put in 56-23-82-34 and take out all the money there. Hell if I know where we're going, but if things don't turn out well we may have to leave Merwin." He grabbed a green shirt off the floor and pulled it over his head.

Faulk angrily threw down the sack he'd filled. "Leave the planet? What the hell for? We didn't kill your dad. Why do we have to be the ones on the lam?"

"Look, let me make this quick for you goody-do-right types. Merwin is populated by Zukar from all different galaxies. Any cutthroat or snatcher that wants a safe haven from the law settles here if they can pass the Zukar's members test. It's a planet full of—well, criminals, hit men, and murderers—people who'll do anything for the right price, get my drift?"

Faulk rolled his eyes. "Uh, well I still don't get the danger here."

Daniel shrugged as he looked under strewn clothes for his vest. "Our new King wants us out, off his planet, and many of the Zukar here won't go without a fight. If we don't find my father's killers before they find us, we'll all be dead or sent to a penal colony on the Planet Uukin. Damned if I know who killed 'im. I just know I don't want us to be next."

"So, we're running from the King and maybe a Zukar?" Faulk asked, raising an eyebrow as he stuffed a knife in his belt.

Daniel put on his vest over his shirt. "My father had a lot of people who hated him—first for his skills and later for his failures. It could've been a Zukar or the King's men. There are different people here every week to gamble. Far as I know, it wasn't even the usual crew, since most of them are out on snatch jobs this time of year. I just thought he was doing his usual weekly gamble bit."

"My parents could help us. They're ambassadors of the Galactic Peace Council."

Daniel pointed at Faulk. "Your parents' power as diplomats for Earth won't help when we get sent to Uukin. Cuz, you came here for an adventure, right? Well it's about time you man up and stop running to your daddy at the first sign of trouble." He grabbed his gun belt and quickly left the room.

He headed to the lower rooms, and climbed down the steep ladder leading downward from the secret door in the floor. "Nick-el? Nickel? You find it?"

Nickel was looking under the couch. "No. Freak! I looked everywhere. We can't leave without it. We gotta find it. Dad made me promise."

Daniel started looking around the room and hastily turned over anything that stood in his way. "I remember walking in on Dad when he was down here. He jumped when I came down, like he was hiding something. He was over there by the mirror."

Daniel bumped into Nickel and then tripped over Nickel's foot. He broke his fall by landing in the middle of the mirror. While he righted himself, he saw the mirror under his fingers glow with a strange blue light.

Nickel pointed. "Look! There, on the opposite wall...the picture moved."

Daniel watched with quiet interest when the picture split in half to reveal a built in shelf. It held a small black book that pushed forward. He took the book out. It felt heavy and thick as the worn pages pushed the black cover up slightly. He flipped it back and forth in his hand for a second and then opened up the first page.

For Daniel and Nick.

Daniel shut the book and put it in his back pocket. He turned to see Nickel staring at him. "Let's go. We've got to get out of here before it's too late." Nickel didn't argue but ran past him to climb up the ladder.

Faulk was waiting at the top of the stairs, and gave Nickel a hand to get up.

Daniel followed Nickel up but purposely ignored his cousin's outstretched arm. "Let's go. Now! Get everything to the door," he ordered, leaping up out of the hole.

Nickel stomped his foot. "We can't leave Dad like that. We gotta do the Zukar ceremony of death. We have to do it or he won't rest."

"We don't have time, Nick. They'll be here soon. We stayed to long already," Daniel said sternly as he pushed Nickel toward the door.

Nickel resisted. He stumbled against Daniel's hard pushes on his back and head to force him forward down the hallway. "No! No, I'm not leaving unless we do it. It's our Dad!"

Faulk looked solemnly at Daniel. "Look, man. I'll pack the car. Give the kid something to remember—a chance for him to say goodbye." With that, he grabbed the bag and left the house.

Daniel gave in and walked with his brother to stand in front of his father's fallen body. "Okay Nickel, let's do it."

They chanted and prayed the Zukar death ritual over their father. Daniel snatched his knife out of his belt and cut off a lock of his hair. He turned to Nickel and did the same. Nickel gathered the pieces and plaited it into his father's long braids.

There was a moment of silence, and finally Nickel dropped down and hugged his father goodbye. He took a deep breath and swallowed hard, trying to be brave. "I'm ready."

Daniel put his hand on his brother's shoulder. He lifted him up and threw him over his shoulder. He tickled Nickel, hoping their old game of capture would take their minds off the grave road ahead of them.

"Put me down! Stop! I'll get you!" Nickel yelled and squirmed.

Daniel slapped him on the leg, a smile tickling his lips. "Keep fighting. You squirt. You'll never be big enough to beat me."

"When I turn eleven, you're going down—you just watch," Nickel replied with a firm smack to Daniel's head. He laughed out as Daniel seized him with another tickle attack.

"Is that so? Then maybe I need to get all my licks in now," Daniel chuckled and slapped Nickel's backside. He forced it out and pushed down the conflicting emotions raging in his chest: pain, anger, and regret filled him whenever he thought of his father. Now, however, all he felt was guilt—and lots of it.

About the Author

LM. Preston is an avid reader. She loved to create poetry and short stories as a young girl. With a thirst for knowledge she attended college and worked in the IT field as a Techie and Educator for over sixteen years. She started writing science fiction under the encouragement of her husband who was a Sci-Fi buff and her four kids. Her first published novel, Explorer X - Alpha was the beginning of her obsessive desire to write and create stories of young people who overcome unbelievable odds. She loves to write while on the porch watching her kids play or when she is traveling, which is another passion that encouraged her writing.